JAMES AXLER

DEATH LANDS®

Prodigal's Return

D0398198

A GOLD EAGLE BOOK FROM
WORLDWIDE®

TORONTO • NEW YORK • LONDON
AMSTERDAM • PARIS • SYDNEY • HAMBURG
STOCKHOLM • ATHENS • TOKYO • MILAN
MADRID • WARSAW • BUDAPEST • AUCKLAND

Recycling programs
for this product may
not exist in your area.

First edition September 2011

ISBN-13: 978-0-373-62610-6

PRODIGAL'S RETURN

Six mistakes mankind keeps making century after century:
Believing that personal gain is made by crushing others;
Worrying about things that cannot be changed or corrected;
Insisting that a thing is impossible because we cannot
accomplish it;
Refusing to set aside trivial preferences;
Neglecting development and refinement of the mind;
Attempting to compel others to believe and live as we do.
                                        —Marcus Tullius Cicero,
                                        63 B.C.

THE DEATHLANDS SAGA

This world is their legacy, a world born in the violent nuclear spasm of 2001 that was the bitter outcome of a struggle for global dominance.

There is no real escape from this shockscape where life always hangs in the balance, vulnerable to newly demonic nature, barbarism, lawlessness.

But they are the warrior survivalists, and they endure—in the way of the lion, the hawk and the tiger, true to nature's heart despite its ruination.

Ryan Cawdor: The privileged son of an East Coast baron. Acquainted with betrayal from a tender age, he is a master of the hard realities.

Krysty Wroth: Harmony ville's own Titian-haired beauty, a woman with the strength of tempered steel. Her premonitions and Gaia powers have been fostered by her Mother Sonja.

J. B. Dix, the Armorer: Weapons master and Ryan's close ally, he, too, honed his skills traversing the Deathlands with the legendary Trader.

Doctor Theophilus Tanner: Torn from his family and a gentler life in 1896, Doc has been thrown into a future he couldn't have imagined.

Dr. Mildred Wyeth: Her father was killed by the Ku Klux Klan, but her fate is not much lighter. Restored from predark cryogenic suspension, she brings twentieth-century healing skills to a nightmare.

Jak Lauren: A true child of the wastelands, reared on adversity, loss and danger, the albino teenager is a fierce fighter and loyal friend.

Dean Cawdor: Ryan's young son by Sharona accepts the only world he knows, and yet he is the seedling bearing the promise of tomorrow.

In a world where all was lost, they are humanity's last hope....

Prologue

With a snap as loud as a gunshot, the rope broke.

"Rona!" Dean Cawdor yelled as the rushing water of the nameless river yanked him off the drowning horse, sending him tumbling helplessly downstream.

Sharona screamed his name, but the crashing waves of the white-water river overwhelmed the sound, until there was only the rumbling thunder of the icy wash. Swimming furiously, Dean fought his way back to the surface, pulling in a desperate lungful of air. Through the spray he saw his horse slam into a boulder, blood gushing from its mouth, its eyes going blank before the animal was swept away—the contents of both saddle-bags floating after it.

Throwing himself forward, he strove to reach the sinking animal. There was still a longblaster in the gun boot alongside the saddle, and a rope coiled over the pommel. If I can just get hold of that, he wished desperately.

But the cold water was quickly sapping the strength from his arms and legs, and his sodden boots felt as if they were lined with lead plate. Realizing the hopelessness of the task, he abruptly changed direction and started slogging toward the rocky shore. The spray made it hard to see clearly, and the speed of the water was making the shore race by in a blur.

Stay sharp! Dean commanded himself. Lose it now and you'll be in a bastard world of hurt.

Just then, something brushed against his leg under the water, and Dean felt a visceral rush of raw terror at the possibility of a river mutie. Kicking furiously with both legs, he felt his combat boot slam into something, and a bubbling roar came up from the muddy depths, heading quickly away.

But his relief lasted only a moment as another boulder loomed suddenly from the blinding spray. Snarling a curse, he grabbed hold of a passing tree and rolled himself onto it a split second before it slammed into the boulder. With a crack of thunder the tree shattered, and Dean was sent hurtling forward, still clutching a broken branch amid a maelstrom of dead birds, leaves, wood chips and pinecones.

Going under again, he almost didn't reach the surface in time, his lungs laboring with the burning need for air. Erupting from the white-water river, he clawed wildly for anything to help him stay afloat. But his clutching fingers encountered only the turgid water and random bits of flotsam. His stomach was starting to hurt now from the cold, a sure sign of reaching the end of his strength. Making a hard decision, Dean started to unbuckle his gun belt, willing to lose the precious blaster to stay alive for a few more seconds, when a line of jagged boulders rose out of the spray.

In a surge of adrenaline, Dean tried to slip between the deadly outcroppings. He made it past the first two, but the third smacked his arm with stunning force, and the entire limb went numb. Spinning about, he lost all track of direction and speed, then cracked his forehead against an unseen boulder. For a brief moment, warmth flooded his face, and the water turned red. Then an undertow dragged him down, away from the air and light toward certain doom.

Even as darkness filled his world, Dean clawed for the knife on his belt and began slashing wildly at his arms and chest. More blood welled from the shallow cuts, but then his heavy bearskin coat fluttered away in the tumultuous river.

Pounds lighter, he felt strength return to his weary limbs, and more determined than ever, the young Cawdor fought to control his passage down the icy river. His world coalesced to chaotic swimming, dodging boulders and trying to reach the shore. Any shore. It made no difference now. Long minutes passed, maybe hours; he had no way of telling. Swim, fight, breathe, live became his only thoughts for an unknown length of time. Then his boot brushed the bottom, dislodging loose rocks, and he dug and clawed his way through the shallows toward the muddy bank.

Grabbing fistfuls of weeds, Dean hauled himself out of the battering water, every inch of freedom gained fueling his will to live. There were trees and bushes only a few feet away.

Struggling out of the sticky mud, he barely managed to crawl onto dry land before collapsing. Totally exhausted, he sprawled on the blessed riverbank, gulping in air.

He had to have dozed for a while, because the next thing he knew a crimson dawn was starting to lighten the cloudy sky. Instinctively, his hands and feet started to tread water again before reason returned. Safe. He had made it onto the riverbank.

Even if I do feel like the loser in an ax fight, Dean thought, grunting at every movement. He had a nuke storm of a headache, his throat was parched and every inch of his body felt bruised and sore. But he was most definitely alive.

Levering himself onto his knees, he patted his clothing to make sure his weapons were still present. His folding knife was long gone, but he still had the big bowie knife, and his Browning Hi-Power .38 was tight in its holster—although a quick check showed the pistol was completely choked with mud. Trying to fire it now would only cause a back blast that would remove his hand. His stomach was rumbling with hunger, but cleaning the blaster was the first priority.

Crawling to the edge of the river, he washed the weapon thoroughly, dropping the magazine to make sure the rush of water reached every crevice. Later on, he would disassemble the blaster and give it a through cleaning and oiling. But his father had taught him that a fast wash would do in times of danger.

"Which this is, since I have no bastard idea where I am," Dean growled, slamming the magazine back into the weapon and working the slide to eject a round. "Much less where Rona is by now."

The memory of his mother screaming his name from the other shore of the wild river filled the youth with a sharp pang of loss. But he knew she was a fighter, and would survive on her own just fine. She had for many years. Sharona had stolen him away from his father and the others, and Dean had been really pissed about that. But his mother had convinced him that she needed him, that Ryan would never have allowed Sharona to stay with the companions. So if Dean would stay with her for a little while, she would let him go back to his father sometime soon. She needed him. The confused youth had given in.

Dean hadn't been alone since he was nine years old. Rona or her old faithful friend, or one of the companions had been around to lend a hand when it was needed.

"But not today," he muttered, shaking the blaster to try to remove any lingering moisture. Until further notice, he would have to fend for himself. Oddly, the idea didn't feel him with unease. He had learned a lot traveling with his father and the other companions; and Dean felt sure there were damn few things in the Deathlands that he couldn't chill, outrun or outthink. Except for a howler, mebbe.

Thoughts of his father, Krysty and the others flooded his mind. He felt bad about what his mother had done. But she needed him, and that was that. He'd had to look after her like he did before. He knew Ryan would never forgive him. Perhaps when he was a little older he'd try to find him—if he lived that long.

Rising to his feet, Dean stomped to help restore circulation while he took stock of the area. The river rumbled steadily along, disappearing out of sight. There were fruit trees and bushes on the other side, but they might as well be on the moon, so he turned his back to the display of inaccessible food. Out of sight, out of mind.

Outcroppings on this side of the river rose to foothills

that were backed by proper mountains. There were a lot of pines and oaks in sight, as well as a wide field of grass. Dean knew a few parts of a pine tree were edible, but reaching them involved a lot of hard work for a small return. Thankfully, he saw a copse of cacti only a few yards away, and lurched in that direction.

Shuffling over to a forked cactus, Dean paused to check for any signs of a feeder hidden under the ground. But there was no indication of the subterranean mutie, and Dean eagerly drew his bowie knife to hack off the crown of the plant. Clear fluids welled up from the juicy pulp within, and he stabbed the chuck of cactus with his knife, carefully removing the needles, before carving out the pulp. It was sticky and sweet, and tasted like life itself. Smelled good, too, like a flower blossoming in the dead of winter.

Most of the cactus was inside his belly before Dean felt some of his strength return. Spearing one last chunk, he walked back to the river to wash the mud off his clothing. Then he knelt on a relatively dry section of ground to carefully disassemble, oil and reassemble the Browning Hi-Power. With internal nylon bushings, the predark blaster supposedly never needed to be oiled, but J.B. had taught him well. It was always better to be safe than buried.

Trying the action on the piece a few times, Dean grunted in satisfaction, then reloaded the blaster and tucked it away. Washed and armed once more, he decided it was time for some real food. Pine trees were a favorite home for a lot of birds, which translated into eggs for breakfast and, with any luck, something roasted for lunch. Falcon was the best, but there was nothing wrong with owl, or even robins—although it took about a dozen to make a decent meal. Plucking that many tiny feathers was something Dean wouldn't wish on a fragging coldheart.

"Afterward, I'll start searching for a ville," he muttered, brushing back his damp hair. He took some comfort in the sound of a human voice, even though it was just his own.

The riverbank was alive with chirping insects and croaking frogs, a virtual chorus of nature. If the trees proved to be barren, he'd eat the bugs and frogs. Food was food. He would honestly much prefer a nice roasted crow over a baked frog stuffed with cicadas. Still, whatever didn't chill you made you stronger, as Mildred liked to say.

Crossing an open field, Dean breathed in the morning air, enjoying the warmth of the sun on his face. Scattered beams broke through the dense cloud cover, causing what Doc used to call the cathedral effect. The air smelled faintly of river moss and punk. A small field of cattails waved gently in the morning breeze, pretty, but useless.

Watching the ground for any sign of animal spoor, or worse, the gnawed bones dropped by muties, Dean was about halfway to the trees when he heard the sound of distant thunder. Fearfully, he looked up at the roiling storm clouds overhead. Swirling black, laced with orange and purple and dappled with shafts of golden sunlight, they seemed normal enough. And there wasn't any sign of precipitation, much less the tangy reek of a dreaded acid rain that could melt the flesh off a person in only a few minutes.

Dean had seen that happen once, and it was something he would never forget. He had made it safe into the wreck of a predark car, the metal roof and old glass windows offering more than enough protection from the deadly rain. But an old man had been caught in the downpour, and had never made it to the wreck alive. In the morning there was only his skeleton lying on the muddy ground, a bony hand outstretched, still trying to reach the door handle.

Shaking off the unpleasant memory, Dean frowned as the thunder sounded once more, much louder this time. Blasting baron, that wasn't thunder, but horses!

Caught out in the open, he knew he wouldn't reach the safety of the foothills in time, so he drew his blaster and knife, and stood waiting for the riders to appear. They might be sec men from a ville, out hunting muties, or slavers trying to recapture an escaped prisoner, or worse, cannies looking for fresh meat for the stew pot.

Grimly, Dean mentally prepared himself to take his own life rather than be taken prisoner and ritually stripped of his skin, then consumed alive by the demented throwbacks. Even barbs treated captives better than that, though not by much.

Just then, a large number of horses galloped over the horizon, the riders bent low in the saddles. Instantly, one of them shouted something, and the entire group changed direction, to head straight toward Dean.

Controlling his breathing so as not to appear frightened, he allowed the riders to come to him. He had five, mebbe six seconds to gauge who these folks were before the confrontation. In life and death, timing was everything.

The riders seemed to be norms, not muties, and there were only men, no women in sight. That wasn't good or bad. The horses appeared to be in fine shape, not underfed or overly whipped, which meant the riders weren't fools. However, their clothing was scraggly and heavily patched, with a wild mismatch of predark fabric, fur and what looked like tent canvas, as if the men had been scavenging through the ruins of some predark city, taking whatever they could find. Only a few of them wore boots. Most were wearing wraparounds, thick animal fur held in place with wide leather straps. It was the kind of clothing Dean would have expected to see barbs wearing.

Or clever folks pretending to be barbs, he thought, which might be the case, as every rider had a longblaster in a gun boot alongside his saddle, and was carrying another slung across his back. They were dressed like outcasts, but armed better than most sec men in a ville. The odd mixture made Dean suspicious of the group, and just for a second he wished that he had made a dash back to the river.

As the pack drew near, he raised his blaster and fired a round into the air both to catch their attention and let them know he had live brass. A lot of people carried empty blasters, and tried to avoid fights through sheer intimidation. Sometimes it worked and sometimes it made you a passenger on the last train west.

Reining in his chestnut stallion, a tall man stopped a dozen or so yards away, and the rest of the ragged group came to a halt close behind. Dean grunted at the display. There was no doubt who was in charge.

The leader was a thin man of mixed Asian descent, his skin faintly golden, but his face heavy with black stubble. He was wearing a black knit cap and buckskin shirt, and had numerous weapons—a Walther PPK .38 in a shoulder holster, an AK-47 slung across his back, and what looked like a Remington shotgun tucked into the boot near his saddle. There were a lot of AK-47 assault rifles in the group, and a few men with 40 mm gren launchers attached. All looked to be in fairly good condition.

"Morning," the skinny man said, resting an arm on the pommel of his saddle. "What are you doing this far from Donner ville?"

Instantly, the gesture put Dean on the alert. It seemed casual, but effectively hid the newcomer's gun hand from observation. These folks like tricks too damn much to be anything but coldhearts, he reasoned, and swiftly changed his tactics.

"Looking for you," he lied, trying to sound like his father. "The name's Cawdor, Dean Cawdor, and I want to join the gang." That statement caused an expected ripple of smirks and snorts.

"Looking for us, way out here, on foot?" the leader asked skeptically, shifting slightly in the saddle.

Sheathing the knife and blaster, Dean shrugged. "Lost my woman, both horses and my best dog, trying to cross that rad-blasted river." Then he patted the checkered grip of the Browning. "Still got my blaster, though. Held on to that like a cross-legged virgin in a gaudy house."

Now the group of coldhearts guffawed, and Dean felt some of the tension ease. It was just like his father had always said—make the other fellow laugh and you're halfway done making a deal.

"Mighty bad luck," the leader drawled, removing his arm from the pommel.

"Sounds more like mutie shit to me," snarled a fat man with a cloth tied around his head in lieu of a hat. He was wearing one ragged shirt over another, clearly too stupe, or lazy, to sew on a patch, and around his throat was a necklace of dried ears, some from norms, a few from muties.

"Wasn't talking to you, tubby," Dean said, not even glancing at the corpulent rider. "So, you them, or not?"

"Them?" the skinny man asked, feigning innocence.

"The coldhearts that have been hounding Donner," Dean continued, struggling to recall the name of the ville they had just mentioned. "I've had enough of the baron, and wanna join." Then he tilted his head as if challenging them to give the correct answer.

Studying the distant foothills and weedy fields as if expecting an ambush of ville sec men, the skinny man said nothing for a few moments. "Yeah, we're them," he said at last. "I'm Wu-Chen Camarillo, and this is my gang, the Stone Angels."

"The Stone Angels," Dean repeated without inflection

"Nuking A! And we rule this fragging valley from Glass Lake to the Iron Mountains!" a bucktoothed man added fiercely, a scarred hand resting on a throwing hatchet sheathed on his thigh.

An old friend named Jak had taught Dean about that

particular weapon, and he now marked the short man as one of the most dangerous in the group. It took a long time to learn how to control the unwieldy weapon, which meant the coldheart had a lot of patience and determination. That was a powerful combination.

As the rest of the coldhearts muttered their agreement to the declaration, Dean nodded along, as if it were a well-known fact, even though he had never heard of the gang before. One blaster against fifty made for triple-bad odds. His only real weapon here was intelligence. He hoped that would be enough to survive.

"Yeah, so I heard," he said. "Wasn't interested in joining up with a bunch of gleebs."

That caused more smiles from the riders. Clearly, they had nothing to fear from one youth, and if he did want to join, well, they always needed fresh boots in the saddles.

"What was your name again?" Camarillo asked, a touch of humor slightly warming the demand.

"Look at them clothes and hair!" The fat man chortled. "Mud Puppy, his name be Mud Puppy!"

"Shut up, Bert," Camarillo snapped. The youth was barely old enough to grow fuzz on his face, yet he stood facing the Angels without the slightest sign of fear. If nothing else, the kid had iron, and that was always in short supply in this line of work. Too many gleebs thought a blaster made a person brave. But a blaster was just a tool, nothing more. Just a tool, like a hammer or a shovel. It was a cold heart that made you truly dangerous.

"Mud Puppy. Funny, that's exactly what your mother called me," Dean said in a smooth, even tone, "just before I parked my tool in her drawer and we fucked in the gaudy house that employed her."

The crowd of coldhearts laughed uproariously at the joke, and even Camarillo smirked, but Bert looked as if he were going to explode.

Reaching into a pocket, Dean withdrew an empty brass shell. "Here. I forgot to pay for her services," he said, flipping the valueless shell toward the red-faced man. "Keep the change."

"Mutie-loving freak! Gonna chill you twice for that!" Bert roared, sliding out of the saddle while drawing a monstrous remade Colt .45 revolver.

As the man landed on the ground, Dean drew and fired the Browning in a single motion. Startled, Bert flinched as his handblaster went spinning away from his grip to land in the weeds. Immediately, the cicadas went silent, and there was only the soft murmur of the river mixing with the gentle snorting of the impatient horses.

"If you didn't have that blaster…" Bert muttered, rubbing his stinging hand.

"I would still have taken you," Dean said, trying to sound bored. "Mr. Camarillo, you want this feeb alive, or not?"

"That's your choice," Camarillo replied, swinging around the AK-47 and working the arming bolt. "But if you want to ride with us, then you gotta chill him without blaster or blade."

Weighing his options, Dean said nothing as the rest of the coldhearts pulled out blasters. He had upped the odds, and now the numbers were falling. Handle this wrong, and the next thing he saw would be an eternity of dirt. Warily, he gauged the adult as twice his size, and easily a hundred pounds heavier. Some of it was obviously fat, but there had to be a lot of muscle, too, as the bastard still moved with the speed of a jungle cat. Big and fast, he'd be a formidable opponent even to somebody with a blaster. Dean wondered if this was this some sort of a test to join the gang, just to see if he had any iron in his guts. Unfortunately, there was only one way to be sure.

"Fair enough," he said, clicking on the safety and tossing aside the blaster, then the bowie knife.

The weapons were still in the air when Bert charged, his huge arms spread wide to prevent the youth from escaping.

For the moment, Dean did nothing.

"Don't get too much blood on his boots!" a laughing coldheart added, cradling a lever-action Winchester. "They look just my size!"

"I want that knife," the ugly coldheart added, sucking on his oversize teeth.

Roaring in victory, Bert closed on Dean, but at the very last second, the young Cawdor ducked out of the way and savagely drove the toe of his combat boot into the groin of his attacker. Gasping in pain, Bert staggered, then unexpectedly pulled a machete from behind his back.

Startled, Dean threw himself backward. Bert almost gutted him anyway, the blade slicing open his damp shirt and leaving a bloody gouge across his chest. Ignoring the minor pain, Dean tried to rush the man and grab his arm, but Bert fended him off, delivering two more slashes across the youth's chest.

"Thought this…was supposed…to be a fair fight," Dean panted, frantically dodging to the left, then the right.

"That wouldn't tell me anything about how good you are, now, would it?" Camarillo replied, tracking the combatants with the fluted barrel of the deadly Kalasnikov.

Constantly shifting about, Bert was swinging the machete as if swatting flies, wild and unpredictable. Ducking out of the way again, Dean bent low, then grabbed a handful of dirt and threw it at the fat man, but deliberately missing. As Bert easily dodged the clumsy attempt to blind him, Dean dived into the cloud and came out with the bowie knife. Spinning, he thrust the point of the blade forward, and Bert backed off with blood on his dirty cheek.

"That be cheating!" the bucktoothed man cried, hefting the throwing hatchet.

"Cheating would have been going for the blaster," Camarillo said, resting the AK-47 rapidfire on his shoulder. "Blade against blade is a fair fight." Then he added, "If that hatchet grows wings, Hannigan, you'll be the first one chilled."

Scowling darkly, Hannigan gave no reply, but his hate-filled gaze never left the frantically moving youth.

Thrusting and lounging, Dean tried to slash the fat man in the belly, or the armpit. Steel slammed into steel with an audible clang as the big knife met the predark machete. The two combatants stood locked together for a long moment, then Bert spit into Dean's face, and the youth brutally swung the knife downward, the razor-sharp blade slicing off several pudgy fingers. Shrieking in pain, Bert dropped the machete and backed away, trying to staunch the geyser of life with his other hand.

Flipping the bowie into the air, Dean caught the blood-streaked blade and threw it. Turning over once, the knife slammed into the fat man's chest, going all the way into the guard. Staggering, Bert gasped and wheezed, crimson spurting from his ruined hand.

"End it," a short coldheart commanded, working the lever action of his Winchester longblaster.

Saying nothing, Dean looked at Camarillo.

"Do as you're told, boot," the chief coldheart ordered.

Dean grunted at the term. Boot as in boot camp. Military slang for a new recruit. He was in. Retrieving the Browning, he inspected the blaster to make sure it was undamaged. Then, from fifty feet, he aimed and fired, putting a single round into the left temple of the floundering Bert. The fat man jerked from the impact of the 9 mm Parabellum round, then dropped onto the churned grass, trembled and went still forever.

Dean was shaken at the coldblooded chilling, but it was survival, plain and simple.

Holstering his blaster, he then retrieved the bowie knife and wisely cleaned it on the grass, instead of using the shirt of the corpse as he usually would have done. A wise man only insulted people he planned on chilling, and he needed the cooperation of these coldhearts for a little while to help him stay alive.

At least until I can get someplace where I can try to build a life, Dean added privately.

"Bert was a friend of mine," Hannigan said through gritted teeth, his fist clenched on the shaft of the hatchet.

"Get better friends," Dean growled, sheathing the

bowie. "Anybody want his stuff, help yourself, blaster included. The clothes are too big, and I have a better knife."

Greedily, a couple of the coldhearts glanced at their chief. Camarillo gave a nod, and they slid off their horses to start eagerly looting the warm corpse.

Going over to the riderless horse, Dean briefly inspected the mare and found her to be in decent shape, just desperately in need of a good curry.

"Easy, girl, easy," he whispered, patting the muscular neck of the animal to try to calm her. Horses didn't like the smell of blood, and he needed the goodwill of the animal even more than he did that of the coldhearts. Still recovering from his ordeal in the river, he was exhausted from the short fight, and way too close to falling over. But he had to appear strong in front of the others. Any weakness now would result in an endless series of challenges, and eventually he would tangle with somebody faster. Or get a knife in the back, which he considered to be far more likely.

Finished with their grisly task, the two coldhearts returned to their horses carrying various personal items from the dead Bert, including the horrid necklace of dried ears.

Dean noticed that a lot of the coldhearts wore similar decorations—ears, tongues, fingers.

"I owe ya one, boot," a scraggly coldheart gushed, tucking away his new possessions. "The name's Natters."

"No prob," Dean replied casually.

The other coldheart said nothing, then gave an open-mouthed grin showing that he lacked a tongue.

"He's McGinty," Natters said with a jerk of his thumb. "Lost his tongue in a bar fight. Nobody seems to know why or how."

"And he ain't talking," Dean finished, climbing into the saddle. He tried not to flinch, feeling the residual warmth of the prior owner. Bert may have been a fat bastard, but he had come closer to acing him than anybody else before.

"What are your orders, sir?" Dean asked, checking the longblaster tucked into the gun boot. Incredibly, it proved to be a remade BAR, Browning Automatic Rifle. Suspiciously, he dropped the magazine. As expected, it was empty. No wonder Bert had used a machete.

"Stay close, boot, and follow us back to camp," Camarillo stated, shaking the reins of his horse. "You fall behind, and I'll personally put lead in your head!"

"Then I get what's left." Hannigan chuckled, patting the edged weapon at his hip.

"Bring a blaster, gleeb," Dean growled in return, kicking his horse into a gallop. "Better yet, bring a dozen to make it a fair fight."

Narrowing his eyes, Hannigan frowned at that, then slowly smiled, displaying his oversize, crooked teeth. "Deal," he whispered, the word barely discernable over the pounding hooves.

As the Stone Angels moved across the wide grassy field, Dean settled into the steady rocking motion of a seasoned rider, and began to wonder exactly how long he might have to stay before he would finally be able to slip away from these people.

Chapter One

Scrambling over the bank of a dried river, six people hastily pelted across the uneven ground, their hands frantically reloading blasters. Their clothing was torn and dirty, their faces gaunt from hunger and exhaustion.

Suddenly, a weird sound came from the riverbed, the noise making them spin fast just as a glowing green mist appeared along the bank.

"Fireblast, here it comes again!" Ryan Cawdor shouted, triggering his longblaster a fast three times.

Instantly, his companions cut loose with a thundering cacophony of weapons. Gray and black smoke billowed from the blazing gun barrels, spent brass flying in every direction.

Rising over the earthen bank, the green mist flowed along the loose sand and rocks, leaving behind a glassy streak of fused ground. Deep within the incandescent fog, something unseen gave voice once more to a high-pitched howl full of rage, pain and unbridled hate.

"What in nuking hell does it take to stop that thing?" J. B. Dix snarled, yanking out the spent magazine from his Uzi machine pistol and shoving in a fresh one. Jerking the arming bolt, he sent another long burst of 9 mm rounds into the cloud. Most of the steel-jacketed lead simply flew out the other side to pepper a low sand dune.

"Hard stop what not see," Jak Lauren muttered, sending off three booming rounds from a massive .357 Magnum Colt Python.

"Not sure we want to see it!" Dr. Mildred Weyth countered, squeezing off a single .38 round from her Czech ZKR target pistol.

"Stinking howler," Jak growled, firing again.

Instantly, the howler inside the billowing cloud doubled the volume of its inhuman keen, and the companions painfully winced at the sonic assault.

"Don't know if that hurt it or just made the mutie angry," Krysty Worth said, dumping out the spent brass from her hammerless Smith & Wesson Model 640 revolver. Pocketing the casings, she dug into another pocket of her bearskin coat and started thumbing in fresh cartridges.

As the creature inside the green cloud flowed by a stand of cacti, the plants began to visibly wither, and by the time the howler was past, they were only shriveled lumps on the fused sand, thin tendrils of smoke rising from the scorched remains.

"Egad, the accursed abomination is like some Dantean monster from the very depths of inferno!" Dr. Theophilus Algernon Tanner announced in a stentorian bass. Thumbing back the hammer on a massive single-action LeMat revolver, the tall man aimed carefully, then stroked the trigger. The huge Civil War-era weapon boomed louder than field artillery, black smoke vomited from the pitted muzzle and a lance of flame extended for almost a foot.

As the colossal miniball hummed through the air to vanish into the cloud, the howler actually moaned even louder, but whether in pain from a hit or pleasure from a miss, there was no way of knowing.

"Shoot it again, Doc," Ryan commanded, shoving another magazine of 7.62 mm rounds into the open breech of the Steyr SSG longblaster. "At the very least, your handblaster slows the bastard thing down!"

"That was my last load, my dear Ryan," Doc replied, his hands already moving in the complex procedure of purging the chambers of the revolver clean as a prelude to packing in fresh black powder, lead and wadding.

"Then we better start using boot leather!" J.B. shouted, grabbing his fedora and turning tail to start a hasty retreat.

After reloading their own weapons, the companions followed suit, running a hundred feet, only to turn and fire, then run again. For the past day they had been fleeing from the unstoppable mutie. They were low on brass and close to exhaustion, but with their wag destroyed there was no other choice. Run, fight, and run again, to survive for a couple more minutes, another precious few yards. But they could do that for only so long. Soon the companions would fall, and be aced. It was just a matter of time.

Ever since the howler had erupted from a predark iron mine to set their wag on fire with a single touch, the companions had been fighting a losing battle, trying desperately to find some way to trap the thing, block its advance or divert it by sending it after slower prey. There should have been a lot of stickies in this region of the Deathlands, and the humanoid muties were oddly attracted to explosions, especially the sounds of blasters firing. The fight should have summoned an army of the things. But so far there had been no sign of stickies, only the endless desert sands.

Charging between two large dunes, Ryan saw the wreckage of some ancient machinery partially buried in the loose sand. Car, truck, helicopter, submarine, he didn't care. It was made of metal, and the location was perfect, which gave them a fighting chance at life.

"Rig it!" he commanded, dropping to a knee to steady his shaking hands.

"Last one!" J.B. countered, pulling a half stick of dynamite from the munitions bag slung at his side.

"No choice!" Ryan yelled, as he looked through the low-power telescopic sights of the Steyr sniper rifle. The howler was tight on their path, never wavering or detouring. That almost made the one-eyed man smile. Stupidity was its own reward.

While the rest of the companions sagged against the shifting sands for a blessed moment of rest, J.B. wearily got to work planting the explosive charge inside the rusted remains of the machine. Unfortunately, his hands shook with fatigue, and he kept dropping loose items. With a snarl, he slapped himself hard across the face, the smacks almost sounding like blasterfire. The pain banished the fog from his mind, and he quickly went back to work. But even as he did, tendrils of sleep began to creep once more through his brain, leeching away his thoughts and offering the sweet release of slumber.

Holding his breath to help steady his aim, Ryan peered through the telescopic sight, adjusted for the wind, then put three rounds smack through the middle of the cloud. There were no visible results. The howler didn't move faster or slower.

However, as Ryan forced himself to stand, he was more than satisfied. The expenditure of brass had been expensive, but worthwhile if it kept the bastard thing coming this way. One of the very first lessons he had ever learned from his old teacher, the Trader, was to never be predictable in a fight. That was the path to oblivion.

"Done," J.B. stated, smoothing out the sand over the trap. He tried to get back up, but stumbled, his strength failing.

Without comment, Mildred grabbed him by an arm, and Krysty took the other to lend some assistance. He nodded in thanks and started shuffling away, searching through the pockets of his battered jacket for anything edible.

Stepping close, Doc offered a piece of smoked fish. J.B. took it with a grunt and shoved the morsel into his mouth. The previous day the delicious smoked salmon had been a very special treat, a gift from the grateful baron who had traded them a functioning wag for the life of his youngest wife, rescued from a band of cannies. Now it was only food, consumed in a swallow and forgotten.

As the companions hurried away from the sand dunes, Jak glanced behind and saw the howler pause before entering the narrow passage. Had it seen J.B. lay the trap? Okay then, time to up the ante. Jerking his hand, the young man caught a leaf-bladed throwing knife as it slipped out of the sleeve of his camou jacket. With an underhand gesture, he sent the blade flying, and heard a solid thump as it hit something inside the swirling cloud.

Instantly, the mutie moved forward once more, and there came the soft snap of breaking string.

"Now!" J.B. yelled, throwing himself to the ground.

A split second later, a bright flash of light washed over the area, and a deafening thunderclap shook the desert. Already in motion, the companions hit the ground half a heartbeat before a hissing barrage of shrapnel passed over their heads. Giving a low grunt of pain, Doc slapped a hand to his shoulder, where the fabric of his coat was soon stained red.

"Please, oh dear God…" Mildred whispered, almost afraid to look backward. Then she cursed bitterly as a greenish light pulsed through the swirling smoke and sand, still moving onward.

"Begone, foul Visigoth!" Doc bellowed, awkwardly firing the LeMat twice with his left hand, his right clenching the wound.

The first miniball hit sand, but the second ricocheted off something metallic, making the howler expand the cloud in a protective gesture.

Startled, Ryan narrowed his eyes in amazement. The cloud could change size? That was a protective gesture, which meant there was something in the world that the nuking thing feared. He had no idea what that might be, but the simple fact that the mutie had any kind of a mortal weakness gave him new hope.

"How far go?" Jak muttered, wiping the sleeve of his jacket across his sweaty forehead. A true albino, the youth was normally pale as new snow, but now he was nearly pink, flushed from the sheer effort of endlessly putting one boot in front of the other.

"Half mile mebbe," J.B. replied in a throaty growl, rising stiffly from the ground.

"W-we're n-not gonna make it…." Mildred sighed, her shoulders sagging.

Grabbing the physician by the arm, Ryan spun her and slapped her across the face. Mildred jerked back from the stinging blow, and placed a hand on her cheek.

"We're gonna make it if I gotta kick your ass all the way!" Ryan snarled, his chest heaving. "Now move!"

Common sense overwhelmed her feelings of rage, and Mildred mutely obeyed, shuffling away from the man as if he had began to issue a green cloud himself.

"Tough love," J.B. said, bumping her with a hip. "Next time, I'll slap you. Then you can do me."

"D-deal," Mildred said with a weak laugh, a touch of hysteria creeping into her raspy voice.

Back in her own time period, the physician would have had access to dozens of chemicals that could have kept the companions mentally alert and physically strong for days. But these blighted days, her medical kit consisted of only what she could find in the ruins of decaying hospitals and veterinary clinics, along with whatever she could cobble together: upholstery needles to sew wounds shut, nylon fishing line as sutures, raw alcohol to clean wounds, razor blades instead of scalpels, and leather straps for tourniquets. There were a few precious drugs hidden among her meager supplies, but they were all soporifics, designed to put patients to sleep so that they could stand the terrible pain of meatball surgery, nothing that would keep the companions awake.

Heat lightning crackled across the stormy sky as they

forced themselves to keep moving. The sand was starting to become mixed with dark earth and rocks, clearly indicating that they were coming out of the desert. That was a good sign, and it put some much needed strength into their heavy legs, their shuffle becoming a brisk walk. But the surge quickly faded, and they returned to a slow stagger, pausing only to fire the occasional round at the howler.

"Any more plas-ex?" Ryan asked hopefully, levering a fresh round into the Steyr. Five more rounds, and he would have to start using his 9 mm SIG-Sauer pistol, which had much less range.

"All gone. Used most of it getting us away from this thing in that box canyon," J.B. answered grimly, his canvas munition bag hanging unnaturally flat at his side. "I'm down to two homie pipe bombs, some firecrackers, a couple of road flares and one, count it, one Molotov that I'm saving for an emergency."

"And this does not qualify, sir?" Doc demanded, askance.

"Not yet," Jak snorted, unscrewing the cap on a canteen to take a fast drink. He offered it to the others, but there were no takers.

Pausing at the top of the dune, Ryan saw that it abruptly ended at a rocky cliff that overhung a large pool of water. Lush green bushes grew in abundance along its mossy banks, along with a couple of juniper trees, and schools of rainbow-colored fish were darting about in the clear shallows. Suspiciously, Ryan checked the rad counter on his shirt, but it remained silent. Fireblast! He had hoped it might be a nuke crater and the rads might be enough to fry the howler. Then he grinned. However, mebbe he still could turn the water to their advantage.

"My dear Ryan, I hope you are not thinking what I think you are thinking," Doc rumbled, sending two more booming miniballs into the misty howler.

"It's only fifty feet or so," Ryan guessed, moving closer to the edge of the cliff.

"That should be enough!" Krysty said unconvincingly, thumbing her last three rounds into the revolver. The cylinder closed with a hollow click.

"Okay, I'll give us some cover," J.B. said, pulling out the Molotov and a butane lighter. "Everybody, get ready to move!"

As the howler started up the dune, the companions cut loose with their blasters, the sheer barrage of hot lead holding the indomitable creature at bay for a few precious moments.

Quickly setting fire to the oily rag tied around the neck of the whiskey bottle, J.B. then dashed it on the rocky soil directly in front of the mutie. As the fireball whoofed into existence, the companions turned and jumped.

The fall was short and they hit the water hard, their shoes and boots actually bumping the bottom of the pond. Bitter cold engulfed them, returning a semblance of clarity to their minds even as it stole some of the strength from their bodies.

Kicking hard, Ryan swam back to the surface and stroked for the nearby shore. Dripping wet, he and his companions moved quickly into the bushes and ducked. A few seconds later, a green cloud appeared atop the cliff. The howler moaned even louder than before, and incredibly, moved away, heading back down the dune.

"Thank Gaia, it worked," Krysty whispered, allowing herself to relax for the first time in a day.

"And we sure needed the bath." Mildred chuckled briefly.

"Hey, where blaster?" Jak asked, checking his empty holster, then looking about on the spongy moss.

"Over there in the shallows, near the lily pads," Ryan said, pointing.

Frowning, the young man dropped to his stomach and began to crawl to the pond, trying to stay as concealed as possible.

"Speaking of which, it seems that I am unarmed once more," Doc muttered, drawing the LeMat, only to slam it back into the holster at his side. Wet black powder was dribbling out of the weapon like ebony blood. The antique blaster would be completely useless until it was thoroughly dried and painstakingly reloaded.

"Here ya go," J.B. said, sliding a scattergun off his back and tossing it over.

Making the catch, Doc checked to make sure the pump-action 12-gauge was fully loaded. At close range the S&W M-4000 could open a person like a tin can. Although what, if anything, the barrage of lead pellets would do to a howler was anybody's guess. However, the scattergun had a much greater range than the sword hidden inside his ebony walking stick.

Just then, the green cloud returned to the little cliff and went straight over the edge to plummet into the pool. It hit with a large splash, and the plants along the bottom of the cliff began to wither and die.

"Run, Jak, it's back!" Mildred yelled, through cupped hands.

Swinging up the longblaster, Ryan started putting 7.62 mm rounds into the cloud until he ran out. Slinging the Steyr, he drew his SIG-Sauer and began hammering the howler just above the surface of the pond. Under the water, some sort of a physical form was visible, more insectlike than norm, along with several mismatched legs, as if the creature had been built from a dozen different bodies.

At the first shot, Jak rose from the water with the Magnum in his grip and fired twice at the mutie, before turning to wade toward shore.

Heading for the pale norm, the howler moved through the pool, the water becoming dull and murky as hundreds of fish rose lifeless to the surface, pale blood oozing from their gills.

"Move fast, my friend!" Doc bellowed, charging out of the bushes to trigger the scattergun at the cloud.

As Jak reached the shore, he slipped in the mud. Reaching out, Doc started to grab the young man by the collar of his leather jacket, then withdrew his hand, unsure what to do for a moment, especially as the collar was lined with razor blades.

"Get him out of the bastard water!" Ryan bellowed, over the gentle coughs of the silenced blaster in his fist.

Firing the scattergun with one hand, Doc thrust out his wounded arm. Floundering in the slippery mud, Jak grabbed the man's hand and just managed to make it onto the shore before an expanding ring of greenish water reached the bank. Instantly, the lily pads began to turn brown and the frogs went silent.

"Incoming!" J.B. shouted, lighting the fuse on a pipe bomb.

Moving with purpose, Jak and Doc sprinted into the bushes. Once they were clear, J.B. tossed the pipe bomb into the discolored water, then turned to join his fleeing companions.

As the howler approached the shore, the water erupted into a boiling geyser of flame, mud and dead fish. Violently thrown backward, the mutie was blown out of the pond, to smack against the rocky base of the cliff. The sandstone facade shattered, sending out cracks in every direction like earthen lightning bolts. The ever-present cloud began to thin as the howler slid back down into the water, and the glowing nimbus of greenish light faded away.

"John, you got him!" Mildred shouted, coming to a stop.

"Mebbe, but I'm not going nearer," J.B. said, adjusting his wire-rimmed glasses.

"Besides, I don't trust that bastard thing any farther than I can piss in the wind," Ryan growled, working the slide on his blaster to eject a misfired round.

"Distance doth make the heart grow fonder," Doc expounded, easing his right hand into the pocket of his sodden coat. "And my dear Jak, please allow me to apologize for not rendering more swift assistance."

"No prob," Jak replied, straightening the collar on his jacket making the deadly razor blades hidden among the feathers and random bits of metal jingle slightly. "How arm?"

"It has been better," Doc admitted, fumbling to reload the scattergun.

"Mildred can fix you up once we're able to stop running," Krysty said, taking the weapon from the wounded scholar. There was a row of spare cartridges sewn into loops along the strap. She eased one free and pulled down the pump to thumb the fat round into the breech on the bottom.

Just then, a low moan sounded from somewhere.

Lurching into action, the companions took flight, pelting through the bushes and shrubbery. In the distance was a proper forest of trees, pine, oak and white birch stretching to the horizon. But the woods was a two-edge blessing. It meant the companions were that much closer to their goal of safety, but going through the trees would also slow them significantly.

"I just hope the howler is chilled and not merely knocked out," Mildred grunted, holding on to her med kit while jumping over a fallen log.

The crumbling wood was alive with termites, and that triggered an old memory from high school biology class. A termite. That was what the howler vaguely resembled inside that bizarre cloud; it looked similar to the intermediate stage of development when a newly born termite briefly possessed both an endoskeleton and an exoskeleton. Bones inside and outside, with muscles anchored in each. Double protection.

My God, no wonder the thing was bulletproof, she realized in growing horror. In the intermediate stage, the insect was virtually unkillable, and a thousand times stronger. Increase the size of the insect from a quarter inch to nine feet tall, and the strength would be multiplied that much more. Bullets and grenades would be no more than minor annoyances to such an abomination.

The companions would need an antitank rocket, or even an implo gren, to have a chance of damaging the adamantine creature.

"Don't waste any more time shooting!" Mildred bellowed, redoubling her frantic speed. "Just run! Run for your motherfucking lives!"

It was her profanity more than anything else that spurred the rest of them to increase their speed, and they were almost at the trees when a greenish light began to pulse into being from the direction of the pond. Then came an inhuman moan, more of a growl this time, followed by the previous low keening.

"Sounds pissed," Jak muttered in an almost conversational tone.

But nobody replied, the rest of the companions saving their breath for the all-important task of leaving the area immediately. When they entered the woods, it took a precious moment for their sight to adjust, but they never stopped moving. They merely slowed a little until able to see clearly again, and then resumed full speed.

The going was tough, with low-hanging branches threatening to knock them unconscious, and exposed roots trying to trip them. But the companions raced on, knowing that death followed on their heels.

Never pausing to rest, the howler relentlessly continued after them through the forest, leaving behind a swatch of decaying trees, the bark turning black before peeling off the trunks. Squirrels and birds dropped lifeless from the crumbling branches, and the leaves fell in droves as if it was late autumn.

"Dark night, what I wouldn't give just now for a bazooka!" J.B. snarled.

"'A horse…a h-horse…m-my k-kingdom…f-for a horse,'" Doc wheezed, his face unnaturally pale and shiny with sweat. His right arm flopped loosely as he ran, the coat sleeve dark with blood.

Seeing his state of near exhaustion, Krysty made a hard decision and called upon Gaia, the Earth Mother, for additional strength, repeating a special mantra. Almost instantly an inhuman power surged through her body, and the woman no longer felt tired or weak. Renewed, she scooped up the much taller man as if he were a small child, and darted ahead of the others, disappearing into the shadows ahead.

"May God grant they make it in time," Mildred whispered, straight from the heart. She knew that Krysty could summon amazing strength in times of extreme need, but it faded quickly, and afterward she would be as weak as a kitten.

"So let's buy them some time!" Ryan snarled, pausing to turn and fire his blaster a fast five times.

In the high branches of a pine tree, a nest exploded with the arrival of the 9 mm rounds. Through the broken twigs, yellowish egg yolk dribbled out as a mother stingwing rose into view screaming for revenge. Launching herself forward, the deadly mutie streaked through the tangle of branches to flash along the nettle-covered ground, searching for the unknown transgressor.

Keeping strategically mum, the companions ran on. But a few seconds later, the howler moaned loudly. Screaming in unbridled fury, the mutie abruptly changed direction and dived at the hellish cloud with both needle-sharp talons arched for a kill. Silently, it vanished into the glowing fog, and never came out again.

"Son bitch ate stingwing. And that was a big one!" Jak gasped in disbelief, glancing over a shoulder.

The trees unexpectedly thinned to reveal an irregular plain of dark crystalline material that gently sloped away. Fireblast, Ryan thought, that's a nuke crater!

"This...isn't on...my map," J.B. huffed, barely able to keep abreast of the others.

"Oh, yes, it is!" Mildred yelled in delight, looking far ahead.

A squat black structure appeared at the bottom of the glass bowl, the satiny smooth metal completely unscratched by the nuke strike from a hundred years ago. It looked to be a redoubt, an underground fortress designed to withstand even a direct strike from a thermonuclear weapon. Lying near a titanic door were two tiny figures, one with flame-red hair and the other with longish silvery locks. Neither was moving.

Glancing at his rad counter, Ryan started down the slippery incline. He nearly fell twice, even his U.S. Army combat boots having trouble finding purchase on the smooth fused earth. Then the companions grabbed one another by the arm and began to glide along like ice-skaters, helping to keep each other moving. It was touch and go in a couple areas, but they finally reached the bottom of the crater.

Scrambling across the glassy surface, Ryan went straight to the blast door. He found a small keypad set into the wall beside the entrance, and slowly tapped in the access code. The one-eyed man breathed a sigh of relief as the colossal door began to ponderously move aside.

But as if on cue, the glowing mist appeared on the slope and began to descend rapidly.

"Here comes," Jak announced, hefting his blaster.

"Screw it, help me with Doc!" Mildred commanded, struggling to hoist the limp scholar over her shoulder.

Reluctantly holstering his piece, Jak moved to lend some assistance, while Ryan simply lifted the supine Krysty in his powerful arms and stood impatiently near the slowly opening door. Live or get chilled; it was all just a matter of timing.

"I've got your back," J.B. stated, pulling out the last pipe bomb, then flicking alive a butane lighter.

Licking dry lips, Ryan wanted to say something to his old friend, but nothing came to mind.

When the crack between the door and the wall was just barely large enough, Ryan roughly shoved Krysty through, then squeezed inside himself, ripping his shirt and losing some skin in the process. Jak went through next, with less damage, and Mildred easily passed him Doc, then followed. Clean air blew from a wall vent. The interior was brightly illuminated by clear fluorescent lights set into the high ceiling.

With a dull boom, the blast door finished opening completely, paused, then began to slowly close once more.

"Come on, John!" Mildred pleaded, watching as the howler reached the bottom of the slope and came directly their way. Somehow, it seemed larger now, and ever faster than before. Then the physician realized that it was merely a fear-induced panic that was altering her senses. Not that it really mattered. Only a moron wouldn't be scared shitless in this situation!

"Not yet, Millie," J.B. answered, biting the fuse on the pipe bomb and leaving only a nubbin.

The disturbing keen of the howler echoed across the irregular expanse of fused earth, making it sound as if a dozen of the creatures were present, and the greenish glow of the cloud reflected off every shiny surface, creating a scintillating display of emerald flashes.

The overall effect was hypnotic, as he lit the tiny fuse and rolled the explosive toward the mutie, J.B. wondered if that was a deliberate ploy of the creature.

Undaunted, the howler flowed over the pipe bomb, which reappeared behind the creature, completely undamaged, the smoldering fuse extinguished a hair away from the lead cap.

"Son of a mutie bitch!" J.B. snarled, stepping back into the mouth of the access tunnel. Swinging up the Uzi, he emptied the blaster into the glass just in front of the howler, sending a spray of broken shards into the cloud.

Appearing alongside him, Ryan, Mildred and Jak opened fire with their blasters, hammering the approaching howler as the massive door continued its slow progress.

Out of brass, Jak started throwing knives into the cloud.

When her ZKR target pistol clicked empty, Mildred backed away. As the SIG-Sauer ran out, Ryan dropped the blaster to grab the S&W M-4000 from alongside Doc. Pumping the choke on the scattergun, Ryan chambered a 12-gauge cartridge and thrust the barrel past his friends to discharge the weapon inside the green cloud. The muzzle-blast of the scattergun sounded oddly muffled, but the howler actually stepped backward as the blast door slid past them to close.

But at the very last second, the writhing tip of a glowing tentacle stabbed through the ever-narrowing opening. With a living being blocking the way, the door automatically paused, then began to rumble open once more.

Chapter Two

Snarling a curse, Ryan triggered the scattergun at the limb, doing no visible damage. Then J.B. lunged forward to attack with a sizzling road flare, and the mutie quickly retreated. However, the blast doors were already in motion.

Rushing to the internal keypad, Jak punched in the access code to try to stop the process. Sometimes that worked, but this time there was no result, and the armored portal continued to open.

On the floor, Doc feebly twitched, and his ebony sword stick rolled over to Jak. The albino teen snatched it up and twisted the silver lion's-head grip to extract a length of shining Spanish steel. As the glowing cloud inched closer, he wildly slashed through the allotropic mist, going for the head, while J.B. did the same with the road flare, much lower. The howler voiced strong displeasure at the attacks, and something shifted about inside the impossible mist, never ceasing its effort to get closer and gain entry.

Inexorably slow, the blast doors finished their programmed journey inside the wall, then once more started across the twenty-foot span to cycle shut.

Finding his pockets empty of brass, Ryan drew his panga, the curved blade gleaming brightly in the fluorescent lights.

"Mildred, drag Krysty and Doc to the elevator!" he snarled, thrusting and jabbing at the terrible mutie. "If we're not there in five, or you see green, get in the mat-trans and jump without us!"

Shocked at the very idea of leaving the group, Mildred started to object, then reluctantly saw the wisdom of the heroic act. If the companions were separated, but still alive, there was always a slim chance of them finding each other someday.

"John, I love you!" she shouted, taking Doc and Krysty by the collars of their jackets.

"Heaven or hell, Millie, I'll see ya there!" J.B. yelled over a shoulder, igniting a second flare with the dying flame of the first.

His heart beating wildly, Ryan started to add something for Krysty, but there was no need for words, and she wouldn't hear him anyway. The two of them were more than lovers and friends, they were soul mates, and he would find Krysty again.

That is, Ryan thought grimly, if I'm still alive in thirty seconds!

As the stocky physician hauled the unconscious bodies around the first turn of the zigzagging tunnel, the howler had to have noticed the departure, and forcibly advanced, uncaring of any damage it might have been receiving from the flame and steel. When the greenish cloud got closer, the three men guarding the door began to feel ill, dizzy and disoriented, their sweaty skin prickly painfully.

"You're not getting in!" Ryan bellowed defiantly, ramming the long barrel of the Steyr into the cloud. He hit something hard, and his hands instantly felt as if they were on fire. A wave of incredible pain rushed up both his arms, stealing the last of his flagging strength. Knife and longblaster tumbled to the floor, and Ryan reluctantly retreated, fighting against the agony racking his exhausted body. His stomach heaved, his vision blurred and he crumpled to the floor, still trying to rise and rejoin the fight.

After kicking the panga back to the trembling man, Jak swung his leg around to slash a sideways kick at the unseen thing inside the cloud. There was a crack as the steel-reinforced toe of his Army boot contacted something breakable, and the howler cut loose with a strident wail that told of serious damage.

"The sides!" J.B. shouted in a burst of sudden understanding. "Dark night, the rad-blasted thing is only armored in front! We gotta hit it from the sides!"

But he was speaking to himself. A shuddering Jak was on the floor, using the sword to frantically hack at the laces of his boot. Half of it was dead white, the military leather crumbling away to reveal the steel support inside, the metal heavily corroded and dissolving.

Torn for a moment between helping his friend and keeping up the defense, J.B. wavered, and the howler slipped into the redoubt.

However, just as the mutie crossed the threshold, the overhead lights instantly changed from a pleasing blue-white to a flashing dark red, and a Klaxon began to sound somewhere deep inside the subterranean fortress. Unexpectedly, dozens of small vents snapped open in the smooth walls, and thick columns of white foam blasted out to slam into the howler. In perfect synchronization, additional vents opened in the floor and hissing torrents of superheated steam exploded forth.

Steadily moving back and forth, the sweeping cascades of foam and steam bodily forced the determined howler back outside, and sent the glowing cloud tumbling along the glassy floor of the ancient bomb crater.

Rigidly, the redoubt maintained the double assault, concentrating on the narrowing opening of the blast door until it finally boomed shut and audibly locked.

Stunned beyond words, J.B. lowered his flare, and was trying to process what had just happened, when the foam and steam abruptly cut off. It was replaced with a medicinal-smelling orange gel that squirted all over the men from new wall vents.

Sputtering and coughing, Ryan awoke. The three companions struggled to get out of the way, but the gel followed along, drenching them thoroughly until every inch of each man's body was soaked. They tried not to get it in their eyes and mouths, but hit from every direction, they found no escape, and soon the gel was everywhere. Oddly, it didn't taste that bad, sort of like overly sweet orange juice, and inevitably some of it even went down their throats.

On and on, the deluge continued unabated, until the Klaxon finally stopped and the ceiling lights returned to their normal color. Then the gel turned off, and down from the ceiling came a gentle shower of soothing, lukewarm water. As the antiseptic gel was sluiced off their bodies, it sluggishly flowed along the floor, to vanish into gurgling drains hidden in the corners. In only a few minutes, the companions were clean again, and soaked to the skin.

"What that?" Jak demanded weakly, looking like a melting snowman. What remained of the bedraggled boot was still on his foot, but the material was no longer disintegrating.

"Musta been one of those antiradiation protocols that Millie theorized about," J.B. said with a weary laugh, casting aside the extinguished road flare.

"Guess so," Ryan muttered, feeling oddly refreshed from the strange cleansing. Actually, it made a lot of sense. The redoubts were designed to survive a nuke war. Mebbe the whitecoats had showed some smarts for once and included some autosystems to keep out anything too hot with rads.

"Never knew could do." Jak sighed, putting his back against the cool armarglas wall. Glancing down, he saw his foot and wiggled the toes. That had been close!

"There's tons of stuff we don't know about these places," J.B. replied, removing his streaked glasses. He tried to wipe them dry, but everything he wore was absolutely soaked, so he was reduced to trying to shake them clean, which accomplished nothing at all.

Just then they heard the sound of running boots. Pulling knives, the men braced for an attack. But it was Mildred who came into view around the corner, her ZKR in one hand and a crowbar in the other.

"Hey, Millie," J.B. said, lifting his chin in greeting.

"I heard the siren…." She sniffed at the strong smell of sweet oranges. "Now, where in the world did you find some antiradiation foam?"

"Gel," Ryan corrected wearily, tucking away the panga. "Came out of the ceiling."

"Protocols," Jak added, as if that explained everything.

"I see you had a close encounter of the third kind," Mildred said, noting his partially dissolved boot.

"Not aced," Jak replied with a philosophical shrug.

Moving closer, she cupped his face with both hands and checked his eyes, then put two fingers on the carotid artery in his throat. The pulse was good, as was his color, pale as it was. "You seem okay," she said hesitantly. "But if you have any stomach pains, or sudden hair loss, let me know right away."

Once more, Jak shrugged. If he ever got rad-poisoning, he was already carrying the only known cure. It was holstered at his hip.

"Where are the others?" Ryan asked, craning his neck to see behind the stocky woman. There was only empty corridor in sight.

"I shoved them into the elevator and sent it to the bottom floor," Mildred said, resting the crowbar on her shoulder. "I figured that even if the howler got inside, it wouldn't be intelligent enough to press the call button."

"Smart move," Ryan told her, rubbing his missing eye with a fist. He honestly couldn't recall ever being this tired before in his life and still be able to move. "Let's go join them. If we don't get some sleep soon, we're going to fall over."

"What about mutie?" Jak asked, looking at the blast doors.

"Sleep is more important," J.B. countered, fighting back a jaw-cracking yawn. "Dark night, right now we're so dead tired we can't even jump out of the redoubt! If we tried to use the mat-trans, the jump would probably ace us."

"Damn near does anyway," Ryan growled, starting forward, his combat boots squishing juicily.

Past the last turn of the zigzagging tunnel, the companions entered the parking garage of the redoubt, which housed several different types of vehicles. Everything was parked randomly, completely ignoring the neatly painted yellow lines on the smooth terrazzo floor, as if the staff had been racing to get inside the redoubt when skydark was about to hit. The companions scowled at the metallic chaos. Whatever had happened in those final moments of civilization had clearly come without much advance warning.

Several of the vehicles were smashed into one another, the windshields badly cracked and the concrete underneath badly discolored from the hundred-year-old fuel spill. There was a LAV-25 armored personnel carrier that had obviously been hit hard by something, the dense plating gashed to reveal the crushed engine.

Only a couple of large black sedans seemed to still be airtight. Grinning skeletons were slumped behind the wheels, their nylon shoulder holsters carrying the rusted remains of what had once been sleek blasters. In the backseats were more skeletons, the tatters of their neatly tailored military uniforms draped over bony shoulder blades. One skeleton had a severely cracked skull, and a burnished steel briefcase handcuffed to his wrist, a pitted Desert Eagle .50 blaster in a bony hand, the slide kicked back to show that it had been fired until the magazine cycled dry.

Annoyed, J.B. grunted at the sight. The poor bastard

had managed to fight his way into the redoubt, then got aced in a car crash. Sadly, the companions wouldn't be able to recover anything from that wag, or from any of the sedans. Each license plate bore a row of stars showing the vehicle was reserved purely for generals, which he knew from experience meant the sedans would be heavily armored, NBC class, proof against any form of attack.

"Think should do sweep?" Jak asked, as they headed down the corridor.

"No need," Ryan stated gruffly.

When they reached the elevator, the one-eyed man pressed the call button. It took two tries. "If there's anybody else in the redoubt, they would have heard the siren and shown up by now."

"True enough," Jak said. Then purely on impulse, he went to a nearby stack of fifty-five-gallon drums and clumsily rolled one over in front of the door as a crude stop. It never hurt to plan for the unlikely. Mildred had an old word for that, *paranoia*. But to him it was just plain common sense.

The companions had to wait only a few minutes, checking their meager assortment of weapons as they did so, before there was a musical ding and the elevator doors opened. Sprawled on the floor inside were Doc and Krysty. She was missing the belt from her pants. It was cinched around Doc's wounded arm as a makeshift tourniquet, a blood-streaked handkerchief sticking out the sides.

"Damn, you're fast," J.B. said with a strong note of pride in his voice.

"Had to be," Mildred replied, kneeling to check her

patients. Each was fine, just so deeply unconscious she felt she could have safely performed major surgery on them without the benefit of anesthesia.

As Jak and J.B. got comfortable on the hard metal floor, Ryan went to the controls and sent the elevator down again, but after only a few seconds of operation, flipped the emergency button, stopping them between floors. The alarm started to ring, and he disabled it with a thrust and twist of the panga into the controls. Done and done. Now if anybody wanted to reach the sleepers, they'd have to pry open the steel doors, or else come through the roof hatch. Either of which would make more than enough noise to wake the companions. He admitted this wasn't a perfect bolthole, merely the best available at the moment. Prepare for the worst, hope for the best.

As sleep began to claim him, Ryan remembered learning that sage bit of wisdom from his father, Baron Titus Cawdor, and then teaching it to his own son, Dean. He wondered if the boy was still alive. There wasn't a day that went by that he didn't think about his son, or wonder why he'd run off with Sharona after all they'd been through together. He hadn't even said goodbye. It had been about three years since he last saw Dean.

A boy could change a lot in that span of time, Ryan thought muzzily, sleep dragging him down into a warm darkness.

Moments later, the elevator was filled with the rhythmic noise of exhausted people snoring, then only the hushed sounds of gentle breathing.

Chapter Three

Dropping the Molotov off the ville wall, Dean Cawdor saw the glass bottle full of shine shatter on a steel hinge and splatter liquid fire across the complex array of ropes and pulleys used to haul the mammoth front gate closed. In only a few seconds, the burning ropes began to snap apart and the pulleys sagged, the main locking bar sliding away from the stout iron hoops set into the gate.

"Angels!" Dean bellowed through cupped hands. Then he quickly dropped flat as a hail of blasterfire tore through the empty space he had just occupied.

While a squad of sec men charged along the top of the wide stone wall, Dean rolled over to fire his Browning Hi-Power a fast five times. Four of the guards jerked, brains exploding out of the back of their skulls as the steel-jacketed .38 rounds cored through. The fifth guard staggered about blindly, a bloody furrow along her temple. As the unlucky woman started to walk off the wall, Dean shot her in the heart to mercifully prevent the her from getting gangbanged to death by the invading cadre of coldhearts.

From outside the ville, a sizzling red flare arched into the sky and gently exploded in a pyrotechnic display of colors.

A moment later, the unlocked wooden gate of

Alpharetta ville violently exploded as the rapidly accelerating steam truck, *Atomsmasher,* crashed through, its chugging engine visibly radiating waves of heat, the steam whistle screaming loudly.

"Angels!" Camarillo bellowed from inside the small control room, both hands operating the mechanisms.

Chorusing the rally cry, fifty armed coldhearts on horseback galloped through the splintery breech, their bodies lumpy from heavy canvas jackets lined with slabs of green wood.

Caught directly in the path of the huge steam truck, a dozen of the ville sec men went under the razor-sharp blades attached to the double row of thirty iron wheels, their high-pitched shrieks of unimaginable agony cut short.

Huffing and puffing, the *Atomsmasher* continued onward, crunching a muzzle-loading cannon, along with the group of sec men trying to aim the weapon. The brass barrel of the cannon visibly bent as it went under the colossal invading machine, the horrified people torn to pieces from the terrible spinning blades.

Reloading his blaster, Dean tried not to cringe at the horrible sight. They were falling like wheat before a crimson sickle.

Charging out of the stables, another crowd of people saw what happened, turned and fled, dropping their own crossbows, spears and zip guns.

Running along the wall, Dean turned his eyes away from the oncoming slaughter. Supposedly working as an advance spy for the Stone Angels, he had attempted to warn the locals of the coming attack. But the baron and sec chief hadn't believed the teenage outlander. The damn fools never did. They were always positive it was just some sort of trick to extract free brass from the ville arsenal.

Stupe bastards. I try to help every ville the Angels attack! Dean raged, reluctantly chilling a sec man struggling to load a crossbow. Why don't the triple-stupe barons ever listen to reason? If the locals could ace the gang, or at least Camarillo, then he would be free from the gang's odious control.

Dean had been riding with the Stone Angels for several months. He had hoped to slip away and head out on his own, but he had made a mistake—he had stopped Hannigan from cutting the throat of a newborn child that wouldn't stop crying. It was just bad luck that Camarillo had noticed the act of kindness. The coldheart boss had kept an eye on the youth from that point on. The prospects of getting away from the gang were greatly diminished. And Dean knew that should he escape, the brutal Camarillo would take it out on the slaves.

Dean was now as much a prisoner of the coldhearts as any of the slaves toiling in the camp's kitchens, chopping firewood or cleaning the outhouses. Unwillingly, he had been forced to help the coldhearts build Camarillo a massive war wag from the assorted wrecks found in the junkyard of some predark ruins. A combination of several Mack trucks, two bulldozers and an antique steam locomotive, the *Atomsmasher* was an iron-plated juggernaught of unbelievably destructive power.

Trying to make amends for his act of kindness, Dean had managed to earn some small degree of freedom from Camarillo by offering to work as the advance spy for the coldhearts. The chief of the Stone

Angels had been suspicious at first, but now seemed to think that Dean was finally becoming one of them. In truth, his hatred of Camarillo grew every day, and the last thing Dean planned to do before escaping would be to ace the coldheart leader by cutting out the heart of the brutal bastard.

Unfortunately, that wasn't going to happen today, Dean sourly noted, discharging the stolen crossbow at a snarling sec man charging his way with a swinging ax. The arrow missed, so Dean used another precious .38 round in the Browning. Dropping the ax, the sec man clutched at his red belly and groaned into oblivion.

With its steam whistle keening, the *Atomsmasher* crashed through a crowd of people foolishly trying to surrender. Laughing inside the control room, Camarillo wiped the spray of warm blood off his face and blew the whistle again. The strident keening noise terrified the horses of the sec men, making the animals throw their riders to the ground. However, the terrible sound had no effect whatsoever on the horses of the coldhearts, who had grown accustomed to it.

Running along the wall, a platoon of Alpharetta sec men fired nonstop at the colossal *Atomsmasher,* and the galloping coldhearts shot back with black powder scatterguns that boomed louder than grens. The sec men were aced, their chests blown open, guts flying to the wind, as they tumbled off the wall.

Suddenly, a sec woman wearing sergeant stripes appeared carrying a pipe bomb, the fuse sputtering away. A dozen coldhearts trained their blasters on her, but all of them missed.

"Alpharetta!" the sec woman yelled, hauling back an arm to throw the bomb.

Snarling in rage, Camarillo thrust the barrel of an AK-47 through the iron bars covering the windows of the *Atomsmasher* and cut loose with a long burst, the hail of 7.62 mm hardball rounds stitching the sec woman from groin to throat. Gushing life from a score of wounds, she collapsed, and a few seconds later a thunderous explosion rocked the wall, a section of the stonework crumbling away as her tattered body went sailing into the distance.

"Damn, so close," Dean muttered in frustration, taking a flintlock from a hand lying on the wall, the arm no longer attached to a body. Nearby lay a bag of powder and shot, the leather splattered with glistening brains. Grimly, he checked to make sure the weapon was properly loaded, then ran for the stairs leading down to the ville. Things were about to get nasty.

As the *Atomsmasher* reached the center of the ville, it was met by the baron of Alpharetta, sitting astride a black stallion. A burly man sporting an enormous beard, he cradled a Thompson .45-caliber rapidfire. As the steam truck turn toward him, the baron cut loose with the weapon, but the soft-lead rounds ricocheted harmlessly off the heavy armor of the converted steam truck, leaving behind only a dabbling of gray smears.

Laughing, Camarillo pulled some levers, and the *Atomsmasher* lurched into motion.

Frantically kicking his horse into a full gallop, the baron tried to escape by going around a building. However, Camarillo drove the vehicle straight into the tavern, coming out the other side in an explosion of smashed adobe bricks. The baron and his horse were hit broadside. Both man and beast were sent flying by the brutal impact, smacking into a nearby tannery. As they slid off the bricks to the cobblestone street, the *Atomsmasher* rolled over their bodies, audibly crushing them flat.

"The baron is dead!" Camarillo bellowed joyously. "The ville is ours!"

Shouting in victory, the Stone Angels climbed off their horses and started running into buildings, shooting anybody they found carrying a weapon—blaster, knife, hammer or pitchfork. Man, woman or child, it made no difference. If the people resisted, they were aced.

"I surrender!" a wrinklie shouted, raising both arms high. "Please, I surrender!"

"What's your job?" a bald coldheart demanded, walking closer, a brace of blasters balanced in his hands.

"Sir, I'm a blacksmith, sir," the old man replied, as respectfully as possible.

"Sorry, already got us one of those." The coldheart sneered, discharging both weapons. The head of the old man exploded, chunks of bone and brain spraying to the littered streets.

"We got a blacksmith?" Dean asked, feeling sick to his stomach.

"Nope!" The coldheart grinned, sauntering away in search of other prey.

Just then, a screaming woman charged out of an open doorway with three coldhearts close behind.

"Gotcha!" one of them yelled in triumph, grabbing her by the ponytail and pulling downward.

With a cry, she crashed to the ground, and two cold-hearts pounced, ripping off her skirt, then grabbed her legs and pulled them apart. Grinning fiendishly, the first coldheart started to unbuckle his pants.

"Better leave this one alone," Dean said quickly. "She's the ville healer. The boss will want her at camp."

Muttering curses, they did as he requested and released the woman, to go back into the building.

"I…I ain't no healer, mister, just a gaudy slut," she stuttered in a whisper, her face tight with fear. "Don't know nothing about healing and such."

"Then lie, or they'll chill you bad," Dean commanded under his breath, helping her to stand. "Wash any wound with clean water, then wash it again with shine, and wrap it with a clean strip of cloth. Now, find a friend, and claim she's your assistant. Remember, clean water only! Savvy?"

"Another healer? Yes, of course, I savvy," she replied, grabbing her ruined skirt off the street and wrapping it back around her hips. Then she asked, "Why are you doing this?"

A piercing scream rent the air as the three coldhearts reappeared with another woman in tow. Plump to the point of being obese, she was wearing a stained cook's apron over a denim dress. Most of her clothing was already gone, ripped to pieces, her large soft breasts flopping about. Tearing off the rest of her garments, the coldhearts hauled the weeping woman into an alley, then her screaming really began.

With no time to explain the value of human life, Dean hauled the gaudy slut over to the *Atomsmasher*.

"Whatcha got there?" Camarillo asked, smoking a cigar inside the control room.

There were several coldhearts stationed around the huffing engine, along with a line of chained people, all of them men. Most of them were badly beaten, with teeth missing and arms clearly broken, judging by the weird angles they hung. But Dean knew these were the lucky ones. The women in Alpharetta ville would suffer much worse before they were finally allowed to be chained as slaves.

"Found us a new healer," Dean said, trying to sound proud as he threw her at the chain gang. "Catch of the day!"

The woman landed in a sprawl.

"A healer, eh?" A fat coldheart chortled, wiping his mouth on a sleeve. "I hear they know all kinda secret things about pleasing a man." The other coldhearts eagerly nodded in agreement.

"Leave the healer be, and do your damn job," Camarillo said, tapping the ash off his cigar. "There'll be more than enough quim to go around later on."

Grumbling in disappointment, the coldheart roughly hauled the woman to her feet and started attaching a collar around her neck.

Confused, one of the prisoners scowled. "Healer?" He started to say more, but stopped at a cold glance from Dean, whose hand rested on the holstered Browning.

"Good job, Tiger," Camarillo said. "Now, go celebrate with the rest of the boys. You've earned it."

"Thanks!" Dean replied, turning away quickly so that the man wouldn't see the open disgust on his face.

Hoping to avoid most of the bloodshed and rape, Dean headed down a relatively quiet street. Turning a corner, he nodded at a group of coldhearts shuffling out of a redbrick building, their arms full of crossbows, gun belts and blasters.

"We found the armory!" one shouted, thrusting out a hip to show the three blasters tucked into his belt. "Not much live brass, but—"

In an explosion of glass, a sec man dived through a window to bury a knife into the back of a coldheart. As the other Angels dropped their loads to claw for weapons, Dean drew and fired the Browning in one smooth motion. With a horrid gurgle, the sec man staggered, blood gushing from the hole in his chest. As he fell, the coldhearts converged on the corpse, kicking it with their boots, and firing their blasters so often the ragged clothing caught on fire.

Taking his leave, Dean felt almost good about saving the sec man from days of public torture for attacking an Angel. The coldhearts knew some tricks that even cannies wouldn't use on their living food, and Camarillo was always happy to find some unlucky bastard to use as an example. Prisoners became more docile and obedient after discovering that any act of rebellion opened a doorway that led straight into the depths of hell.

Heading across the ville, Dean encountered several people hanging from trees, some alive, some not. But without a legitimate reason, any effort on his part to ease their suffering would only have put him in their place. He wanted to help these people, but not at the risk of his own life. If they were family, of course, kin helped kin. But not total strangers. Survival came first in Deathlands.

Trying to ignore the screams coming from every direction, Dean turned a corner to find a chilled sec man splayed in the street, his body severed in two from the spinning blades attached to the wheels of the *Atomsmasher*. Looking around to make sure nobody was watching, Dean quickly knelt to search the corpse. The holster was empty, but flipping over the lower half of the torso, Dean found the loops of the gun belt full of brass in a caliber suitable for his BAR longblaster. Taking it all, Dean continued on while stuffing the precious ammo into different pockets to prevent it from jingling together when he walked. Clinking brass could chill your ass, his father, Ryan, used to say. Words of wisdom, indeed.

Something exploded in the distance, throwing a dozen bodies high into the sky. Dogs howled, a woman screamed and coldhearts cheered in delight.

Discovering a tavern, Dean slipped inside, hoping it hadn't been looted yet. Usually, he wasn't a drinker, but this day was surely the exception. However, he was too late. The shelves behind the counter were empty, and the limp bodies of sec men and ville people lay everywhere, the sawdust on the floor lumpy with spilled blood. Ah well. He was just about to leave when a pretty woman came racing down the stairs, chased by Hannigan.

"Come back here!" Hannigan growled, and he dived forward to tackle her around the knees. She slammed into the floor, throwing up a small cloud of dirty sawdust.

"Get the fuck off me!" she yelled, kicking out and beating at him with her fists.

"Shut up, bitch!" Hannigan laughed, punching her in the belly.

Going pale, the woman struggled to breathe as the coldheart pulled a knife and grabbed the front of her blouse.

"Well done, brother! Thanks for catching her for me!" Dean said with a fake grin, hauling the limp woman to her feet. "The stupe bitch got away from me before. You're gonna pay for that, slut!"

"Mutie shit, I found her!" Hannigan growled menacingly, his throat tight with barely repressed lust.

"Sure, but only after she got away from me!" Dean pointed at her broken nose, with no idea how the damage had happened. "That's my mark on her face."

Narrowing his eyes, Hannigan weighed his options, then wisdom took control, and he moved his hand away from the sawed-off scattergun at his side. As a raw recruit "Mud Puppy" hadn't been frightened of him, and now, months later, "Tiger" Cawdor, a blooded Angel, was one of the toughest bastards in the gang, and greased lightning with his fancy blaster. Only a triple-stupe droolie would challenge him in a fair fight.

"Take her." Hannigan sniffed, hitching up his gun belt. "The bitch is too old and stringy, anyway."

"Thanks, brother!" Dean chuckled, slapping the hated man on the shoulder in a friendly manner. "I owe you one!"

His face a mask of repressed fury, Hannigan lumbered out of the tavern, firing his blaster at a corpse in the gutter for no valid reason.

"Thanks, but I've never seen you before," the woman said, wiping the blood from her face with a sleeve. "I broke my nose running away from the first wave of coldhearts as they came over the wall."

In case somebody was watching, Dean drew back his arm as if to cuff the woman. "He would have raped you, girl," he whispered urgently, "and I won't." He stepped closer and she flinched. "Now come with me if you want to keep sucking air!"

Unsure for a moment, she looked into his eyes and was startled to see only kindness there. Nodding in understanding, she did nothing as Dean grabbed her by the collar to roughly drag her to an undamaged house across the street.

As Dean approached, a coldheart walked out with a skinny, bucktoothed young woman. She was dressed in rags, most of her body fully exposed and covered with dark bruises.

"Hey, Tiger, done found me a virgie!" The coldheart laughed. "That be a first."

"Good work, Natters!" Dean complimented the man, feeling sick to his stomach for the woman. Her shoulders kept moving as if she was crying, but there were no tears on her cheeks. "You done in there?"

"All yours, brother!" Natters laughed, leading his captive away like a dog on a leash.

Going inside, Dean checked over the house. It was small, with just one room and a single door, no windows. Perfect. Closing and locking the door, he sighed in relief. "Okay, this buys us some time," he said. "Wish I could help your people more, but I've been treading water with these bastards for a while, and they still don't completely trust me yet."

Silently, the woman stared at him, not sure what to do.

"Come on, scream," Dean ordered, taking a chair and sitting. "If somebody passes by, it has to sound like you're fighting for your bastard life, or we both get aced. Savvy?"

"You…a roughrider?" she asked hesitantly, clutching the front of her ripped shirt.

Though he'd never heard the slang word before, Dean could make an educated guess to the meaning. "No, I like women in my bed," he said honestly, and then for some unknown reason felt compelled to add, "Not that I've had that many."

That comment caught her totally by surprise. Suddenly, she decided to trust the handsome stranger.

Taking in a deep breath, she cut loose with a blood-curdling shriek.

Startled, Dean blinked from the sheer ferocity of the cry, then smiled as he heard a couple of coldhearts laugh outside, and somebody thump the locked door.

"Not so hard, Tiger!" a voice called. "Let her breathe some, unless you like riding the peach off a corpse!"

"Shut up, I'm busy!" Dean shouted back, punctuating each word with a grunt.

Chuckling, the coldhearts walked away, singing and firing their blasters.

"I'm Althea," she said. "Althea Stone."

"Dean Cawdor."

"Tiger?"

"Just a nickname," he said with a scowl.

"What should we do?" Althea asked, sitting on the bed.

"Better rip those clothes some," Dean replied, pulling out a knife and tossing it over. "Then cut me on the cheek. Gotta make this look real."

Making the catch, Althea tested the balance of the blade, then slashed out, her hand a blur.

Caught completely off guard, Dean jerked at the stinging touch of steel, then used fingertips to check his face. There was a shallow cut along his jawline. Damn, she was quick!

Flipping the knife over, Althea slashed at her clothing, then added a few cuts to her legs. Dean was impressed. The blood would make folks think he had been her first, which would prevent most of the other coldhearts from bothering her, acknowledging an unspoken rule that she was his. He would have to keep a watch out for Hannigan. Someday soon, he would have to chill the man.

Finished, Althea threw the knife back. It thudded onto the floorboards between his boots. "Can't let them find me with a weapon," she said, starting to remove her clothing.

"Hey now, that's not necessary," Dean said, raising a palm.

"Gotta make this look real if somebody checks," she replied, letting the tattered garment flutter to the floor.

As she finished disrobing, Dean said nothing, transfixed by the unbelievable beauty of the young woman. She had scars, of course—everybody alive did—but her skin was beautiful anyway, glowing with health.

Her breasts were pert and firm, her stomach flat, and the delta between her legs was completely hairless.

"You shave down there?" he asked, his throat oddly tight.

"Never had no hair there," Althea replied, sitting on the bed, which squeaked slightly. "Guess mebbe I got a little mutie blood in me. Most of the people in this ville do. We had a former baron who… Well, to say that he was crazy as a shithouse rat wouldn't half load the blaster on that story."

"Reckon so," Dean said, crossing his legs. The little cabin felt uncomfortably warm.

"Now what?" she asked, pulling a blanket to cover herself. She wondered how it was possible that she was feeling an attraction to the coldheart. He had a kind face and intelligent eyes, but he was still an invader destroying her home and everybody she loved. Yet he had gentle ways, and the mixed messages confused her greatly.

"Now we wait for the chilling to stop. That should be sometime around dawn," Dean said, removing his gun belt and laying it on a rickety table mostly held together with duct tape. Then he hesitated, not really wanting to take off his shirt or his pants, although for vastly different reasons. Choosing the lesser of two evils, he pulled off the buckskin shirt.

Inhaling sharply, Althea felt a visceral surge at the sight of his powerful chest and broad shoulders. Dean had the muscles of a blacksmith, and his wide chest was thickly matted with black curly hair, except for three white strips that looked like old knife wounds.

"I can see why they call you Tiger," Althea said,

starting to reach for the scars, then stopping herself. She was inexplicably drawn to the gentle killer.

"Anything's better than Mud Puppy," Dean snorted.

"What?"

"Never mind. Spent brass." Turning away, he took off his combat boots and pants, then paused again, unwilling to turn around in his turgid state.

Guessing the cause of his unease, Althea turned down the oil lantern.

Relaxing slightly in the darkness, Dean padded barefoot across the cabin to sit in the wooden chair alongside the little bed.

"Mebbe you should join me under the covers," Althea suggested.

Finding it difficult to think, Dean cleared his throat, trying to choose the correct words and not offend. He felt dizzy, almost drunk, and his heart was pounding.

Moving onto the bed, he sank into the ancient mattress as he lay next to the young woman. He could feel the heat coming off her naked body.

After drawing up the covers, he didn't move for a long time. Then Althea whispered his name, and he pulled her close. Hugging each other tightly, they both tried to ignore the pitiful screams and wails coming from outside. Unexpectedly, there was a prolonged chatter of blasterfire, followed by an ominous silence that was infinitely more disturbing than the previous shrieks of terror.

Chapter Four

Groggily coming awake, Krysty started to reach for her blaster, then saw where she was and gradually relaxed. They'd spent the night inside the elevator? That was clever!

With her prehensile hair flexing and moving, she checked for any damage from the fight, but found only some bruises and scrapes, nothing serious. Her belly was empty and audibly demanding food, but aside from that she felt just fine, and not in the least bit tired from the previous day's exertions.

With a snort, Ryan came awake, his good eye snapping open, then narrowing as he looked about, making sure the companions were alone.

"Morning, lover," Krysty said, reaching out to straighten his leather eye patch. "I take it the howler didn't get inside."

"Not for long, anyway," he replied, giving a half smile. Then he frowned. "Fireblast, what's that awful mucking smell?"

"Me, I think," Krysty said hesitantly, taking a sniff of her soiled shirt and grimacing. "Yes, it's me. Probably Doc and Mildred, too. How did you and the others get so clean?"

As he briefly explained, the rest of the companions

began to stir, yawning and stretching, then immediately checking their blasters.

Levering himself erect, Ryan checked to make sure the access panel in the ceiling hadn't been disturbed while they slept. Meanwhile, J.B. did the same thing to the elevator doors and control panel.

"Clear," Ryan announced.

"Same here," J.B. replied, adjusting his wire-rimmed glasses.

Holstering the blaster, Ryan grunted. "Okay, our first task will be to recce the redoubt. We need to make sure that bastard howler is still outside, and that there is nobody else inside the base with us."

"Then food," Jak declared. "Feel like been drinking acid rain belly so empty."

"Indeed, my dear Jak. I heartily concur," Doc stated, moving his tongue around the inside of his mouth with a dour expression. "Although I would think anything we consume to break our morning fast would taste infinitely better if the ladies, and myself, took a quick trip to the showers."

"Smell like bayou," Jak admitted honestly.

"Hey, Doc, I'll scrub your back if you scrub mine," Mildred said with a straight face. Then she burst into laughter at the scholar's shocked expression. "Silly old coot, you fall for that joke every time!"

"That is because, madam, I am always terrified that someday you may actually carry through with the vile threat," Doc replied haughtily, retrieving his sword stick from the floor. Twisting the handle, he inspected the blade. There were some minor stains on the steel, but otherwise the sword was in fine shape. Especially considering the situation.

The companions waited patiently a few minutes for Doc to reload the LeMat, then dutifully returned to the garage level. Warily advancing along the access tunnel, they were greatly relieved to see that the blast doors were tightly closed, and there was no fresh dampness on the walls to show that the howler had gotten inside again, only to be repelled by the auto-defense systems.

"The big ugly bastard might very well be standing right on the other side of this," J.B. said, thumping the black metal door with a fist.

"Good," Ryan stated bluntly, over a low rumble from his stomach. "Let it rot out there. Come on, let's finish the sweep, then have some food."

"How are our supplies, madam?" Doc asked with intense eagerness.

"We lost a lot of stuff in our mad dash across the state," Mildred said with a sigh, pulling out an ancient yellow notepad. She kept track of the supplies these days, even though everybody carried some of the foodstuffs. That way if one backpack was lost, the entire group didn't go hungry. There was a lot of wisdom in not putting all your eggs in one basket.

"And?" Ryan prompted impatiently.

"And we should still have two cans of beans, four self-heats and nine MREs. That's three days' worth, five if we stretch it."

"We're a lot lower in brass," Krysty said, opening her blaster to check the cylinder. "I've got three live rounds left, and a pocketful of spent brass for reloading."

"Got nothing," Jak snorted. "And down five knives."

"Well, my Uzi is out, and the scattergun has one, count it, one remaining 12-gauge cartridge," J.B. added glumly.

"The Steyr is empty, and I'm down to six rounds in the SIG-Sauer," Ryan said, not bothering to check. He would have to be aced and buried for at least a week before he didn't know the exact amount of live brass he was carrying.

"Two live rounds," Mildred said, hefting the target pistol. "That's why I came running with the crowbar."

It had been a very long time since the ZKR was this light, and Mildred hated the feeling of vulnerability. Safety meant a loaded blaster in your hand, with good friends standing alongside.

"Alas, I am also down to only two rounds," Doc stated, displaying the massive LeMat. "I have lots of lead miniballs, primers and cloth wadding, but most of my black powder seems to be missing. Lost in our hasty egress across the desert." He paused. "But I do still have my sword stick."

"Okay, we're going to eat before anything else. Empty bellies make for weak arms. Then we scav for anything usable as a weapon, before checking the armory down on the third level."

Everybody nodded in agreement.

"At least here in the tunnel we know one direction we won't be attacked from," Krysty said, glancing at the huge blast doors. "That's something, anyway."

"Prefer more brass," Jak countered, hunkering down to rip open an MRE pack. He passed around the cheese and crackers to give everybody a taste, then split the envelope of beef stew with Doc. Ryan did the same thing with Krysty, and Mildred shared an MRE of spaghetti and meatballs with J.B.

The food was cold but filling, and tasted absolutely wonderful, especially after their last few meals consumed on the run.

The companions made their way to the service bays and checked the abandoned vehicles. They located no weapons inside the trucks, which was rather odd, since most predark soldiers kept some sort of a handgun in their vehicle. J.B. found a box holding a dozen road flares behind a front seat. Eight of them were useless, split open from internal corrosion, but the remaining four seemed in decent condition.

"Better than nothing," he said glumly, tucking them into his munitions bag. "But not by much."

Turning their attention to the workbenches, Doc stood guard with the LeMat and his sword while the rest of the companions carefully chose some of the larger wrenches and pry bars. Several acetylene welding torches still held a small amount of charge, but the tanks were prohibitively heavy, and while the flame was lethally hot, the range was pitifully short.

"Lots of juice in the gas pumps," Ryan said, checking a pressure gauge. "But without any glass bottles, we can't make Molotovs."

Tightening the jaws on a massive Stillson wrench, Jak scowled. "This mil base. No beer in fridge?"

"Sure, lots of it. In cans."

"Damn!"

"We'll find some whiskey bottles in the CO's office," J.B. stated confidently. "Never yet found a commanding officer who didn't have a private bar hidden somewhere."

"Rank doth have its little privileges," Mildred stated.

"Speaking of rank," Doc said, lifting a small plastic envelope from a box on the workbench. Using his teeth, he opened it and extracted a scented pine tree, which he hung off a button of his shirt. "Until we hit the showers," he explained unnecessarily.

Everybody smiled at that, and even Ryan almost grinned.

"We don't smell that bad," Krysty scoffed, crossing her arms.

"Yeah, do," Jak stated honestly, looking apologetic.

Fed and somewhat better armed, the companions took the stairs down to the third level, pausing several times along the way to try to hear if anybody else was moving around in the redoubt. But aside from the gentle murmur of the air vents, the base was quite literally as quiet as a grave.

On the third floor, the main corridor was lined with doors. Each office was full of furniture and not much else, aside from stacks of government forms, the ancient paper much too scratchy to even use in the bathroom. Then Krysty smiled, remembering how once a desperate Dean had tried using carbon paper as toilet paper, the results of which had been with him for almost a full week.

At the end of the corridor, the hulking steel door to the base arsenal was ajar, which was almost always a bad sign. Sure enough, the cavernous room proved to be empty, the shelves and gun racks containing nothing but a thin layer of dust, the scuffed floor littered with empty mylar bags and mounds of excelsior stuffing.

"Okay, five minute recce, then we move on," Ryan said, pulling out the SIG-Sauer and taking a guard position near the open door.

As the rest of the companions spread out, J.B. headed straight for a repair station in the corner. There was nothing usable in sight, all of the reloading machinery empty of anything being processed. Then he spied a plastic box marked R&R. Inside the "repair or reject" container, he found a pile of ammunition magazines with busted springs. Sure enough, several of them had a round jammed inside. Using a screwdriver, he gently forced out the live brass, and soon had a small pile of 9 mm rounds. Sorting out the bullets too badly corroded with age to risk using left him ten good brass. Since the SIG-Sauer and the Uzi took the same caliber, J.B. split the find with Ryan, both men dutifully reloading their weapons with the meager supply.

Probing with his sword into the mounds of foam peanuts, Doc located an unopened crate of M-60 machine guns. The weapons were thickly coated with Cosmoline protective gel and in perfect condition. Unfortunately, there were no belts or ammo boxes or even loose brass, so Doc turned his back on the stash of deadly manportable rapidfires. A blaster without brass was only deadweight.

Sighing in disappointment, Mildred closed the door on a first-aid cabinet. Aside from a box of elastic bandages, which she took, everything else on the shelves was over a century old and couldn't be safely used, even in an emergency.

J.B. opened a cupboard and removed a couple glass bottles of vinegar from a shelf. "These will do fine for Molotovs!"

"Why do they store that in here?" Mildred asked, clearly puzzled.

"Nothing cleans off Cosmoline better than vinegar," J.B. stated, already turning away to continue the search.

Deciding to check the drawers of the wooden desk, Krysty found a metal box bolted into place inside. Now, that was curious. The box was locked, but as a small child she had learned how to open such things with only a knife and a slim piece of wire. The trick didn't always work, but this time it did, and inside the lockbox were a pile of laminated security passes, a dusty S&W .38 revolver and a plastic-wrapped cardboard box marked Remington.

Eagerly, she removed the airtight plastic to find the box full of rounds.

"Over here!" she called, waving an arm. "Fifty live rounds!"

"What caliber?" Jak asked hopefully, looking up from a trash barrel.

"Thirty-eights."

"Hot damn, back in biz!" he exclaimed, turning and pulling out his .357 Magnum Colt Python. The cylinder could accommodate both standard .38 bullets and the much more powerful .357 Magnum rounds. Firepower was good, but versatility was even better.

Eagerly, Krysty, Mildred and Jak divided the contents of the cardboard box, each of them promptly reloading their blasters. Since she had found the stash, Krysty got the extra few rounds, then Jak checked the revolver in the drawer to find six more live brass. He started to remove them, then paused with a frown.

"Here, Doc, you take," he said, walking across the room. "Six of something better than nine of nothing."

"I still carry two charges," Doc corrected, accepting the modern-day revolver. "But as always, my friend, you are the very epitome of pragmatism."

Jak frowned. "That good?"

"Indeed it is." Opening the revolver, Doc made sure the bullets were in good shape, then removed them to dry fire the weapon a couple of times, checking the action. The trigger was tight and light, the hammer smooth, the barrel clear of any obstructions. Perfect! But then, considering that the military-grade weapon had been tucked into a locked box, sealed inside a desk that was located within a vault situated at the heart of a nukeproof fortress, he would have been highly surprised to find the weapon in anything but perfect working condition. However, bitter experience had taught him that the first time a person took such things for granted was always when they failed spectacularly, usually sending the person straight into the grave.

Doc reloaded the weapon before tucking it into his canvas gun belt. The S&W revolver actually weighed less than the ammunition for his LeMat, and he made a somber mental note to aim higher at a target in compensation for the lack of a proper recoil.

Eventually, the companions were done searching the armory, locating nothing more interesting then a roll of fuse for J.B. to use, even though he didn't have any explosives to attach it to at the moment. Continuing the interrupted sweep of the redoubt, they were soon satisfied that there was nobody else present, and finally headed for the much needed showers.

"At last!" Krysty sighed, shrugging off her filthy bearskin coat before starting to remove her shirt.

While everybody got undressed, Doc went off to shower alone. In his time period, any form of nudity was totally unheard-of, strictly forbidden, tantamount to devil worship, and even though he now knew better, he simply couldn't shake off the strict lessons of childhood. There were times that his nudity in front of the others was unavoidable, but they were few and far between.

"Call if you need anything!" Mildred shouted, as he disappeared around a tiled corner.

"Only the absence of your alleged wit, madam!" Doc yelled back, the words echoing slightly along the hallway.

Carefully putting their blasters on a nearby shelf, the companions padded naked into the huge communal shower room and turned on every faucet, then got out again fast. A few seconds later, the rattling pipes disgorged a bubbling torrent of thick brown sludge. But that soon change into a murky flow that finally became a steady downpour of hot, clean water. The bars of soap had remained intact, and soon the companions were covered in glorious suds.

After toweling dry, the men shaved, and J.B. stuffed several empty shampoo bottles into his munitions bag, along with a handful of rusty razor blades recovered from the garbage.

"These will make excellent shrapnel for when I cook

up more pipe bombs," he explained, at a puzzled glance from Mildred.

Next, everybody went to the laundry to wash and repair their bedraggled clothing and undergarments. Finding officer uniforms stored inside dry cleaning bags, everybody got a new shirt, while Krysty and Mildred were each delighted to acquire a new sports bra, their threadbare old ones mostly held together with the power of positive thinking.

Taking some of the plastic garments bags, J.B. then rummaged among the dry cleaning machinery to locate a couple unopened containers of spot remover solution, plus a small tin of desiccated shoe polish. The cracked material inside resembled a fried hockey puck, but J.B. beamed at the dried lump as if it were manna from heaven.

"You'll need this, too," Ryan said, passing over a small bottle of bleach and a handful of loose pennies.

"Thanks! Now, if there's a working microwave in the kitchen, we'll soon have some pipe bombs again." J.B. grinned, tucking away the assorted items.

"And disassemble some pipes," Jak added, checking through a shelf of shoes and boots waiting to be repaired. With a grin, he found a combat boot in his size, and for the correct foot. Happily removing the tattered remains of his old boot, he slipped on the new boot, and tied it firmly. It was a different color than his own, the right boot solid black, the left camouflage-green, but his only concern was that it was a comfortable fit.

After getting dressed, the companions found a well-scrubbed Doc drinking coffee in the kitchen. The room was huge, and well supplied with a dozen ovens, a score of refrigerators and a row of dishwashers, the largest, in the corner, chugging softly.

"There's coffee on the stove," he said in greeting, sipping from a cracked mug bearing the logo of the Green Berets.

"French roast or Viennese cinnamon?" Mildred asked playfully, taking a sniff.

"U.S. Army, regulation grind, coffee, for drinking of."

"Oh. Well, better than nothing."

Just then, the dishwasher chimed. Rising from the table. Doc opened the machine and used a dish towel to withdraw the LeMat, the metal shining brightly.

"I'll never get over you washing a blaster that way." J.B. chuckled, placing his munitions bag on a dining table.

"Why not, John Barrymore? There are no nylon bushings like those in a modern weapon to dissolve from the heat," Doc said, setting the steaming-hot blaster on a wood cutting board. "Besides, after I greased the cylinder to prevent a cross fire, it needed a good cleaning, and this way is much easier than scrubbing it by hand."

Then he paused in confusion. "Did…did I ever mention that J. E. B. Stuart used to boil his LeMat at least once a week, as did Ulysses S. Grant? There was an article I just read in the *New York Herald* about Grant using whiskey instead of water, but I think it was a joke…." His voice trailed away.

Used to the time traveler's occasional ramblings, the companions merely dropped their backpacks on the floor and went to get some coffee.

"Anything in the freezer?" Ryan asked, wandering over to yank open a stainless steel door. Inside the unit were numerous shelves piled high with an assortment of objects, all of them so heavily covered with ice it was impossible to tell what was hidden underneath the translucent layers. He scowled at the sight. Fireblast, everything in there would have such bad freezer burn it would be less edible than boiled boot.

"There's some salt in the cabinets," Doc said softly, making a vague gesture. "Along with some rice, but that is all, my dear Ryan. This horn of Cornucopia has blown its last note."

"Rice will stretch out our supplies for another day or two," Krysty said, opening the cabinet doors to find the plastic container. As she took it down, a small jar of honey was revealed tucked into the corner. Probably the private reserve of some member of the kitchen staff. The honey had dried to a hard golden crust the consistency of stone, but she knew it could easily be reconstituted with a little boiling water. As long as they were kept away from air and moisture, honey and rice would never go bad.

"No food, no brass, howler at door," Jak said, pouring himself a mug of coffee. He took a sip, scowled, then took another. "How soon jump?"

"The sooner, the better," Ryan stated, glancing upward as if he could see the savage mutie pounding on the blast doors. If it got inside again, the antirad alarms would give them plenty of warning. But then their only course of action would be to jump, so why delay the inevitable?

"Agreed. The sooner we reach another redoubt, the

better our chances of finding some food or brass," J.B. said, picking up his munitions bag.

After having coffee and a meager breakfast, the companions left the kitchen and took the elevator to the gateway level, marched along the corridor and entered the comp room. Banks of computers hummed softly, several control panels blinking different-colored lights, relaying volumes of information to technicians no longer alive to interpret the data.

Crossing the room, the companions then passed through an antechamber that led to the mat-trans unit. The armaglas walls of the unit were a dark blue, streaked with gold and edged with an emerald-green diamond pattern. The mat-trans unit of every redoubt had a different color, for reasons lost in time. The companions had assumed it was for easy place identification. But if it was for identification, why not simply use a sign that gave the name of the redoubt, or the latitude and longitude, or put a fragging map of North America on the wall with one of those little you-are-here arrows? It just didn't seem practical.

Stepping into the mat-trans unit, the companions sat on the floor while Ryan closed the door, which would start the jump. He went to join the others.

Traveling from one redoubt to another took only a few seconds, even when the other base was a thousand miles away. The "journey" usually caused blinding headaches, and in some of the companions induced vomiting.

Mildred had a theory that this was because they were not using the mat-trans properly. There was an alphanumeric panel set into the wall, obviously there to enter a destination code. But since the companions didn't know any of the codes, they had discovered that closing the door without entering a destination code would initiate a random jump.

A strange mist filled the unit, the floor plates glowed, then they were sent hurtling through a swirling sub-atomic vortex to arrive at another redoubt, unconscious on the floor. Weak and battered, but alive.

"Dark night, I hate to lose my breakfast so soon," J.B. muttered, removing his glasses to tuck them safely into a shirt pocket.

Agreeing wholeheartedly, Krysty wanted to say something comforting to her friend, but after so many jumps, she knew exactly how long it took the chamber to activate, and there was no time. Drawing a deep breath, she prepared to be torn into her component atoms.

Moments passed, and nothing happened.

Growing uneasy, the companions began to exchange nervous glances as long seconds flowed into impossible minutes, and still the white mist didn't engulf them. The mat-trans chamber remained as cold and quiescent as a sealed tomb.

Chapter Five

Muttering a curse, Ryan looked around the antechamber, wondering if they had just experienced a painless jump. Where they remained conscious. Unfortunately, it was the same chamber, blue and gold with little green diamonds.

"What happened?" Jak demanded suspiciously.

"Mayhap the computer is broken," Doc muttered, worrying the handle of his ebony stick. "Or do you think the arrival of our noisy green friend outside may have something to do with this deplorable display of dysfunction?"

"Damned if I know," Mildred said, brushing a beaded lock of hair off her face. "That mainframe is over a century old, and survived a nuclear war. I've always been a little surprised that it ever worked."

Doc scowled darkly. The redoubts and the mat-trans system were supremely important to him, more than to any of the other companions. They were his only way to return to his beloved family. If the redoubts were breaking down and the mat-trans system collapsing, then he was truly stranded in this future time, never to see the past and home again. Alone, forever.

"Mebbe if we try again," Krysty suggested, standing to open the door and step out the unit. The other companions followed suit, and after a few moments, they all walked back into the chamber and sat, except Ryan, who shut the door. He hurriedly went to sit beside Krysty.

Nothing occurred.

"Okay, now what?" J.B. growled, putting his glasses back on. He had tucked them in his pocket for safekeeping.

His temper flaring, Ryan slammed a fist into the armaglas wall. "Fireblast!" he snarled furiously, massaging his stinging hand. "With the mat-trans dead, and a howler at the door, we're caught down here like a jam in a breech!"

Opening the door and marching out the mat-trans unit, the one-eyed man started across the antechamber. "Okay, the Trader always said that when you're caught in an ambush, then do the unexpected and dive out the window."

"Fair enough, but where's the window?" J.B. demanded, tilting back his fedora.

"The front door," Ryan stated. "There's nothing we can do about the mat-trans, so we're going to find a way to chill that howler. Afterward, we travel overland to the next redoubt."

"Chill a howler? I've never heard of that being done before, lover," Krysty said. "And we've been trying."

"First time for everything," Ryan stated, keying in the code to open the door that led to the corridor, his face a dark mask of somber concentration.

"We might be able to smash past the howler if there was a working APC, or a tank," J.B. said, cracking his knuckles. "But with only civilian wags, I don't know…." He chewed a lip.

"Come on, John, I've seen you make bombs out

of bedsheets and silver jewelry," Mildred chided in a friendly manner, as they reached the elevator. "There must be something we can do. Some sort of explosive, or poison."

"We do not know if poison can kill a howler," Doc interjected, as the doors opened. "Or even if the cursed thing can be chilled!"

The companions stepped inside, and the doors closed.

"Anything get aced," Jak retorted, then he frowned. "Course, not really know if howler alive, or just a thing, like tornado, or dust devil."

As the elevator started moving, Mildred arched both eyebrows. She had never considered the possibility that a howler might not even be a living creature, but some sort of a freak occurrence, like Saint Elmo's fire—a ball of lightning that chased after people, not to eat them, but merely because human beings had a magnetic field, and it was drawn to them like steel filings to a magnet. It was a sobering thought.

Just because the thing sort of looked like a hellgrammite, she noted dourly, didn't mean that it was.

The elevator doors opened with a musical chime, and Ryan strode across the garage level, studying the array of crashed vehicles. "We'll start with that motorcycle," he said, rolling up his sleeves.

WHEN THE WORK was done for the day, the companions had dinner and hit the showers again. However, this time everybody was free to use the private stalls reserved for officers.

Standing with his head bowed under the warm spray, Ryan let the water wash away the day's accumulation of sweat. They had almost exhausted the meager supply of acetylene in the welding tanks, finishing the job, but it was done and as good as what could be achieved under their present circumstances. But as the Trader always liked to say, the proof of the plas-ex was how far the bodies flew. The next day would tell if the plan worked or not.

As Krysty removed her sweaty shirt in the changing room, she noted the collection of new scars on his body. They were almost lost among the host of others earned from a thousand battles, hard fought and won. The puckered circles of bullet wounds, the freckling from shrapnel, the straight line of a knife slash… Ryan wore the history of his life etched into his living flesh.

Just for a moment, she recalled the first time she'd seen him, charging through the billowing smoke of that burning barn, bodies strewn across the ground. She had been positive that she was going to die, but Ryan had changed that, saved her, and asked nothing in return, not even to share her bedroll for the night.

And he had certainly earned the right to ask, if nothing else, she thought, sliding off her pants. But he had waited until she approached him first. *Gallantry* was a word few people understood these days, and she loved him all the more for it. Deep inside, Ryan was a gentle man who wanted nothing more than to live in peace. But when trouble came, he shook the world until its teeth rattled. He was the ultimate Deathlands warrior. In her opinion, he was the only real man she had ever known.

Gathering a fistful of soap residue from a plastic container, Ryan started lathering his hair, the excess suds cascading down to flow across his hard muscular frame. Krysty felt a visceral surge of excitement at the sight, as she removed her bra and panties.

"Care for some company, lover?" she asked, looking over the frosted plastic door of the stall.

"Always room for you," he said, smiling through the dripping suds. Her shapely form was only a vague blur through the distorting plastic, and for some reason that seemed to make her even more desirable than usual.

Swinging open the door, Krysty stepped into the stall and closed it behind her. Ryan shifted to the side to allow her to get wet, her prehensile hair flexing almost happily in the misty warmth as her fingers gently massaged apart the filaments.

"Been a long day," he said, watching as she soaped up a washcloth to build a lather.

"Tired?" she asked, washing her face. The suds flowed down her body, clinging to every curve like the finest lace.

"Never been that tired." He chuckled.

Suddenly, the washcloth fell, and she bent over from the waist to retrieve it from the floor.

"You sure?" she asked, maintaining the tempting position.

Reaching down, he cupped her chin and drew her up until they were inches apart. Silent words were exchanged in the intimate moment. Moving closer, they kissed, tenderly at first, savoring the delicious contact, then with a growing passion as their naked bodies touched, hands roaming over slippery skin, caressing, holding, stroking....

With the warm water cascading over their bodies, the couple became lost in their sex play. Then they parted, and Ryan gently set Krysty on the tiled floor. Spreading her legs, he moved closer and eased himself inside her, the heady contact of rock hard and velvet soft combining with the rush of intimate heat to invoke a visceral sensation beyond words. And so began their dance of love, an affirmation of life and devotion in the harsh reality of the Deathlands.

Chapter Six

The next morning, a yawning Dean opened the door to the little cabin to be hit by a tumultuous roar of men whooping, dogs barking and blasters firing.

For an instant, he thought the ville had been taken back by the baron, and the sec men had come to chill him. But as the last dregs of sleep left his mind, he saw the crowd of people was composed entirely of Stone Angels, along with a scattering of women wearing chains. Dean recognized each of the men: Natters, Bradshaw, O'Shay, Durante, Lutz, Shapario, and oddly, Hannigan, his expression unreadable.

Behind the beaming throng of coldhearts, wrinklies and small children were loading buckboard wags with barrels of taters, jugs of shine and wicker baskets full of dried fish. Dean knew that had been the main reason for the attack, supplies for the coming winter.

"How was she, brother?" Natters asked, striding from the mob. Although he was unshaved, his face streaked with blood, the man was wearing clean clothing, without patches, and two blasters jutted from his wide leather belt, a revolver and a flintlock.

"Better than your sister," Dean said, forcing a wide grin while hitching up his belt.

Laughing in delight, Natters moved fast to throw a punch. Having experienced this sort of thing before,

Dean didn't dodge or duck. Instead, he caught the fist in his palm, and they stood locked together, both straining to shift the other.

"That's our Tiger!" Natters smiled, relinquishing the attack. Throwing his arms wide, he embraced Dean, then draped an arm across his shoulders. "Let's hear it for the new Angel!"

As the grinning crowd gave voice to their approval, Dean felt his stomach turn as he pushed off the friendly arm. Was this what they had been waiting to happen before he was fully accepted into the gang—for him to rape an innocent girl? The famous Cawdor anger boiled inside him, and Dean let loose with a full-throated bellow of rage, the ferocity and volume surprising even him.

Shocked at first, the coldhearts then redoubled their joyful cries, obviously mistaking it merely as a defiant roar.

"Nuking hell, that's what a good slut can do!" Bradshaw chortled. He had an arm draped across an older woman, his bloodstained hand openly fondling her breast. "Turn a boy into a man!"

"So where is the bitch?" Hannigan muttered softly, almost as if speaking to himself.

On cue, Althea stepped out of the cabin. Saying nothing, she stood behind Dean, her head down and her hands meekly folded.

"Come on, let's see what she's got!" Shapario chuckled, uncoiling a bullwhip from his shoulder.

Dean stopped him with a raised palm. "No need to bruise the goods," he said with a humorless laugh. Over a shoulder, he added, "Strip, girl."

Quickly, Althea disrobed, letting her clothing fall to the dirt until she was completely naked. Shivering in the morning cold, she stayed mute while the coldhearts voiced their various opinions about her physical attributes.

"Black dust, Tiger's got her trained like a dog already!" Natters grinned in frank approval. "Well done, brother. I still have to beat mine with a club just to make the bitch open her mouth."

"Wouldn't mind having a ride on that myself," Hannigan growled, the throwing ax tight in his fist. There were grisly new souvenirs on his necklace, most of them still oozing life.

"Nobody rides my horse but me," Dean answered back, the Browning Hi-Power instantly leveled at the man. "And that goes double for my slut."

"Just asking," Hannigan replied, the muscles in his arm visibly tightening as he turned to walk away from the celebration.

"All right, get dressed," Dean commanded, not bothering to turn around. "Don't want you catching the black cough."

Obediently, Althea put her clothing back on and stood barefoot in the dirt, waiting patiently.

Just then, the *Atomsmasher* chugged into view from around the ruin of the former baron's home. With a police gun belt now draped across his chest, and a bloody cloth tied around his head, Camarillo was still standing inside the control room. More iron bars had been added to the narrow windows, the raw welds still shiny, and the armored roof was festooned with new coils of razor wire. In the tender behind the engine, a sweaty pair of chained slaves maintained a steady rhythm as they threw chunks of wood through the open fire door to feed the ravenous machine.

"All right, mount up!" Camarillo ordered, removing the cigar from his mouth. He flicked ashes into the breeze. "We're heading for camp! Be sure to pack everything you want, because we're burning this rad pit to the ground."

"That seems a waste, Chief," Dean said, with a frown. "If we leave the ville standing, more pilgrims will come to rebuild, plant crops, and eventually we can hit it again for new supplies."

"Sort of like planting winter corn for the summer harvest," O'Shea said, nodding.

"Makes good sense to me, Chief," Lutz added, scratching at his arm inside a leather sling. He had caught an arrow during the fight, but the new healer had done a good job getting out the shaft and patching him up. Tiger had been triple-smart to save the woman, he thought. Her assistant had been useless, though, so was thrown to the troops. She hadn't survived the night, but nobody was really complaining.

Blowing a long stream of dark smoke out his mouth, Camarillo inspected the soggy end of the cigar. "Yeah, that does sound smart," he admitted, putting the cigar back into place. "Hate to not torch the place, but Tiger makes a good point. Which is why—" Just then, a valve on the engine discharged a thunderous blast of steam.

"What was that again, Chief?" Durante asked, cupping an ear.

"I said, that's why I have changed my mind, and instead of Durante, I'm promoting Tiger to be my new lieutenant." Camarillo shifted the cigar to the other side of his mouth.

Grinning widely, Natters pounded Dean on the back, while Shapario let loose a war whoop.

"The newbie?" Durante gasped. "B-but he's just a kid!"

"A kid smarter than most," Camarillo said, resting an elbow out the window grill. "He figured out how to fix the *Atomsmasher*. He helped D'ville make the black powder we used to blow up the ville gates, and he walked into the damn ville as a scout with only a blaster at his side." Camarillo removed the cigar to stab it at the coldheart. "Didn't you refuse to do the job because it was too dangerous?"

At the pronouncement, Althea glanced sideways at Dean, her eyes alive with hatred. If Dean noticed, he gave no sign.

"But...I...that is..." Durante stammered, turning red in the face.

"On the other hand," Camarillo continued, "if there was somebody tough enough to take him out—"

Snarling, Durante spun, clawing for his blaster.

With the Browning Hi-Power already in his hand, Dean fired once, and blood erupted from the older man's upper arm. Clutching the flesh wound, Durante reeled backward, then made a feeble grab for his own blaster. Coolly, Dean shot him again, in the upper thigh. With a cry, Durante toppled over to lay sprawled in the hard-packed dirt, his breath a puffy mist in the cold morning air.

"Why'd you let him alive?" Camarillo asked, crossing his arms.

"Be a waste of lead to ace him, Chief," Dean countered, holstering the weapon. "He's just drunk from all the shine and chilling. Besides, the Sarge is the best damn gunsmith we have. Those don't grow on trees, ya know."

"That's for sure," Camarillo said softly, the words almost lost in the huffing of the steam truck. "However, during the fight last night, I saw him hide among a pile of corpses when the ville boys staged a rally." Pushing up the cloth on his forehead, he exposed an open wound. "I got this because that yellow piece of mutie shit ran when the lead started flying hot."

"A dirty coward," Natters whispered, putting a wealth of hatred into the last word.

Hawking loudly, Lutz spit on the wounded coldheart, while O'Shea and Bradshaw pulled out knives and started walking forward.

"Wait, don't ace him!" Dean commanded.

"What?" Bradshaw said in a throaty growl, his knuckles white on the handle of the knife.

"You gonna let him live?" O'Shea asked incredulously.

"Th-thank you, brother," Durante wheezed, tears streaming down both cheeks. "By the Sacred Eagle God of DeeCee, I promise that—"

"Shut up, slave! Strip the bastard naked, and break both arms so that he can't defend himself," Dean stated without emotion. "Then chain him with the other sluts. The ladies can play with him on the trip back to camp… where we're going to nail his stinking bones to the lashing post!"

As the coldhearts gave voice to their savage approval,

a pale Durante fumbled for the knife on his belt and started to cut his own throat. Before anybody could move, a blaster cracked, and the blade went spinning away, a mirror in the sunlight, to bounce off the armored side of the hulking *Atomsmasher*.

"Natters, take his boots," Dean said, holstering the Browning. "Shapario, you get his horse. Lutz, his blaster. I'll take half his brass, and the rest goes into the war chest."

Screaming hysterically, Durante tried to fend off the coldhearts as they descended upon him, brutally using their blasters and boots to pulverize his shoulders and arms. Mercifully, the feebly struggling man fell unconscious long before they were done and dragged him away to certain doom.

"You could have taken everything," Camarillo said, pulling a home rolled cigar from his shirt pocket. He tossed it over.

Making the catch, Dean tucked it into the side of his mouth. "That would have made it seem personal, instead of biz," he replied, flicking a wooden match alive with a thumbnail. He started to hold it to the end of the cigar, then paused. "Is this tabacca?"

"Mixed with a little Mary Jane and wolfweed."

Flicking aside the match, Dean tucked the cigar into a pocket. "Then I'll save it for later, when I'm not in front of the troops."

"I'm smoking one," Camarillo stated gruffly, his eyes narrowing dangerously.

Dean gave a half smile. "Yeah, but I'll bet that yours is just broadleaf tabacca, and not a damn thing else."

"As I said before, smarter than most," Camarillo

grunted, the fumes of the cigar rising into the air exactly like the dark smoke exiting the iron-bound chimney of the *Atomsmasher.*

"What good is a feeb as XO?" Dean asked, drawing the Browning to drop the clip. He started thumbing in fresh rounds.

"XO?"

"Old speak for executive officer, a lieutenant."

Camarillo nodded. "Nice, I like it. But the troops would prefer lieutenant." With a squeal of rusty metal, a riveted door in the control room swung aside, and he stepped onto a short set of stairs. "So, Lieutenant Cawdor, what's our next move?"

Easing the clip back into the handle of the blaster, Dean worked the slide to chamber a round, then clicked on the safety. "We leave for camp, and along the way accidentally let a couple of the wrinklies and some of the little ones escape."

Camarillo frowned deeply at that. "What in nuking hell for?"

"They'll head straight for the nearest ville. That will spread word of the massacre, and put fear of the Stone Angels into the bones of every civie and sec man across the whole damn valley."

"I see," Camarillo muttered, removing the cigar to inspect the soggy end. "That way, the next time we charge a ville shouting our name, most of the civies will run away in fear, weakening the wall defense."

"Mebbe some of the sec men, too. Then we keep doing it. Each time, making it easier for us to take over a ville, and the next one after that."

"Winter corn again, eh?"

Dean shrugged. "Gotta plan for the future, Chief. Besides, the wrinklies wouldn't be good for anything but target practice, and now we have Durante for that."

For a long minute, Camarillo looked hard at the teenager, then slowly smiled. "Well done, Lieutenant. There's a sealed jelly jar of .308 brass that'll fit your BAR longblaster in my bunker back at camp. Stop by for dinner tonight. We'll talk some more biz, and you can pick it up afterward."

"Thanks! But you better make it after dinner. I plan to do some hard riding with my new slut as soon as possible," Dean said, smacking the girl on the butt. Althea jumped at that contact, but stayed mum, her face oddly blank.

"Fair enough," Camarillo relented, going back inside the iron room. "Now go choose your wrinklies. Two should be enough."

"Better make it an even dozen."

"Five, and make triple-sure they're strong enough to run away from any mutie, but not in such good shape that they'll try to come back and rescue any friends." The door slammed shut, and Camarillo scowled through the grille. "If even one of my coldhearts gets aced by them, you pay the price. Understand?"

"Yes, sir!" Dean said, snapping off a smart salute.

Snorting in reply, Camarillo returned the gesture much more cavalierly, then started working the controls of the steam truck. Slowly, the huge machine began to inch forward, gradually building speed.

"Come along," Dean commanded, and Althea rushed to obey.

Once they were away from the other coldhearts, she

moved in closer to whisper, "You helped these monsters raid my ville," she said, "yet you saved those wrinklies. I don't understand."

"I have to pretend to be a part of the gang, or else it will be my ass nailed to the lashing post," Dean stated bluntly, slowing his long stride to match her smaller steps. "I helped the wrinklies because it's the right thing to do. An old friend of mine named Doc always used to say that the only true definition of civilization was the strong helping the weak. That sounds about dead center to me." He shrugged. "I can't save everybody, but if I manage to rescue even one poor bastard from a life in chains, that seems worth doing."

Walking alongside the teenager, Althea said nothing until reaching his horse. Climbing into the saddle, Dean reached down a hand. Without hesitation, she took it, and he pulled her up to sit behind him.

"Hang on tight. The sons of bitches like to ride fast," Dean growled, his hatred for the other coldhearts readily evident. "It takes the fight out of the slaves, and makes them easier to train."

Wrapping her arms around his waist, Althea rested her head against his back.

"Got any family?" Dean asked in a whisper.

"Some," she replied in confusion. "My mother got aced on the wall, but my father used to be the ville potter, and I have a cousin named Bill."

"Old?"

"Young. A sec man."

"Too bad for him. We'll find your father, and he'll be the first of the five set free."

Hot tears welled in her eyes, and Althea hugged Dean a lot tighter than necessary to merely stay on the horse.

"Yeah, I know." He sighed, shaking the reins to start the horse into an easy walk. "Wish I could free everybody. But at the moment there's nothing we can do but wait, and stay sharp." Dean kicked the horse into a hard gallop and headed toward the long line of chained slaves.

Chapter Seven

Checking over everything one last time, the companions prepared their meager supply of weapons.

"Everybody ready?" Ryan asked, loosening the panga in the sheath at his side.

"Born ready," Jak said confidently, flexing his hands.

"That must have surprised your mother immensely," Doc quipped,

Jak grinned. "Nope. She born ready, too."

"Okay, we go on my mark," Krysty said, stepping out of the cobbled-together war wag, and walking over to the keypad alongside the blast doors. "Three…two…one…go!" Slowly, she tapped in the access code.

At the sound of working hydraulics, she turned and ran for her life back down the tunnel as the blast doors started to ponderously move aside.

As the first thin crack between jamb and door appeared, a glowing green mist issued into the redoubt, and the howler cut loose with a hellacious wail, the noise echoing along the tunnel until it sounded as if there were a thousand of the things waiting outside.

Scampering up the front grille of mismatched car bumpers, Krysty reached the top of the chrome-plated barrier, and just barely managed to squeeze between it and the ceiling. The fit was deliberately tight and, for a split second, Krysty thought she wasn't going to make it. Then her snagged belt buckle came free and she slid forward to land on top of the domed cage.

Grabbing a bar, she swung through the open roof hatch and dropped into her seat as Jak moved forward to close the hatch. He then rammed home a thick bolt, locking it tight.

"Welcome aboard Flight 666, leaving for the ninth level of hell," Mildred muttered, tightening the safety harness around her chest. "Please extinguish all cigarettes and prepare to kiss your ass goodbye."

"What did you say, Millie?" J.B. asked, furiously working the hand pump on a pressurized container.

"Nothing, John. Keep working," she said, raising the modified broomstick. "I've got your back!"

"Hope so," he replied, redoubling his efforts.

As the flexing tip of an armored tentacle crossed over the threshold, the antiradiation systems surged into operation, hammering the howler with powerful streams of orange foam and blasts of live steam. Shrieking insanely, it struggled to gain entrance, but as the door continued to move, additional wall vents added their contents to the disinfectant torrent. Once more the howler was forced out of the entrance, but no farther. Its writhing tentacles latched on to any irregularity in the fused earth outside, holding the creature in place, until it started to inch forward once more.

"Fireblast, here we go!" Ryan cried, stomping on the gas pedal and shifting into gear. The rumbling diesel and gasoline engines struggled to synchronize their speeds, then the transmission engaged with an audible grind, and the wag lurched into action, the dozen exhaust pipes issuing thick plumes of oily smoke.

At barely a crawl, the cumbersome vehicle inched forward, the grille of the car and truck bumpers scraping along the walls and throwing off sprays of bright sparks.

"Onward, the mighty *Hercules!*" Doc bellowed, waving a fist.

"What Hercules?" Jak asked with a scowl.

"From Greek mythology, a famous slayer of demons!"

"Would have preferred *Xena,* myself," Mildred snorted.

Doc blinked. "Who is that, madam?"

"Lucy Law… Tell ya later!"

Sitting among the laboring engines, the companions were tightly strapped into chairs firmly bolted to the corrugated floor. They were draped in crude ponchos made from plastic shower curtains, and completely surrounded by a lumpy metal cage composed of driveshafts and axles, reinforced by dozens of shock absorbers.

In spite of the cascading deluge from the walls and ceiling, the green mist began creeping around the bumpers, extending tiny tendrils into the *Hercules.* With a sputter, the front two engines died, and the rear four struggled to take up the slack. After checking the play on their hoses, Doc and Mildred stabbed out the broomsticks to sweep the cloud with the acetylene welding torches duct-taped to the ends, the thin stilettos of blue flame brighter than the sun. As the cloud retreated, the engines struggled back to life.

"Goggles!" Ryan shouted, pulling a sheet of window glass into place.

Moving fast, everybody did the same, with J.B. peering

owlishly through his double layer of wire-rimmed glasses and car window.

As the makeshift war wag entered the defensive jets, the wall vents tried to change their angle to stay concentrated on the howler. However, that was soon impossible, and the powerful torrents of deadly steam eased, leaving only the sticky orange foam. In seconds, the companions were drenched, and a welding torch went out with a pronounced hiss.

Keening louder than ever, the howler shambled over the threshold and into the redoubt, only to slam into the moving wall of car bumpers. The *Hercules* jerked at the collision, and the companions were almost torn from their seats, but their safety harnesses held. Then a diesel engine coughed and stopped.

Kicking the starter on the Harley-Davidson motorcycle, Krysty got the Twin-V 88 auxiliary engine working, and a set of car generators attached to the tireless wheels revved into furious operation.

As the chrome started to peel off the bumpers, exposing the soft iron underneath, Ryan flipped a switch on the dashboard, and the full power of a dozen car batteries cut loose, augmented by a score of alternators and generators. Fat electric sparks snapped and crackled across the grille, and the moaning howler hesitantly retreated.

"Holy shit, it's working!" Mildred shouted, using a road flare to ignite her torch once more. Then she glanced at the pressure gauge. The repaired tank was already down a third. Damn it, the hose was leaking again! At this rate they'd never reach the nuke crater.

"Only hurt, not chilling!" Jak shouted, trying to get

the diesel working once more. A wrench slipped from his hands and dropped through the open gridwork of the floor.

"Don't need to ace it! Just move the big bastard back a hundred feet!" Ryan replied, frantically working a choke, a throttle, stepping on a clutch and finally shifting into high gear.

The wag was almost at the blast doors, but a glance at the dashboard told Ryan the bad news. The power was dropping again, almost as quickly as the fuel supply. If there had been just one fragging nuke battery among the crashed mil wags, the *Hercules* would have been unstoppable. Now it was a contest between mutie and machine, with all of their lives riding on the outcome.

Reaching down among the complex array of controls on the floor, J.B. twisted a valve, then pressed a button. There was a low hiss of gas, then the gasoline engines revved with power, the *Hercules* surging forward as if jet-propelled to slam into the howler with prodigious force.

"Nitrogen gas!" he shouted, keeping a hand on the valve in case the engines started melting. "Found a bottle in the dentist office! Only a few pounds of pressure, but while it lasts…"

With a lurch, the howler fell back. The companions' wag erupted from the redoubt and started streaking across the glass bottom of the nuke crater.

Twisting the steering wheel hard, Ryan banked sharply in a tight circle and headed straight back at the howler as it tried to reach the closing blast doors.

"You're not getting inside!" he snarled, sweeping in from the side.

Just for a second, the world disappeared as the companions were engulfed by the swirling cloud. Then the grille of bumpers exploded off the front of the *Hercules* as they rammed the unseen mutie at full speed. Yellow blood splashed across the front of the wag as a pale, misshapen mutie flew through the air to land sprawling amid a cluster of crystal spires. Twinkling shards blasted everywhere, masking the mutie, and before the companions could get a clear view of the creature, the strange green mists returned to obscure it once more.

Covered in golden blood and orange foam, Ryan swung the war wag around again for a second pass, the four car tires losing traction on the slippery surface, but the six military tires holding on tight. However, at the very last moment, the nitrogen ran out and the engines decelerated, the wag drastically slowing as if hitting an invisible wall. Easily, the howler moved aside. But there was a smear of inhuman blood on the fused soil behind, a contrail of lost life, and the protective cloud was much smaller than before.

Circling the creature, Ryan deliberately slowed this time, and the companions cut loose with their blasters. Then J.B. added a Molotov that had been poured into a vinegar bottle. Sounding almost human, the howler screamed in pain from the rear assault, and more blood spurted from the cloud, splashing across the crystalline earth.

Jouncing over a shallow ravine, Ryan snorted as he studied the dashboard. Every dial was either busted or giving wildly inaccurate data, with engine temperatures showing in the thousands of degrees, the wag's speed at less than five miles an hour. The ground underneath flashed by in a blur.

"Blast doors?" Ryan shouted, swinging past an outcropping of slagged bronze that bore a vague resemblance to a man riding a horse. It had to have been an airburst for anything on the ground to survive a thermonuclear explosion.

"Almost… Okay, they're closed!" Krysty answered. "There's no way it can get inside now!"

Grunting in reply, Ryan turned away from the howler and started across the bottom of the blast crater, soon leaving the wounded mutie far behind. Even if they had the spare brass, there was no reason to waste it on something they could easily outrun.

"Then good night, wretched boy, parting is such sweet sorrow!" Doc yelled, triumphantly brandishing the broomstick. "Let us say good night, till be it morrow!"

"Stop misquoting Shakespeare." Mildred laughed in relief, turning off her torch to save gas. The cracked dial said that the tank was empty, but the flame was still bright and strong.

"Ah, but the Bard of Avon had no objection to his actors doing a bit of ad-libbing," Doc replied haughtily, doing the same to his own torch.

"You're old, but not that old!"

He grinned mischievously. "Am I not, dear lady?

"Not unless your real name is actually Dr. Methuselah Tanner," Mildred answered back.

With a roar, the *Hercules* raced across the nuke crater, Ryan effortlessly dodging the spiky, jagged crystals that rose irregularly from the vista of rad-fused soil. Soon the rad counter on his lapel eased out of the red zone.

"Go left!" J.B. commanded, pulling out his compass to check the heading.

Shifting into a lower gear, Ryan took off in that direction. The sloping walls of the crater were noticeably lower there, and he started up the glass. But the going was extremely treacherous, and every couple of yards the top-heavy wag slid back a little. Only the military tires gave the *Hercules* any purchase, the civie tires spinning uselessly on the slick material.

"Walk faster," Jak declared, removing his face shield to wipe the sweat off his face. Then he caught a reflection in the glass and turned around. "Incoming!" he growled, pulling the Colt Python and thumbing back the hammer.

"I see it. Save your brass!" Ryan ordered, both hands white on the steering wheel. "Only shoot when—if—the bastard gets close!"

"Lead doesn't do anything unless we shoot it in the back!" Mildred reminded them.

"I know that!" Ryan snapped. "But mebbe we can…" However, he was out of ideas. If they didn't reach the crest of the crater before the howler got ahold of them, it would be all over.

Only one choice then, Ryan dourly noted. He'd shift into Reverse and ram the bastard mutie, driving it all the way back down to the redoubt, then try to crush it between the machine and the blast doors. He would buy the farm, but the others could jump out along the way and might survive. Unlikely, but possible.

"Lighten the load!" J.B. commanded, ripping free

the useless nitrogen tank and shoving it through the bars of the cage. It hit the fused soil outside with a ringing clang, then skittered away, rapidly increasing speed until it vanished in the distance.

"Doc, get the rear hatch open!" Krysty added, unearthing a wrench and kneeling alongside the Harley. She started undoing the restraining bolts.

"At once, dear lady!" Slapping open the buckle on his safety harness, Doc slipped free and lurched to the rear of the war wag by holding on to the overhead cage.

Ryan fought the shuddering, fishtailing wag yard by yard up the wall of the blast crater. The howler continued after them, steadily moving faster, as if its wounds were healing.

With a creak of tortured metal, Doc got the rear hatch open and pushed it aside, only to have it come swinging right back and almost clip off his hand. Scowling in annoyance, he pushed it open once more, and J.B. tied the hatch to the bars of the cage with a length of fuse.

"Give me a hand," Krysty grunted, trying to lift the Harley-Davidson from its cradle.

The other companions stumbled over to assist, then awkwardly manhandled the motorcycle to the rear door.

"Careful! We only get one chance at this…" Krysty said through gritted teeth, trying to estimate trajectory and speed amid the constant waggling.

By now the howler was only a hundred feet behind the war wag, the green cloud pulsating as it expanded.

Suddenly, Jak shoved the bike through the door. It hit with a crash, loose parts breaking off to fly randomly away as the machine tumbled down the smooth slope, rapidly building speed. Caught between a ravine and a stand of crystal spires, the howler paused for a spit second in confusion, and the Harley slammed into the creature, pushing it down the crater wall, careening helplessly through an endless array of shattering crystals. Reaching the bottom, the cloud slid along for quite a while before finally coming to a rest near the bronze statue. The ancient metal immediately began to change color.

"Nice shooting, Tex!" Mildred said, patting him on the shoulder. "Ever done any professional bowling?"

Arching a snowy eyebrow, Jak could only stare at her in a complete lack of comprehension.

"That was a compliment," J.B. told him, pushing back his poncho. Then he grinned. "At least, I think so."

Slowly rising, the howler shambled forward once more, as unstoppable as the dawn.

"How very annoying. Shall we try the chairs next?" Doc asked, brushing back his long silvery hair.

"Let's use one of the diesels," Krysty suggested, flexing her hands.

Jak nodded. "Sounds good."

Just then, the *Hercules* stopped fishtailing and with a hard jerk went level again, the speed increasing dramatically.

"Made it!" Ryan sighed, easing his grip on the wheel. Flipping switches on the cracked dashboard, he attempted to turn off a few of the engines to save fuel, but they continued running. "Somebody ace those things!"

"On it!" J.B. replied. Walking over to the nearest engine, he placed a hand on top of the air filter, then reached down and yanked out the distributor cap. With a gasp, the machine stopped, and then he did the same thing to both diesels. There was a lot more juice for the car engines than for the big Detroit power plants, which was a shame, since they got much better mileage.

The hard ground was fused and cracked for hundreds of feet around the nuke crater, something the Trader used to call the dinner-plate effect, but in the distance Ryan could see a vista of growing plants, and past that a scattering of trees.

"We'll go slower in the woods," Krysty stated, removing her splattered poncho. "But it sure will be nice to see green again."

"On the other hand, we better not stop until we are very far away from here," Mildred advised, gratefully dropping into her chair.

"Now, that could prove to be most unwise, madam," Doc said, loosening the knotted fuse and closing the hatch to lock it tight. "We should briefly halt to remove as much of this cage as possible. While iron bars do not a prison make, the sheer mass of the metal is slowing us considerably."

"Agreed," J.B. stated, wiping his glasses clean. "Speed is our best defense against that mutie."

"That's brass in my blaster," Ryan agreed, pulling throttles and pushing in chokes before applying the brakes. The wheels squealed in protest, and smoke rose from the front tires, but gradually the rattling vehicle came to a full stop near the edge of the grasslands. The ground below was a mixture of fused earth and rich loam.

"Okay, Krysty and Mildred on guard," Ryan directed, gratefully releasing the steering wheel to flex his sore hands. "J.B. and Doc, cut the cage. Jak and I will do the engines."

As everybody got busy with their assigned tasks, Ryan took a few minutes to try to massage some life back into his aching muscles. As a young man, he had once killed a cougar with his bare hands, the bastard fight of his life, but trying to control this ramshackle piece of homemade salvation was starting to rate a close second. He felt as if he had been beaten with a club. Even his bones ached from trying to control the machine. With six different engines all running at the same time, it was a miracle his arms hadn't been yanked out of their sockets.

It took J.B. and Doc almost an hour to cut away as much of the cage as they dared without weakening the structural integrity of the *Hercules*. Meanwhile, Ryan and Jak removed both of the big diesel power plants and their fuel tanks, then did the same thing to one of the gasoline engines, which had cracked its block sometime during their escape. The engine was still running, but it wouldn't for long at the rate it was losing oil. The removal cost them a lot of horsepower, but hopefully, the decrease in weight would balance everything out.

"Done, and done!" J.B. announced, turning off the acetylene torch. "We cut away anything more from the frame, and the wag might fall apart."

"It might anyway," Doc said in disdain, tossing aside an empty fuel tank. Then he softly added under his breath, "By Gadfrey, we should have named this the vehicle *Frankenstein* instead of *Hercules*."

"The doctor was named Frankenstein, not the creature!" Mildred replied smugly.

"No, madam, the creature was called Adam and took the last name of Frankenstein for himself. Go read the book again."

"Sure, just let me pull a copy out of my ass!"

Sliding his leather jacket back on, Jak scowled. "How far next redoubt?" he asked, returning to the subject at hand. He really didn't give a damn about predark white-coats and their bastard experiments.

"About six hundred miles or so, as the crow flies," J.B. replied, not bothering to check the map in his munitions bag. "And we have a lot of bad country to cross, too,"

"Want me to take the first shift driving, lover?" Krysty asked, sitting on a nearby tree stump.

"No, I'm good for a couple more hours," Ryan replied, wiping his greasy hands clean with a gasoline soaked rag. "Just let's have… Fireblast!"

A glowing green cloud was rising over the rim of the crater, and the wind carried to them a low, inhuman moan.

Chapter Eight

Scrambling back into the stripped-down *Hercules,* everybody grabbed a seat, and Ryan quickly got the wag moving. The handling was much easier for him with only three engines to contend with, and the speed was considerably faster. He had no accurate way to gauge the velocity, but the grasslands were crossed in only a few moments, and soon the crater was lost in the distance behind them. Out of sight, but never out of mind.

Entering the forest, Ryan discovered the remains of an ancient road and followed it deeper into the woods. The trees were well spaced, with lots of sunlight coming through the branches, so lack of headlights didn't slow them in the least. Miles passed in restful quiet. It was cool among the trees, with squirrels darting about on the ground, and birds singing in the upper branches. The companions smiled at the sweet sounds, as it meant there were no major predators in the area, which was always good to know. There were a lot of bushes alongside the road, blueberry, hydrangea and laurel, along with the occasional wreckage of a partially melted skyscraper, the windows smashed and the interior alive with insects and weeds.

Startled, Mildred sat upright as something flashed by the hurrying wag. "This was a park!" she said, spotting the rusted remains of a wrought-iron bench.

"Most excellent news! Parks indicate the presence of a major city, or even a metropolis!" Doc said with a grin. "And we shall need an abode for the evening. It would be far too dangerous to risk driving across open country at night without working headlights."

"Even if I had put in a set, they never would have survived ramming the howler," J.B. said with a dismissive shrug.

However, noon came and passed without any sign of a city. Eventually, Krysty replaced Ryan behind the wheel, and then Jak took his turn wrestling with the mighty *Hercules.* Coming across a babbling creek, the companions stopped for a break, but then quickly decided against it and moved onward as the creekwater registered hot on the rad counters.

"Lover, what are we going to do if the mat-trans in the next redoubt is also down?" Krysty asked, unscrewing the cap from a canteen to take a drink.

"Check another," Ryan replied gruffly, rubbing his bristly, unshaved jaw. "But we gotta consider the possibility that the whole bastard system has crashed, and that we walk from now on."

"Or find someplace to stay," Doc countered, unwrapping a stick of gum from an MRE food pack. "Perhaps Vermont was not very badly damaged during skydark, and we know there are friendly villes in Virginia, Nevada, and New Mexico." Starting to chew, Doc frowned. "Not many, but a few."

"N'Orleans," Jak added proudly, making it one word.

"Okay, four villes out of hundreds." Mildred sighed, shaking her head.

"Better than naught, madam."

"Sad, but true."

"How to get there would be the next problem," J.B. said, neatly sidestepping the whole issue of finding a permanent place to settle down. "This rolling heap of mismatched parts wouldn't last for an hour in the desert, or trying to cross the Darks."

"Horses," Jak stated, as if that settled the matter.

"Horses," Ryan said in somber agreement.

It was late in the afternoon when the companions stopped to take a break alongside a narrow brook. Getting out of the wag, they stretched cramped muscles, while Doc ambled off to relieve himself in the bushes.

"Hey, smell shine cooking," Jak said, sniffing the air.

"There might be a ville nearby," Krysty said hesitantly, resting a hand on her blaster.

"J.B. and I'll go check it out," Ryan said, getting the Steyr and hanging it over a shoulder. "Everybody else stay here, and be ready to run."

"Sounds good to me," Mildred said, rubbing her mouth with the back of her hand.

Following the pungent aroma of bubbling mash, the two men wandered through a forest of birch trees until coming to the swell of a low hillock.

A large log cabin stood across a woody glen, dark smoke spiraling from a stone chimney. A split-rail fence edged a vast expanse of neatly trimmed grass, where a small herd of sheep contentedly munched away. White vapors rose from a small hut near a cord of split wood, the breeze carrying the familiar smell of cooking shine.

Netting was draped over the front porch, and rocking in a chair was a busty teenage girl in torn pants, and a patched denim shirt tied under her breasts for some much needed support. She was smoking a pipe and carving something small out of a block of wood.

"Hello!" Ryan shouted through cupped hands, and then gave a friendly wave. "Mind if we come over to talk some biz?"

Laying aside the knife and wood, the young woman spoke to somebody inside the cabin, and a hulking man appeared at the front door. Dressed entirely in tanned leather, he was bald with a beard that went down to his belt. He held what appeared to be a remade predark Barrett .50 longblaster.

Instantly, Ryan and J.B. became alert, but kept their weapons pointed at the grass. A drawn blaster wasn't the way to start a negotiation.

Bellowing something in an unknown language, the huge man swung up the Barrett and worked the arming lever. Diving for cover, Ryan and J.B. hit the grass just as the man cut loose, and a birch tree shook violently as a section blew off the trunk.

"Hey, we just want to talk!" J.B. yelled from behind a fallen log.

Peering between some weeds, Ryan saw a pair of adult women join the man on the porch, both also cradling longblasters, one of them working the lever to open the breech and insert a bullet. The teenager smoking the pipe appeared bored, and had started whittling on the piece of wood once more, as if this sort of thing occurred every day.

The three adults triggered their weapons in unison, and branches were blown off the birch trees, missing the companions by inches as they came crashing down.

"Mighty unfriendly folks," J.B. observed, removing his hat and stuffing it inside his jacket.

The longblasters boomed again, the trio of concussions rolling across the grazing land to shake leaves off the trees.

"Bastard good shots, too," Ryan added with a grimace. "They're not even using the telescopic sights, but just firing from the hip. Not sure I could do that."

The grim family fired another synchronized volley, the rounds slapping into the side of the hillock, throwing out puffs of dirt.

"These are warning shots," Ryan snarled, pressing himself lower against the ground.

The ancient longblasters spoke again, and the log exploded, nearly breaking in two, loose chips and bit of bark flying everywhere.

"So I figured," J.B. grunted, squinting through his glasses. "If they like blasters so much, what do you say we show them what we got, old buddy?"

"Fine by me," Ryan replied. "On my count of three... two...one!"

Rising slightly, both men cut loose with their blasters, but the range was too great, and the hardball rounds only rustled the tall grass and startled the sheep, not even reaching halfway to the sharpshooters.

As she worked the bolt on her longblaster, the shirt of the younger woman got caught and ripped free. Uncaring, the topless woman fired the longblaster again, her full breasts jumping from the titanic recoil. Her face was sweaty and smiling, and now both of the companions understood that these were chill thrillers, crazies who liked to ace folks purely for the pleasure of taking a life. There would be no negotiations with these people, and since there was nothing the companions wanted except for some shine for the wag, it was pointless to expend any more brass.

"Time to go," Ryan muttered, and crawled away until the natural curve of the hill took the log cabin out of sight.

Returning to the other companions, Ryan and J.B. brushed the leaves off their shirts, and tousled their hair to remove any lingering wood chips or bark.

"We heard blasters," Krysty said, scanning behind them for any danger.

"What happened?" Doc asked, hefting the LeMat and looking around in a circle.

"We got a lesson in marksmanship," J.B. snorted, climbing back into the wag.

"Let's get moving," Ryan said, squeezing in through the cage. "And if any topless women appear, shoot to chill."

Hours later, the sun was nearing the horizon when the companions saw several columns of dark smoke on the horizon. They seemed to be rising from behind a long narrow band of tan stone. The regular pattern clearly showing it was a wall.

Driving closer, they could see that the surrounding land was laid out in neat squares of different colors— the dark green of some leafy vegetable, the tall golden shafts of wheat. There was even a barren field where nothing had been planted, to let the soil rest and recharge for a season.

"By the three Kennedys, that's crop rotation!" Doc

said in delight. "Clearly, these are not uneducated hill-billies such as those people you encountered!"

"Which only makes them that much more dangerous," Ryan growled, pulling an object from his coat pocket about the size of a soup can.

Extending the antique Navy telescope to its full yard in length, he surveyed the place. "Can't see much from this angle," he muttered. "Just some wooden guard towers, a gallows and what looks like a brick water tower in the center of ville. No signs of a slave pen."

"At least there are none in sight," Mildred retorted.

Squeezing out of the cage, Krysty stepped away from the wag and drew in a deep lungful of air. "No smell of long pig, if that helps any," she said softly, trying to sense anything unusual. Sometimes she could detect a trap, or an ambush, before it was sprung. But most of the time she couldn't.

"Well, we can't go much farther, anyway," J.B. said, bending over to rap a fuel tank with a knuckle. It responded with a hollow boom. "This is the last of our juice, and it's almost gone. Another fifty miles or so, and we start walking."

"How far do you gauge it is to the ville?" Doc asked, testing the draw on his new revolver. The 6-shot .38 S&W felt unnaturally light in his grip, almost like a toy in comparison to the massive LeMat handcannon.

"Twenty miles or so," Ryan said, collapsing the telescope. "That's cutting it close, but this is our best chance to get some supplies."

"We going to barter, or go for a nightcreep?" J.B. asked, stressing the first option to clearly show his preference.

"I'd rather cut a deal with the local baron," Ryan said gruffly, adjusting the Steyr to hang across his chest. "But if he's not interested in doing some biz, we still need those supplies. Juice, horses, food, whatever they got."

"Ain't got much barter with," Jak noted, starting forward.

Checking the magazine in his blaster, Ryan grunted. "Yeah, I know."

Following the road down the hill, Jak steered around several potholes large enough to swallow the wag whole, one of them with a small tree growing from the depths.

As they drew closer, a gong began to sound from the ville, and there seemed to be a lot of activity along the top of the wall. Suddenly, dozens of previously unseen people poured out of the fields to race toward a large dark area set into the wall. As they approached, the dark area swung aside, revealing it was a gate. The farmers raced into the ville, and the gate closed immediately.

"That was professionally done," Mildred said. "They've been attacked before."

"Who hasn't?" J.B. asked rhetorically, adjusting the meager contents of his munitions bag so that a length of fuse dangled in sight. It wasn't attached to anything but the rest of the roll, but the mere fact that he owned a predark mil fuse would make smart folks think twice about trying something.

Suddenly alert, Krysty looked sharply about, feeling as if she was under direct observation, even though there was nobody in sight. Could the ville have a doomie? Just in case, she decided to keep her thoughts under tight control. Better safe than chilled.

Abruptly, the wild countryside ended at a split-rail fence that edged the cropland and followed along the road. The wood was old and splintery, but studded with jagged pieces of glass that sparkled like diamonds in the setting sun. Next came a wide band of punji sticks, wooden poles jammed into the earth, the ends sharpened like spears.

Cradling the empty Steyr, Ryan nodded in approval at the layered defense. It was a good design. The punji sticks would ace anything from trying to jump over the outer fence. Triple-smart. The baron here was clearly no feeb.

In passing, the companions could now spot a couple raised platforms set among the crops to offer the field workers somewhere to fall back to in case of an attack. The base of each also bristled with punji sticks, and every one possessed a brass bell of some kind.

"Those are warning bells," Doc said, allowing himself a small smile. "They must have scavenged those from the ruins of a firehouse, or mayhap a school. This speaks well for the local baron. Clearly, he cares about his people."

"On the other hand, Hitler loved the German people," Mildred countered. "Only them and nobody else."

Just then, the *Hercules* passed by a crucified scarecrow, its arms outstretched, the bleached bones of a grinning human skull perched on top of the sagging, rag doll body. Though they surreptitiously checked their weapons, nobody made a comment.

"May I suggest that we swap blasters, my dear Ryan?" Doc asked, proffering the S&W .38 revolver. "It would be unwise for us to demonstrate the unique acoustic properties of your SIG-Sauer at this early a stage of the negotiations."

Passing over his blaster, whose built-in sound suppressor sometimes worked, Ryan said nothing as the exchange was made.

The farmland stopped at another set of fences, leaving a broad field of flat dirt that extended to the outer wall. That was pretty standard for any ville. This was a shatter zone, leaving invaders no place to hide or take cover, making them easier to chill. This close, the companions could clearly see the sec men stationed along the top of the wall. They were dressed in assorted clothing: flannel shirts, buckskins pants, leather jackets, fur hats and lots of faded denim. The only unifying item was a dark blue vest marked with a white star on the right side, and red stripes along the left. The companions easily identified that as a version of the American flag, which wasn't a good sign or bad, just something to take into consideration. The founders of the ville might have been military personal who survived skydark. That would explain the orderly fields and multiple layers of defenses.

The wall was composed of large stone blocks, some neatly cut into precise rectangles, while others were lumpy and irregular, clearly replacements added to effect repairs. There were more punji sticks along the bottom, but also more along the top to discourage climbers. The gate proved to be a collection of sheet metal bolted together into an overlapping pattern. In spite of numerous dents and scratches, it was a formidable barrier.

"Dark night, we'd need a lot of grens to blow a hole

in that," J.B. muttered, covering his mouth with a hand just in case of the sec men on the wall could read lips.

Braking to a halt at the end of the road, Jak turned off each engine individually both to save gas and to demonstrate how well equipped the *Hercules* was. A lot of people had never seen a working engine of any kind before.

Holding their blasters and crossbow clearly in sight, but not actually pointing then at the companions, the sec men and women on the wall did nothing, and several minutes passed before a woman appeared, wearing dark green fatigues. Her blond hair was tied back in a long ponytail, and a puckered scar crossed her face, ending at a badly broken nose. Blasters rested on each hip, and her battered leather gun belt was shiny with polish, the loops full of brass. A pinkie was missing from her left hand, and she wore a decorative bracelet on the right wrist, the wood covered with intricate scrollwork. A white scarf was tied around her throat, one end tucked into her shirt, the other blowing free in the wind.

Instantly, Ryan identified that as a wind marker to aid the other sec men in shooting. His respect for the woman increased. Obviously, this was the sec chief for the ville. He had a gut feeling that whoever gave her that scar was breathing dirt, and had been about a split second after her nose was broken.

"Welcome to Alton!" she bellowed, through cupped hands. "What are ya looking for, outlanders?"

"Trade!" Ryan replied, lifting both hands from the Steyr before stepping from the wag. Then he added, "Although I wouldn't mind a cool summer rain if ya got one!"

Although she clearly tried not to, she grinned at the joke, as did most of the other guards.

"Sorry, used the last one yesterday to wash the dog!" she replied, hooking both thumbs into the gun belt. "Anything else you need? We got some food to barter. But no room in the barracks. We're full up on gaudy sluts, and we don't got no slaves!"

"Glad to hear it!" Ryan said, taking a single step forward. "The name is Ryan Cawdor. We're looking for juice."

"Abigail Ralhoun, sec chief for Alton ville," she yelled back, then tilted her head to the side. "And this is Sergeant Constantine Hohner."

Standing next to the sec boss, the big man lifted his chin in a silent greeting. Heavily muscled, Hohner had a tattoo of an American bald eagle on his face, and stars on the back of both hands. A .22 longblaster was slung across his back, and holstered at his waist was a Webley .445 handblaster in good shape, the grip covered with notches.

His boots crunching on the loose dirt, Ryan walked to the edge of the punji sticks, and Ralhoun squatted to bring them closer together. Immobile, Hohner stayed off to the side, his hands splayed, poised and ready for a fight.

"Okay, Cawdor, we got some juice. Good stuff, too. What do you have for trade?" Ralhoun asked. "Always could use more brass, and you boys have enough blasters showing to start a major war, and that's the honest truth of the eagle god." She squinted. "Or are they empty?"

Moving slowly, Ryan drew the borrowed .38 revolver

and fired a single round into the air. The bang echoed off the stone wall and out into the fields.

"Now, that might have been your last," Ralhoun said, rubbing a finger along her scar. "But I don't think so." She turned. "Stand down, boys! We're talking biz!"

Relaxing their stance, several of the sec men rested their longblasters on a shoulder, and the archers eased the tension on their crossbows. Only Hohner didn't move. There was no visible sign of life except for the subtle rise and fall of his wide chest.

"So, a wag like that must have a mighty thirst. What ya got to trade for the juice?" Ralhoun asked, smiling widely.

"The wag," Ryan said, jerking a thumb in that direction.

That seemed to catch her totally by surprise. "Ya wanna barter the wag...for juice?" she asked in confusion.

"Nope," Ryan answered. "We'll trade the wag for six horses, tack and saddles, food for a week."

"Horses and tack? Then what the nuke did you ask about juice for?"

"To see if you could run a wag."

Slowly, Ralhoun smiled. "Triple-smart, there, Blackie." Shielding her face with a hand, she looked at the wag. "She's battered some, but I heard all three of those engines running, and she got here, sure enough. But I don't know...."

Grandly, Ryan gestured toward the fields. "Add on a plow, and with a gallon of shine you can plow more dirt in a hour than a hundred people in a day."

"Turn a war wag...into a field plow?"

"Triple the yield, easy."

"Mebbe yes, mebbe no," Ralhoun said warily. "But I prefer horses. Never yet seen a wag that could make more wags." Standing, she dusted off her pants. "Sorry, no deal."

"You sure? Lots of uses for engines," Ryan continued doggedly, wondering how the deal went sour so fast. "Pumping water from a deep well, moving that bastard big gate…and, of course, with this many engines, you could take the wag apart and make three smaller war wags. Or one big war wag covered with lots of armor."

"No, not interested," Ralhoun said, hitching up her gun belt.

"We can still barter brass for food—" Ryan started.

"Better move along, outlander," Ralhoun said with a scowl, resting a hand on the grip of a blaster.

Instantly, the companions swung their weapons around, and the sec men did the same, with Hohner in the lead, the pitted barrel of the Webley looking as big as a tunnel entrance. A long minute passed slowly, the tension in the air almost palpable.

"Fair enough," Ryan said carefully, taking a step backward. "We'll leave right now. No corpse, no crime, eh?"

Nobody laughed this time.

"Wise move," Ralhoun growled. "And don't be hanging around here waiting for any handouts! We've got nothing to spare."

That was clearly a lie, and suddenly Ryan knew why the deal had gone flat. He hoped that he was wrong, and the locals were just suspicious folks, but if he was correct, then the next thing they would do was offer some friendly advice.

"Hey, Chief!" Hohner called out. "Aren't there some ruins to the north of here?"

"Yeah, y'all can camp up there, Blackie," a sec woman added. "There be fresh water, and some game about. Squirrels and such. Not much, but better than chewing grass, eh?"

Nodding his thanks, Ryan walked backward to the wag and carefully got in, while Jak got the engine working. Shifting into Reverse, Jak drove the wag into the fields, and didn't stop until the companions were near the scarecrow and far out of longblaster range.

"That didn't go well." Mildred sighed, holstering her ZKR target pistol.

"It could have been worse," Krysty agreed with a scowl. "But not by much."

"Nightcreep?" Jak asked, twisting his hands on the steering wheel.

"So it would seem, my young friend," Doc muttered, as he returned the blaster to its proper owner. "As I have so often said, stupidity is its own reward."

With a shrug, Ryan passed back the S&W and checked the magazine in his own blaster. Stupid and greedy were pretty much the same thing to him.

"I just hope it's a dark night," J.B. growled, pulling out the thick roll of fuse.

"It will be for some," Ryan replied grimly, holstering the blaster.

Chapter Nine

By the time the companions found the ruins, night had fallen across the land, and the ringed moon slowly rose above the horizon. The so-called ruins turned out to be only a burned-down warehouse with one of the walls missing. But most of the roof remained, which was good enough to keep out the rain.

Parking the *Hercules* alongside the ancient warehouse, Ryan kept guard while the others went into the fields and woods to find as many dry sticks as possible. Then they got busy with the fuse.

Several hours later, a dying campfire was crackling softly in a shallow pit. Six bedrolls lay positioned around the small blaze, the moss-covered walls reflecting back the reddish light, making them appear to be painted in blood. Combats boots lay next to each bedroll, and there came the muted sound of snoring.

A dozen people carrying crossbows silently emerged from the darkness, their faces and hands blackened with charcoal. As soon as the lumpy bedrolls came into view, the attackers raised their crossbows and fired. The barbed arrows hissed through the night and slammed into the patched blankets with dull thuds. There was no reaction.

"Sorry about this, Blackie," Hohner said with a laugh, walking over to the first bedroll. "Just biz, as they say." But yanking aside the covering, he gasped in shock at the sight of a large bundle of twigs, bound tight with fuse.

"Nuking hellfire, it's an ambush!" Hohner shouted, tossing away the crossbow to claw for his blaster. "Grab iron, boys!"

But only one of the sec men did as he commanded, the rest horribly gurgling as dark fluids gushed from their throats. As the attackers toppled over, a companion was revealed standing behind each one, faces and hands dark with mud, sharp knives dripping with the dark rubies of life.

Snarling a curse, Hohner swung up the Webley hand-cannon, but Ryan fired first, the built-in baffle of the SIG-Sauer working, reducing the discharge to no more than a hard cough. Groaning, Hohner crumpled over, his blaster shooting randomly, the lead ricocheting off the brick wall and smashing the remnants of a dusty window.

"Don't shoot! I surrender!" the last sec man yelled, dropping his weapon and raising both hands.

Disgusted at the action, Ryan withheld triggering his blaster, and looked at Jak.

Instantly, Jak jerked his hand forward and let fly a knife. It turned over once, and the handle slammed into the forehead of the sec man. With a throaty sigh, he collapsed to the ground, twitching, but still alive.

"Perimeter sweep," Ryan commanded. "Mildred, ten yards. Doc at twenty. J.B., do fifty. Go!"

As they disappeared into the darkness, the rest of the companions starting gathering blasters and ammunition from the corpses.

"We really shouldn't have let this man live," Krysty said, scowling. "The local baron is going to be triple-mad over this, and he'll need somebody to punish for his mistake."

"Surrender, can't ace," Jak replied, recovering his knife.

"It would be a mercy."

"Not my prob," he said, sheathing the blade. "Cowards get what deserve."

She shrugged. "Fair enough."

Using a blanket from one of their bedrolls, the companions had assembled quite a pile of weapons when a whippoorwill sounded in the night. Quickly drawing his blaster, Ryan replied with a call of a seagull, and the other companions emerged like ghosts from the thick shadows alongside the sagging brick wall.

"All clear," J.B. announced, slinging the Uzi over a shoulder. "We found eight horses, and there are eight of these feebs."

"Okay, grab the bedrolls and let's go," Ryan said, holstering his blaster. "We want to be far away from here when the local baron figures out his nightcreep failed."

"Indubitably, sir," Doc said. "Hell hath no fury like a baron scorned."

Ignoring that, Mildred knocked away the bundle of sticks to gather up an armload of blankets. "What should we do with the wag?" she asked. "Burn it, so they can't follow?"

"No, just drain the fuel tanks, nothing more," Ryan growled, hoisting the blanket full of blasters. The clicking bundle sounded like an army preparing for battle.

"We offered Alton ville a fair trade, the wag for

horses and tack," J.B. added, watching the night for any suspicious movements. "Well, we got what we wanted, so the *Hercules* belongs to them now. Fair deal."

"Better deflate the tires, too," Krysty said, slinging a crossbow over her shoulder, then lifting another. "Remember they have juice. Or at least Chief Ralhoun said they did. But pumping up a flat tire is an entirely different matter."

Following Jak through the gloomy forest, the companions soon reached the horses. They were tethered to some bushes on the outskirts of the ruins, near what resembled the congealed remains of a melted aircraft. The weapons were stuffed into the saddlebags, then everybody chose a mount. The spare two horses were left behind to nibble on the low grass, as the companions walked their new horses over to the *Hercules* and finished transferring their meager supplies.

While J.B. drained the fuel, Doc and Jak let the air out of every tire. Both men secretly wanted to slash the tires to make any chance of pursuit absolutely impossible, but a deal was a deal. Mildred liked to say that honor was a binary state, either yes or no. There were no gray areas.

"Okay, we rendezvous in an hour, five miles due north," Ryan said, climbing into the saddle of his roan stallion. The horse nickered softly from the unaccustomed weight, and he reached out to gently scratch the animal behind the ear. It snorted at the unexpected pleasure, then shivered slightly, flexed its muscles and accepted the new rider.

Heading out in different directions, the companions did what they could to confuse any trackers—riding around in overlapping circles, doubling back over their own tracks and crossing streams. Riding a young gelding, Doc even sprinkled some of his precious black powder on the ground to deter any dogs, and Mildred did the same with a small amount of black pepper. She was very pleased with her choice, an Appaloosa mare that was clearly bridle-wise, and promptly responded to her every command.

"Okay, I'm not Clayton Moore, but Silver will do for a name, eh, girl?" Mildred whispered, gently patting the muscular neck.

Catching only the last part, Girl responded with a friendly nicker, her fear of the new master starting to fade at the easy tones, and the lack of spurs.

BACK IN THE RUINS, the little campfire dwindled away completely, and as darkness fell, creatures eased from the shadows to feast upon the corpses. The lone Alton ville sec man still alive came rudely awake with something sniffing at his face.

With a scream, he tried to bat it away, while also going for a blaster. Terrible pain filled his universe for a very short time, until it abruptly ended with the brutal crunching of his skull. Silence returned to the ruins, followed by the juicy gnawing of fresh meat, and low contented purring.

IN THE DISTANCE, Ryan could see riders coming his way, and he pulled out the Navy telescope. But the shadows were too thick for him to make a positive identification. Tucking away the device, he loosened the panga on his belt and thumbed back the hammer on his blaster to save a half second of reaction time. Just in case of trouble.

He didn't relax as Krysty came into focus, her animated hair endlessly moving, the red filaments seeming oddly black in the silvery moonlight.

Reining in her mount, she stopped a few yards away, one arm draped across the pommel of her saddle. "Hey, Adam," she called out in a monotone.

At that, Ryan allowed himself a half smile. The use of a name starting with that letter was her way of asking if he was bait in an ambush.

"The name is Charlie," Ryan replied, telling her the area was clear.

"Glad to hear it, lover." Krysty grinned, rode closer and leaned forward.

Thumbing the hammer back down, Ryan briefly kissed the woman. Then they both turned in the saddle, their blasters out and ready as three more riders approached, the beat of the hooves masked by the nearby turbulent river.

"Hey, Arnold," Mildred said, scratching her belly, her fingers only inches away from the deadly Czech ZKR.

"Yo, Adam," J.B. added, the Uzi openly held in his fist.

"Salutations, Abraham!" Doc hailed with a grin, giving a crisp salute.

The proper exchanges were made, and everybody eased their stance some when Jak suddenly rode into sight from around a copse of maple trees. He was bent low in the saddle, the Colt in his fist, his horse racing at a full gallop.

"Hey, Daniel!" Jak bellowed, continuing past the others without slowing.

Muttering curses, the companions kicked their horses into fast action just as the first howl was heard, the noise eerily cutting through the rumble of the river.

"Any riders, or just dogs?" Ryan demanded, loosening his grip to let the horse have free rein.

"Just dogs!" Jak replied, his long hair streaming in the wind. "But huge. Pit bulls!"

"Any wags or bikes?" Krysty asked urgently,

Jak gave a hard laugh. "No need!"

Fireblast, the bastard dogs were that large? Weighing their limited options, Ryan made a fast decision. "Fuck it, we ace them here!" he snarled, reining in the horse and turning.

"In open country, my dear boy?" Doc demanded askance, his S&W .38 at the ready. "We should retreat to the ruins, or engage the beasts among the foothills, funnel their attack and take them out individually, one at a time!"

"But if they're as big as Jak says," Krysty added, drawing the Colt .38 revolver, "we'd be wise not to let them get that close!"

"And here they come," J.B. added, working the arming bolt on the Uzi rapidfire.

Moving fast, a pack of pit bulls was streaking across the field. The dogs were enormous, easily three or four times the expected size.

Ryan grunted at the sight. Clearly, there was a little mutie blood in the dogs, which also explained their protruding fangs.

"Sabertooth pit bulls," Mildred whispered, feeling

her heart flutter at the sight. "Why didn't the baron simply send out those instead of risking sec men?"

"Were there any sec women in the group sent after us?" Krysty asked with a grimace, her hair coiling tightly.

"Not that I recall…oh," Mildred said, her expression turning nasty. So it had been a ride-and-raid party, eh? Now she was sorry that they had let one of the sons of bitches live. Her father had been a Baptist minister, a truly gentle soul of the Lord, but even he believed that the only proper way to handle any sexual predator was a firmly knotted rope and a short drop off a tall tree branch.

"Dark night, I wish those sec men had carried more ammo," J.B. said, hefting the Uzi, its weight telling him exactly how many rounds there were in the magazine. "A couple of spare nines would come in mighty useful right about now. I'll have to start conserving ammo. Had to share with Ryan."

Dourly, he cast a fast glance at the longblaster in the gun boot of his saddle. It was a Remington 30.08 bolt-action, perfect for this type of a fight, but until it was checked, it was a last-ditch weapon only. More than once when entering an ambush he had jammed the barrel of a spare blaster into the dirt to block the barrel, just in case it was taken away and somebody tried to use it against him. The back blast destroyed the weapon, but also took off the arm of the cannie, and let him escape alive. J.B. considered that a more than equitable trade. A blaster for his life.

"Woulda, shoulda, coulda," Mildred muttered. "Want me to find a cow?"

J.B. grinned. "No time, babe, but thanks for the offer."

"Here, take spare," Jak said, pulling a blaster from inside his jacket and tossing it over.

Catching the weapon, J.B. saw it was Hohner's Webley. Excellent! Letting the Uzi hang by its strap, he cracked open the top-break revolver to check the brass in the cylinder, then snapped it closed again with a jerk of his wrist.

"Look at them move. These are trained hunters, sec dogs!" Ryan said, pressing the SIG-Sauer flat against the saddle where it couldn't be seen. "Quick, everybody hide your blasters!"

"What for?" Jak asked through clenched teeth, stuffing the Colt into a pocket of his leather jacket.

"These dogs will be trained to avoid blasterfire," J.B. answered, swinging the Uzi behind his back. "But they won't do anything until we show iron. Understand?"

"Softly, softly, catchee monkey," Doc muttered, his hand jammed inside a saddlebag.

"Translation, don't shoot until you can see the whites of their eyes!" Mildred growled for the rest of the companions, who most likely had never read anything by Rudyard Kipling.

Moving low and fast, the monstrous dogs hurtled across the ground. Their clawed paws churned the dark earth, leaving behind a contrail of dirt, dust and dandelions. None of them barked or howled. They came on like machines.

"Horses not scared, must see a lot," Jak said smoothly.

Fingering her blaster, Krysty snorted. "Just not from this side of the fight."

"Easy now. Once we fire, they'll separate, each one attacking individually," Ryan said in a deceptively calm voice. "They'll be triple-hard to ace then, so we gotta chill all of them in a single volley. We go on my command."

"Aim for the mouth in case the half-breeds are armored like a hellhound," J.B. added, "and don't stop shooting until you're damn sure they're aced."

"Then shoot again," Jak said, his muscles tightening.

Suddenly, the panting of the pit bulls could be heard over the river, the padding of their paws sounding like impatient fingers drumming on a table.

"And…now," Ryan whispered, whipping out the SIG-Sauer.

In ragged unison, the companions swung around their blasters and cut loose with a thundering fusillade. The hail of soft lead rounds hammered the monstrous dogs, breaking their charge and sending several of them to the ground. Gushing scarlet, the bullet-riddled animals shuddered into death. But the rest kept coming, veering sharply away from one another to converge upon the companions from different directions.

Pulling around his empty Steyr, Ryan dropped the longblaster and vehemently cursed. Instantly, the largest pit bull charged, obviously thinking he was now unarmed and vulnerable. As it got close, he brought up the SIG-Sauer again, and shot the thing twice in the open mouth. Jerking backward as if it had swallowed a wasp, the pit bull mouthed broken teeth, and Ryan put another round into its side. Whimpering in pain, the wounded dog turned to limp away, and he ruthlessly fired once more, directly in its rear. With a yip, the pit bull froze, then fell sideways, gushing life from both ends.

Triggering the Uzi in short bursts, J.B. tried to track a hulking dog, riding the bucking blaster until it cycled empty. Then he pulled out the Webley and started placing his shots. A glancing round wounded the pit bull in the hindquarters. It whined from the pain, then turned to face the man, its eyes full of hate. His heart pounding wildly, J.B. did nothing as it raced forward and launched itself into the air, its huge mouth turned sideways to remove J.B.'s throat. At point-black range, he triggered the Webley, the huge round punching through the black nose to come out the back of the dog's head in a grisly spray of bone, brains and blood. A split second later, the corpse slammed into the man, and he nearly went out of the saddle, but grimly held on to the Webley.

With a loud whinny, Krysty's mare reared on its hind legs, throwing off her aim and sending a round harmlessly into the night. A pit bull lunged for the vulnerable belly, and the horse came down again, both its iron-shod hooves slamming into the back of the beast. There was a crackle of splintery bones, and when Krysty could see the dog again, it was lying on the grass, jagged pieces of bones sticking out of the dark hide, blood everywhere.

Coming out of the darkness like a stealth missile, a pit bull violently slammed into Jak, knocking him to the ground. He hit hard, then the dog was upon him, clawing and biting. The albino teen rammed his blaster into the animal's mouth, then slashed it across the throat with a knife and kicked it away. Shaking its head, the dog threw off a spray of crimson, then charged again, going for Jak's groin.

Twisting out of the way, Jak then threw his knife, which missed. The pit bull lunged for him again, stopped when a lance of silver speared the beast in an eye, the needle tip of the Spanish blade coming out its mouth.

"And thou, wretched boy, shall with him hence!" Doc bellowed, twisting the sword before yanking it free.

Blood gushed from the enlarged holes, and the dog wobbled away, only to arc back, still trying to reach Jak, but barely able to stay erect.

Contemptuously, Jak grabbed it by the scruff of the neck and slit its throat from ear to ear, then shoved it aside. "Thanks," he growled, flipping the blood from his blade.

"My pleasure," Doc replied, doing the same thing with his sword. "Now, cry havoc, for these are the dogs of war!"

"Not anymore," Ryan countered, setting a boot onto a dead pit bull to extract his panga. The blade came loose with a brittle sound, a piece of white bone stuck on the end.

"Any more of them?" Krysty demanded, her hair flexing wildly.

"This was the last," Ryan said, knocking the bone off the blade with the SIG-Sauer.

"Are you sure?" J.B. asked, squinting into the night to see if there were more colossal beasts coming their way. But the landscape was as peaceful as before, with the nearby river rushing along, splashing and crashing.

"I counted nine earlier," Mildred panted, holstering her blaster. "And we have that many bodies. Yeah, this is all of them."

"Good to know," J.B. said warily, not relinquishing his grip on the Webley handcannon as he got back into the saddle.

"Krysty, watch for anything else coming this way," Ryan commanded, recovering the Steyr. Briefly, he inspected the longblaster, then slung it across his back.

"Got your back, lover," Krysty replied, patting the neck of her horse as she stared into the night. The mare loudly chuffed in pleasure at that and stamped gory hooves.

"J.B., do a fast check on a couple of the longblasters. I'm out of brass again," Ryan said gruffly, wiping the panga clean on a chilled dog, before sheathing it again. "Mildred, inspect the bodies. Jak and Doc, get some of those crossbows loaded and ready!"

As the men got busy, Mildred slid to the ground and warily walked over to the nearest pit bull. She had to be sure that the wounds had completely stopped bleeding before she knelt to cut open the belly and inspect the internal organs.

"This is just a dog!" she announced with a note of surprise. "No sign of any serious mutations."

"Hot damn, steak for dinner!" Jak said with a grin, notching an arrow into a crossbow. The steel cross arms had been made from the leaf springs of a car, the bow made from a braided cable, and it took all his strength to load the weapon. It was crude, heavy, cumbersome, and would probably chill a bear at a hundred yards.

"Better make that breakfast," J.B. countered, looking at the moon through the barrel of the Remington. Satisfied that it was safe, he began to reassemble the weapon.

"Yeah, agreed," Ryan said, throwing a pit bull across his saddle. The stallion grunted from the impact. "It wouldn't be wise to stop and light a fire until we are far away from here!"

"Very far away from here," Krysty corrected, reaching out a hand in the windy night. "I think...I think the ville knows that we ambushed their men."

"How can they?" Ryan demanded, climbing into the saddle. "They got a doomie?"

"Somebody does...." she whispered, the fleeting images in her mind fading away as fast as they had come.

She struggled to see more, to again push back the ethereal curtains of time and space, but it was a useless effort.

"What direction doomie?" Jak asked, slinging a quiver of arrows across his back.

Shaking herself, Krysty came out of the reverie. "To the south, toward Alton. But we should go east."

"What for?" Mildred asked, looking in that direction. There were black mountains on the horizon, nothing more.

"Because the doomie doesn't want us to," Krysty replied, mounting her horse.

"Any idea why?" J.B. asked, working the bolt on the Remington.

She shrugged. "None whatsoever."

"Forgive me, dear lady," Doc said, shifting uneasily in his saddle. "But I feel compelled to remind everybody that the next redoubt is to the north. Due north."

"What do you think, old buddy?" J.B. asked, resting the Remington longblaster on a shoulder. "The Trader always used to say that when you're not sure what to do, at least make it something the enemy doesn't like."

"That loads my blaster," Ryan stated, kicking the stallion into an easy gallop. "East it is!"

Chapter Ten

Standing near the open doorway of the noisy tavern, Sec Chief Ralhoun leaned on a wooden railing and sipped from a plastic mug full of frothy beer, her loose hair fluttering gently in the breeze. Soon enough, the ville would have a wag, a real working war wag! It was a day for celebrating, yet she felt oddly anxious, the same way she did when the acid rains came early.

Inside the Greasy Eagle, a party was in full swing, with the ville folk singing and dancing, putting on a real show for the sec men chowing down for dinner, while others were off celebrating upstairs with the gaudy sluts. Ralhoun had already sampled both pleasures, and now just wanted to relax with a mug of beer, icy cold and fresh from the root cellar. However, the back of her neck was starting to prickle every time she thought about the sec men doing the nightcreep.

She had given them some extra time to have a little fun with the female outlanders before returning with the war wag. That sort of thing was just one of the perks of being a sec man. But when they seemed to be taking too long, she had unleashed the bulls as backup, in case there had been any unforeseen trouble. The outlanders did have a lot of blasters, and that one-eyed bastard named Ryan looked meaner than a shit house rat. But still…

Caught in the act of taking a swallow, Ralhoun gagged on the beer and spit it out into the street. Her mouth was filled with the taste of blood. Something bad had just happened.

Lowering the mug, Ralhoun tried to listen to the wind for any blasterfire, explosions or howling, but could not hear a thing over the raucous music from the tavern.

"Everybody shut the fuck up!" she bellowed over a shoulder.

In ragged stages, the party inside the tavern grew quiet.

"What's up, Chief?" a sec man asked, walking closer. A greasy napkin hung from his neck, and he held a partially eaten roasted lizard leg.

"There's something wrong with the bulls," Ralhoun said in a low, dangerous tone.

"Think they're snacking on the outlanders?" he asked, taking another bite of the greasy meat.

"My dogs know better than to eat longpig," Ralhoun muttered, setting down the mug. "No, the nightcreep must have gone sour. I can feel it in my bones."

That gave the sec man pause. Everybody knew that the chief was the daughter of a doomie, and while she didn't have the full powers of her deceased father, her gut feelings about things were almost always correct. That was how the ville had survived being betrayed by their former baron. He had secretly offered to trade everybody in Alton to a wandering band of cannies for some predark meds to cure his rad sickness. When she was just a lowly boot, Private Ralhoun had alerted the other sec men to the plan, the cannies got aced and the baron was chilled. Now Abigail Ralhoun was the sec chief, and the baron, although she only liked to be called chief.

Turning sharply, the sec man strode back into the tavern and cut loose with a long, loud whistle. "Get ready, people!" he bellowed. "The chief smells blood on the wind!"

Instantly, the party atmosphere was gone, and every sec man and woman in the place pushed aside their drinks or food to start checking their blasters.

"Hey, honey, we're in the middle of a game," a fat gaudy slut said, lowering a hand of cards. In the middle of the table was a large pile of cheap items, a plastic comb, a bit of a mirror, a golf tee....

"Later, sweetcakes," the sec man growled, holstering his remade Colt .45 blaster. "Biz, first."

"Hey, Bobbie!" a sec woman yelled up a flight of stairs.

On the second level, a door slammed open. "What?" a man demanded. He was stark naked except for a gun belt cinched around his waist.

"Something is wrong! We're gonna go check on the crew!"

"Shitfire...now?" He grimaced, glancing back at the slut behind him.

"Right bastard now!" Ralhoun insisted, reaching back to start tying her hair into a ponytail.

The sec man scowled, then sighed. "Okay, okay. I'll be right down." The door slammed shut.

"Schwartz, Faroot, Kleinova, saddle the horses!" Ralhoun ordered brusquely, pulling a strip of rawhide from her shirt pocket to lash her hair tight. "Muncy and

Caramico, get the grens! All of them! I want a posse ready to go in five minutes!"

"We'll ace those outlanders, Chief!" a sec woman boasted, brandishing her longblaster.

"Cut that crap! I want them to go to the lashing post alive and kicking!" Ralhoun growled, marching into the dark street. But almost instantly she paused, and looked to the east with a sick feeling in her stomach. Oh, no, anywhere but there....

BATHED IN MOONLIGHT, the companions rode on through the night, pausing only briefly to let their horses drink from a small pond, and feed on some apples in what had once been an orchard.

"Not too many," Krysty warned, filling her canteen from the pond. "Horses get stomach cramps very easily."

Wiping a finger behind his ear, Doc displayed it to the woman to show a complete lack of moisture.

Closing the canteen, Krysty chuckled in response.

"Smart-ass," Mildred snorted, stepping away from a bush to wash her hands in the little creek trickling away from the pond.

"Better than being a dumb-ass, I suppose." Doc grinned, stuffing some of the apples into his pockets for later. Delicious and nutritious, apples were food for both man and horse. The good Lord had done some mighty fine design work there.

"Here, this blaster is fine," J.B. said, passing over a battered M-16.

"How's the ammo?" Ryan asked, dropping the magazine, before sliding it back into the breech.

"Only two mags. So don't go trigger happy."

"Never have before." Working the arming bolt, Ryan was careful not to catch a finger when it snapped into place. "Any shells?" he asked, scowling at the stubby gren launcher attached just below the main weapon.

"None in the saddlebags. They probably save those for emergencies," J.B. replied, removing his glasses to clean them on a rag. "Thankfully, doing a nightcreep didn't come under that particular criteria."

"Criteria?"

"Criteria. Millie has been trying to improve my vocabulary."

"Seems to be working, old friend," Ryan said, giving a rare smile. "Trade you for the Remington? That's more my speed."

"Sure. I like rapidfires," J.B. said, patting the Uzi hanging from the pommel of his saddle.

The exchanged was made.

"All right, mount up!" Ryan stated, climbing onto his horse. "There's still plenty of night remaining."

"Woods lovely, dark and deep," Jak said, hoisting himself onto his stallion. "Have promises keep, and miles go before sleep."

Everybody was a little startled at such a long speech from the normally taciturn albino teen.

"Well done, me dear Jak!" Doc said beaming a smile. "Where did you learn that poem? It is one of my favorites."

"Learn from you," Jak replied. "Say all time."

"Do I really?" Doc asked softly, his voice starting to fade away.

Recognizing the telltale signs, Mildred spoke quickly.

"Now, the first time I heard it was in a Charles Bronson movie. Telephone, telethon, something like that. You sure the poem wasn't written by him?"

"An actor, madam?" Doc snapped furiously, the fog leaving his eyes. "It was penned by Robert Frost. One of the greatest poets of all time!"

"Better than Shakespeare?"

"Well, no, actually." Doc relented. "But I did say he was merely one of the best, not the grand master."

"In your opinion," Mildred said, using both knees to nudge her horse into motion.

Riding alongside, J.B. gave a telling nod.

Feeling herself blush under his frank approval, Mildred merely shrugged in reply.

As the companions continued eastward, the land began to rise and fall in gentle swells, indications of a massive earthquake.

Slow miles passed as they endlessly traversed shallow rivers, or rode through vast fields of clattering bamboo. With each breeze, the tall stalks smacked into one another, making a deafening clatter.

"Sounds like a million wooden wind chimes," Krysty yelled, maintaining a firm grip on her blaster.

"Or just one really big mutie crab," Ryan shouted back, keeping a finger on the trigger of the rapidfire.

Just then, a frog leaped out of the muddy water to land on the dead pit bull lying across his saddle, and took a tiny bite. Annoyed, Ryan knocked it away, only to have dozens more come flying out of the darkness, croaking defiantly. Kicking their horses into a full gallop, the companions soon left the infested field of bamboo, and the leaping army of frogs disappeared in the distance.

Smiling broadly, Jak removed a large frog from his knife and stuffed the it into a pocket for later. Down in N'Orleans, frogs were a staple item on the dinner table, and he knew how to fry the tasty little legs to perfection. That was when he noticed that the frog had teeth, and eight legs. Mutie! With a frown, he tossed the body away. He had never been hungry enough to eat a mutie, and never would. Starvation would be preferable to an agonized death of screaming dementia and shitting blood.

With the coming of dawn, Ryan stopped the companions in a small glade in a hollow. The combination of empty stomachs and lack of sleep was finally starting to take its toll. There was plenty of dry branches around for a fire, but the hollow would help hide the blaze from sight.

While J.B. and Jak did a perimeter sweep for anything dangerous in the area, Doc gathered firewood and Ryan used his panga to butcher the dog. He took extra special care to remove the area bitten by the frog, just in case the little mutie had been poisonous.

Since it was their turn, Mildred and Krysty unloaded the saddlebags, then Krysty laid out the campsite while Mildred walked the horses to a nearby stand of green grass. As they settled in to eat their fill, she checked the animals and found several of them with scrapes and bruises from the fight with the dogs. She treated the minor injuries as best she could with sterilized water mixed with shine. It wasn't much, but the best that she had. Her med kit hadn't been this empty since she first found it.

When J.B. and Jak returned, Krysty started to cook breakfast. Soon their campsite was awash with the delicious smells of rice and beans, and roasting dog meat, flavored with apple slices.

Taking along the aced pitbull had been a smart move. The saddlebags held little food or water, and absolutely nothing for the horses, not even a salt lick. That really wasn't surprising, since the sec men had fully expected to be safely back behind the ville walls within a few hours. This had only been a sortie, a smash and grab, as Mildred liked to call such things. But the companions had brought along all their bedrolls and other supplies from the *Hercules,* including the rice and honey from the redoubt.

"Nothing rare or medium, only well-done," Mildred warned, wrapping a bandage around the fetlock of a palomino. "We can't risk internal parasites."

While Ryan washed up in a nearby creek, Jak went to help with the cooking, and Doc joined J.B. at the task of inspecting the newly acquired arsenal. Soon the men were busy disassembling blasters, oiling springs and making piles of brass.

Their earlier caution had been wise. Many of the sec men had rigged their longblasters, leaving only their handblasters fully operational. However, the caked dirt jamming the barrels was easily removed, and soon the companions possessed a small arsenal: two M-16/M-203 combo rapidfires, a plain M-16, the Remington bolt-action, a Winchester lever-action, a Jackhammer 12-gauge scattergun, and six handblasters with gun belts. There were four crossbows, a hundred arrows and more knives than they could ever possibly need. Brass was in short supply, but that was to be expected.

Since Ryan had the Remington, Jak took the battered M-16, Krysty and Doc each took an M-16/M-203 combo, Mildred choose the Winchester, and J.B. stayed with his Uzi, and S&W scattergun.

Unfortunately, the Jackhammer was in terrible shape, with the barrel slightly bent and the firing pin worn down to a nubbin. Extracting the cartridges, J.B. simply tossed the weapon away and slid the fresh rounds into the loops sewn along the strap of his own S&W M-4000.

"Waste not, live another day," J.B. said with a grin, setting the scattergun aside. "At least if more dogs come our way, we'll be ready."

"Indeed we will, John Barrymore," Doc said, lifting a familiar handcannon into view.

"Is that…that's not your LeMat, is it?" J.B. asked.

"No, it is not," Doc replied, turning over the massive handcannon. "Mine is on my hip."

"Another bastard LeMat," Ryan scoffed, drying his hands by shaking them in the air. "We have a hard enough time finding black powder and shot to keep that prehistoric hogleg you have loaded. Better just harvest the ammo, and toss it."

"Oh, no, my dear Ryan," Doc countered. "This is a twentieth century reproduction. An exact working duplicate of a LeMat from my time period, only this one uses bullets instead of black powder, miniballs and wadding. I had one before, if you recall, and I quite liked it."

"You gonna upgrade?" Jak asked, using a green stick

to stir the rice to keep it from burning on the bottom of the pan. "We find lot more .44 rounds than black powder!"

"I know that. But you see…" Doc paused to chew a lip, trying to find the correct way of saying what he had to say. "My LeMat was made in 1878, the time I originally came from. This is a physical part of my past. It is… I mean, to say…" He paused, frowning.

"The LeMat is a piece of home," Mildred said softly, stepping forward to rest a hand on the tall man's shoulder. "You carry that handcannon to remind you of better times. Hearth and home. Safety and sanity."

"My wife and children, actually," Doc replied, drawing the older model and holding them both out for inspection. Aside from a few minor details, the weapons were identical.

"Then keep them both," Ryan said, sitting on a saddle resting on the ground. "Or will that much weight slow you down?" He already knew the answer to that question, but this was a personal matter Doc had to decide for himself.

"The weight would be considerable," Doc muttered, hefting the two revolvers. Although they were the same size, the reproduction model was significantly lighter, nearly half the weight. Plus, it wouldn't be vulnerable to misfiring if it got wet, and would load infinitely faster.

"I lost family, too," Jak said, staring deep into the fire. "Wife and baby girl. Never get mine back. They aced. But mebbe you can go back someday." He looked at the man. "If you still alive."

Pursing his lips, Doc gazed at the two weapons. Hold on to the past or concentrate on living? He wanted both, but there was only one choice. Whipping his arm forward, he threw the antique LeMat into the pond. It hit with a splash and disappeared.

"Dark night, why did you do that?" J.B. demanded, resting a fist on each hip. "At any ville that blaster would have purchased all six of us a week of room and board!"

Opening his mouth to speak, Doc paused, the complex emotions involved in the decision too complex to explain.

"After crossing a bridge, sometimes you have to burn it to make sure you never go back," Ryan said, touching the patch covering his missing eye. "I'm proud of you, Doc. That was a gutsy move."

Spreading out a handkerchief, J.B. started making a pile of loose .445 brass, most of it from the Webley. The sergeant had been very well armed. The privileges of rank, and all that dreck. Only a few of the rounds were originals, most were reloads, and a few were even dumdums, but expertly done.

"It was simple necessity, nothing more," Doc said, holstering the reproduction and walking over to the pond. "I swore to do whatever was needed to return to Emily. If nothing else, I am a man of my word." Opening the pouches in his canvas gun belt, he began tossing away the small jar of axle grease, plastic bag of dry cotton wadding, the miniballs, bullet mold and copper percussion caps. Years of scavenging vanished in only a few seconds.

"Just be careful using that thing," Mildred warned gently. "Even a modern-day .44 kicks like a mule on steroids, and your shoulder is far from being completely healed."

"Truly, madam, I do not think such a precaution is needed for such an elegant piece of hardware as this," Doc murmured, slapping his hands together to knock off any lingering residue of the black powder. "But I shall defer to your normally sage medical wisdom, and use a two-hand grip until further notice."

"Dinner! Come and get it!" Krysty announced, walking away from the campfire. Sitting down on a log, she balanced a Boy Scout mess kit on a knee and started digging into the steaming rice and beans, along with an enormous hunk of roasted dog meat, covered with apple slices and honey.

The heady aroma was intoxicating, and getting their own mess kits, the rest of the companions quickly followed suit, using wooden spoons to fill their metal plates.

Taking a bite of the meat, Ryan nodded. "Good dog," he said, then snorted at the double meaning.

"Needs garlic," Jak said, taking a sniff.

Lowering her knife, Krysty frowned. "You always say that."

"Not mean not true." Jak grinned, tearing off a chunk with his teeth. As he chewed, his face brightened. It *was* good dog!

For almost an hour there was no further conversation, the hungry people concentrating on the meal. The smoke from the campfire rose lazily into the air, thinning away to nothing on the morning breeze. In the pond, a frog gave voice to its famous cry, and one of the horses started to loudly snore. High overhead, the orange-and-black clouds of pollution began to flow across the clear blue sky, masking the sun, and sheet lightning crackled on the horizon.

"That was wonderful, dear lady!" Doc said, putting down his mess kit. "Doubly so, considering the rather incongruous arrival of the main course." A belch bubbled up from within, but he politely held it in check.

However, J.B. didn't. "Any coffee?" he asked, taking out a toothpick and starting to clean his teeth.

But before she could answer, there came the unexpected sound of blasterfire from somewhere nearby, immediately followed by the dull boom of a gren, the rattle of a rapidfire and the piercing scream of a child.

Chapter Eleven

Dropping his plate, Ryan grabbed the Remington and dashed up the gentle slope of the hollow. Nearing the crest, he dived forward and landed flat on his stomach. Crawling forward the last couple of feet, he peeked over the top.

There was nothing in sight but more rolling hills. The grass moved as J.B. appeared, then the rest of the companions.

Just then, the scream came again, closely followed by the roar of a cannon. A moment later a puff of gray smoke rose into the sky from behind a hillock far to the north.

"That must be at least a thousand yards away," Krysty said, squinting into the distance. "These hills must carry noises forever, like an underground cavern."

"Then it is a good thing that we have taken the righteous path of the church mouse," Doc whispered, the M-16/M-203 tight in his grip. "Shall we investigate?"

A chattering rapidfire, accompanied by numerous blasters, made up Ryan's mind.

"No, let's go," he replied, lowering the longblaster. "With any luck, we should be able to ride away without being heard."

"None of our biz," J.B. agreed, starting to crawl back down the slope.

The scream came again, full of pain and madness.

"But they're killing children!" Mildred cried, her face flushed with suppressed fury.

"What makes you think that?" Ryan asked, just as the scream come again. "You don't mean that noise, do you?"

She grimly nodded, tightening both hands on the Winchester.

"That cougar," Jak stated. "Sometimes sound like kid screaming. Fool newbies into becoming meal for cat."

"Are you sure?" Mildred demanded. "Absolutely positive?"

Brushing back his snowy hair with the barrel of his M-16, Jak frowned. "Not know for sure unless see. But…"

However, Mildred was already in motion, crawling down the crest. Reaching a grassy plateau, she scrambled erect, to start running along the slope toward the distant battle.

The others hesitated for only a moment, then took off after her. Following the sounds of battle, the companions moved along the sloping hollows until they began to clearly hear voices, people shouting, horses whinnying, the muffled rumble of engines.

Easing up the next slope, Ryan again crawled to the top and used the barrel of his longblaster to carefully part the tall grass. In the next hollow, men were fighting, screaming, cursing and dying, blasters firing, and flights of arrows whistling through the smoky air, leaving behind swirling contrails.

Forming a circle around a campfire, situated next to a sparkling azure pool of bubbling spring water, were

a dozen horse-drawn wags made completely of wood.
The things were huge, thirty feet long, with six wheels.
The curved roofs were covered with punji sticks, the
edges frothy with barbed wire, and the sides were composed entirely of louvered slats. The people inside were
steadily firing blasters out of hinged blasterports, or releasing arrows through the narrow openings between
the slats. At the front of each wag was a team of two
horses harnessed to the flexible yoke, obviously designed to handle particularly rough or uneven ground.

"Nice," Jak said with a grin.

"Strong, light, durable and easy to repair," Doc rumbled, clearly impressed. "Behold the Conestoga wagon
of the new millennium!"

Unfortunately, the lead pair of animals for each
wooden wag had been aced, their bellies ripped out
and their throats completely gone. Unable to move with
the dead bodies in the way, the rest of the horses were
trapped, whinnying in fear and jerking against the re-
strictive reins.

Darting back and forth among the wags were a brace
of cougars, the big cats only tan blurs as they went from
one team to another, terrorizing the animals into immobility, their wild screams sounding eerily like a dying
child.

Racing around the trapped wags were a score of
armed men riding weird three-wheeled motorcycles.
Shooting black powder blasters as if ammo grew on
trees, the riders of the machines were wearing lumpy
canvas jackets that bristled with arrows, but there was
no blood visible.

"Body armor," Krysty stated. "See how lumpy they

are? Those bastards must have slabs of wood strapped on for protection."

"Well, it seems to be working, madam," Doc noted. "I observe several dead bodies, but they are all travelers. None of them is wearing one of those peculiar canvas jackets."

"Coldhearts not fools," Jak growled. "What they on, some kinda modified bike? Fast."

"Those are sandhogs," J.B. muttered. "Dark night, I haven't seen one in years!"

"Used to have one myself, long ago," Ryan stated in a low voice. "A sandhog will go through sand, mud and swamp that even a Harley can't cover."

"The actual name is an ATV, all-terrain vehicle," Mildred said out of the blue. "Stability was their greatest weakness. They tip over easily if unbalanced."

"How do that?" Jak asked eagerly.

"Riding sideways on this slope would do it."

"That why stay where flat."

"Guess so."

He grunted. "Smart."

"Well, no children are being chilled," Ryan said, looking hard at Mildred. "So let's go back. Coldhearts ace travelers every day. This isn't our concern." Both Doc and Mildred liked to tell tall tales about heroes who tried to save the world, but those were just stretches to entertain children, not life lessons. Nobody had enough brass to try to save everybody they met. That was just nonsense.

"Then again, if we could jack some of those sandhogs, we'd be able to reach the next redoubt in a couple of days, mebbe less," Krysty said smoothly.

"That's sure enough," Ryan said, thoughtfully rubbing his jaw. Privately, he wanted to help the travelers. The poor bastards were getting slaughtered. But without a good reason, he simply couldn't risk the lives of his friends. Kin helped kin was the only unbreakable law, and the travelers were strangers.

"Cougars and sandhogs are tough combo to beat," J.B. said slowly.

Just then, the rear wooden door of a wag slammed open and out raced a group of travelers firing blasters and crossbows. As some of the coldhearts turned that way, the running people yanked out some lengths of curved wood, and whipped them forward hard.

Ryan was astounded. Boomerangs? He hadn't seen those oddball weapons in many years! The desire to leave was strong in him, but the need to know more about these coldhearts was even greater.

Whizzing along low and fast, a boomerang slammed into a coldheart, knocking him off the sandhog. He hit the ground, clutching his belly, blood gushing between his fingers. On the ground nearby, the 'rang lay sparkling in the sunlight, the edge clearly studded with chunks of broken glass.

"Nice," Jak whispered, smiling widely.

Without a driver, the sandhog continued onward, splashing through the shallow pond to roll into a campfire. Hitting the logs, it toppled over into the flames.

The other coldhearts veered away from the travelers as the cougars attacked. The man fell, burying his knife into the throat of one cat, and the woman was mauled across the belly by the other, her guts slithering out like greasy ropes. But as she fell, she drew a squat blaster, the barrel composed of a dozen smaller barrels held together with iron rings. As the cougar leaped for her throat, she fired, and all twelve barrels discharged together. Slammed aside by the barrage, the cougar limply fell, minus its head. Then the first cougar attacked her from the side, and she died screaming under the fangs and sharp claws. In perfect harmony, the sandhog exploded into flames, sending out a spray of loose parts that rattled harmlessly against the wooden sides of the wags.

More travelers dashed out, heading for the teams of horses, their hands full of axes. As they started cutting away the dead animals, a swarm of coldhearts came howling down the slope of the hollow, screaming, and whirling petards over their heads.

The travelers in the wags cut loose with thundering volleys of blasters, arrows as thick as swarms of bees. Most of the coldhearts were hit, but not a man fell. Reaching the floor of the hollow, the coldhearts released the ropes of the petards. The small jugs lofted high to gracefully descend through the smoky air and crash into the top of a wooden Conestoga. But there was no explosion, only a burst of some watery substance that dripped into the louvered slots. Almost instantly, the people inside the wag stopped shooting and went deathly still.

The travelers working to free the horses suddenly started to wobble, then lay down.

"Poison! These bastards want the wags intact!" Krysty snarled.

"No, it's probably just an anesthesia, such as ether," Mildred guessed, chewing her lip. "That's easy enough to make, if you know how."

"Catch fire?" Jak asked casually, laying aside the M-16 rapidfire and swinging a crossbow from behind his back.

"Hell, yes. Even more than gasoline!"

"Let's see," he whispered, levering in an arrow and releasing it immediately.

Twirling a petard, a coldheart running past the burning sandhog jerked as an arrow lanced through his neck. Gurgling crimson, he staggered into the flames and dropped the ceramic jug. As it crashed, a fireball engulfed the coldheart. Shrieking insanely, he began to run about, beating at his burning head with flaming hands.

Braking to a stop, a coldheart on a sandhog shot the dying man in the back to end the pitiful wails of agony.

"Fuck taking prisoners!" a skinny man of Asian descent bellowed, brandishing an AK-47 rapidfire. "Chill them all!"

Yelling something inarticulate, the coldhearts on foot charged toward one side of the ring of wooden wags. Revving their engines, the coldhearts on the sandhogs went to the other side and began hammering the wags with blasterfire.

"Divide and conqueror, eh?" Doc growled, kneeling in the tall grass to trigger a long burst of 5.56 mm rounds from his M-16/M-203 rapidfire. "Not this time, my dear Julius!"

Preparing to throw a petard, the skinny Asian man dropped the jug to jerk wildly as the hail of 5.56 mm rounds arrived. Blood spurted from his arm, but aside from that minor wound, he appeared undamaged.

"Doc, this isn't our fight," Ryan said with a scowl.

"Is it not, sir?" Doc retorted, jerking the arming bolt on the rapidfire to clear a jam.

Suddenly, a small boy appeared from underneath a wag and ran barefoot to the team of horses. Pulling a huge knife, he began sawing at the tangled reins, until a sandhog drove by and the coldheart fired a 12-gauge scattergun. With most of his face removed, the boy was violently thrown backward to land in a crumpled heap. Still horribly alive, he lay twitching, covered in gore, as the laughing coldheart drove away, waving the scattergun in victory.

A surge of visceral rage swelled within Ryan at the callous act of chilling, and he struggled to control the urge to ace the coldheart in return.

More petards crashed on top of another wag, and the people inside stopped fighting. The travelers in the others redoubled their outpouring of arrows, but the blasters were shooting slower, as if the defenders were low on ammo and carefully placing their shots.

Carrying a small hatchet, a teenage girl dashed out from underneath another wag. Promptly, the travelers inside cut loose with a sustained barrage of blasterfire, the dark billowing smoke masking her completely.

As she started hacking away the reins, a fat coldheart scurried across the uneven ground to throw a net. Caught in the strands, the young woman tried to cut herself free when the coldheart braked to a halt and shot her in the wrist. Blood erupted from the hit, and the hatchet went spinning away. Pulling out a knife, she started sawing at the net, but the coldheart hopped off the sandhog to race over and slam her in the back with the butt of a longblaster. She collapsed with a cry,

then stabbed her blade into his boot. Screaming obscenities, the coldheart shot her in the other hand, then proceeded to bludgeon her with the barrel of the weapon.
She threw dirt into his face, even as an arrow took him
in the arm. As the longblaster fell, the coldheart drew
a knife and grabbed the young woman, to haul her up
and hold her in front of him as a shield.

"Stop fighting or the slut gets aced!" he bellowed,
drawing the blade across her chest, cutting open the
blouse. The material started to turn red along that path.

"Chill us both!" she screamed, ramming an elbow
into the belly of the fat coldheart.

With a grunt, the man released her and she kicked
him between the legs. As he doubled over, she grabbed
up the knife from his hand and slashed his throat from
ear to ear. Turning, she started back toward the horses,
when black holes appeared across her shirt and red
blood erupted from her chest. Staggering onward, she
reached the reins and feebly hacked at them until going
still.

Saying nothing, Doc looked at Ryan and waited.

"Okay, Doc, you're right. Let's nuke the bastards!"
he snarled, working the arming bolt on the Remington.
Standing, he aimed and fired.

Far away, a coldheart jumped backward from the
trip-hammer arrival of the 30.06 round. He landed in
a crumpled heap directly in front of a speeding sandhog. Jerking the handlebars, the driver tried to avoid
the corpse and failed. The front wheel hit the dead man,
and the bike flipped over, the driver briefly screaming
as the machine came crashing down on his head. There
was a crunching noise, and the screaming stopped.

Moving steadily down the grass slope, the companions cut loose with a hellstorm of hot lead from their blasters as they ran from tree to bush, always staying behind some sort of cover. For several moments, the chattering rapidfires went unnoticed amid the raging battle, and a dozen coldhearts died. Then a skinny coldheart pointed in their direction and triggered a long burst from his AK-47. A swarm of sandhogs wheeled sharply about, the riders unleashing a barrage of handblasters and scatterguns.

Diving for cover behind some chilled horses, the companions waited a moment, then returned fire, their blasters blowing off the knees of several coldhearts. As they fell, Mildred used her ZKR target pistol to administer a coup de grâce into the unarmed top of their heads with surgical precision.

"Reinforcements?" a bald coldheart yelled, triggering a cobbled-together Ruger .44. "Must be mercies!"

"Ace 'em all!" a bucktoothed coldheart snarled, wildly waving two blasters, the twin streams of spent brass arching away

"Save me the redhead!" the skinny leader of the coldhearts added, slapping a fresh clip into his AK-47. "Tiger, chill the rest!"

Spinning to get behind a wag, Ryan tried to figure out where the sniper had to be hidden, when he spotted movement. Instantly, he swung up the Remington just as a colossal musket stabbed out of a blasterport. Somebody was pointing a flintlock longblaster his way.

"If you can't tell a friend from a coldheart, then best to use that on yourself," Ryan said, taking his finger off the trigger before lowering the longblaster.

"Reckon I can at that, Blackie," the shadowy man said, and the musket moved aside. "Who are you anyway— Duck!"

Dropping low, Ryan heard the flintlock discharge, dark smoke bellowing outward as the muzzle-blast slapped his face. Glancing over a shoulder, he saw the body of a coldheart twitch into death, a hole in his chest the size of a fist.

"Thanks," Ryan muttered, shooting the Remington. The report was much less noisy, and a coldheart riding a sandhog flew off the seat to land sprawling on the ground with most of his throat gone.

"These old friends of yours?" the man inside the wag asked, busy ramming in a fresh load of powder.

"Just lending a hand," Ryan said, blowing off the arm of a coldheart swinging a petard. The shrieking man staggered away, blood gushing from the ragged end of his shoulder. The jug lay unbroken on the soil, a hand still clutching the knotted rope.

"You helping us for free?" the unseen man asked suspiciously, tapping the butt of his longblaster on the floor to expertly set the charge.

"Well, I wouldn't mind having those sandhogs," Ryan said on the spur of the moment.

"Fuck that noise. Half the hogs, and half the brass."

"Plus one of the aced horses."

"For steaks, I guess. Fair enough. Deal?"

"Deal!" Ryan said, thrusting a hand into the darkness.

The men shook, then separated, their weapons dealing harsh justice to the thinning crowd of coldhearts.

Raking 5.56 mm rounds across a group of coldhearts

taking cover in some laurel bushes, Krysty frowned as the M-16 combo rapidfire jammed with a bent brass stuck in the ejector port. Kneeling, she struggled with the arming bolt, and nearly lost a finger when the spring snapped back with deadly force. With no time to clear the jam, she cast the useless weapon aside and drew her S&W Model 640 revolver just as a hulking coldheart advanced, shoving a fresh 12-gauge cartridge into the open breech of a rebuilt scattergun.

"Stupe-ass slut. You gonna ace me with a broken blaster?" He laughed, closing the weapon with a snap of his wrist. "That piece of shit don't even got no fragging hammer!"

Realizing the futility of trying to explain the mechanics of a compact blaster with an internal hammer, Krysty simply waited until he was a little bit closer, then stroked the trigger. The muffle flash of the snub-nose S&W .38 revolver actually entered his smiling mouth, and bloody lead came out the side of his head, carrying along bits of teeth and hair. The coldheart stopped short as if hitting an invisible wall, his sagging face rapidly draining of color. Conversing about ammo, Krysty grabbed the scattergun from his limp hand and sprayed the laurel bushes with buckshot and bent nails, generating a chorus of screams, before moving on for fresh targets.

Lighting the rag on a Molotov, a grim J.B. threw the vinegar bottle high, to land with a fiery crash in front of a running group of coldhearts. As the flames rose, they hastily backtracked, undamaged, and more angry than before.

Taking careful aim with the Winchester, Mildred cut

down a coldheart sitting astride a sandhog. As he fell, the vehicle went racing past and she stepped out of the way just as a cougar raced by, its claws missing her by only inches. She actually felt the wind of its passage.

Feverishly working the lever, Mildred spun and hammered the crouching cougar with soft lead rounds until it collapsed at her boots, the fur riddled with holes. Ramming the wooden stock into its face to confirm the kill, Mildred then shot a coldheart coming her way, and ran behind a nearby wag to start thumbing in fresh shells. But her pocket was empty. The rest of the brass had fallen out somewhere in the fight.

Unexpectedly, a cupped hand came out of a blaster-port holding a dozen 9 mm cartridges.

"These help you any?" a gruff voice said.

"Wrong size," Mildred replied, drawing the ZKR with a free hand. "But thanks for the offer."

"I'll take those," J.B. said as he strode forward, gathering up the brass and shoving them into the pocket of his pants. "How you doing, Millie?"

"Never better, John!" she replied, walking back into the fray, her two blasters throwing flame and death.

Staying behind the woman, J.B. maintained a regular barrage of double aught buckshot from the M-4000, wounding coldhearts and driving away another cougar that had been hiding.

Dust and gun smoke filled the air, the roar of the sandhogs mixing with voices of the dying. The travelers in the wags had taken heart at the arrival of the companions and now were shooting their crude blasters with renewed vigor. The huge miniballs hummed through the cloudy air, smacking into trees on the opposite slope with the sound of a lumberjack ax.

As his M-16/M-203 cycled empty, Doc cast it aside and drew the LeMat. The reproduction blaster felt ridiculously light in his grip, which threw off his aim, the first shot completely missing the target. The recoil made his wound hurt something fierce, and Doc felt a trickle of warmth start down his arm.

Sneering at the poor marksmanship of the old man, a coldheart revved the engine of his sandhog and raced forward with chilling on his mind.

Holding the new LeMat with both hands, Doc took aim at dead center and fired once more. The big bore .44 boomed, and the coldheart flew from the sandhog, leaving most of his internal organs behind on the plastic seat.

Doc gracefully stepped aside as the driverless sandhog raced by, leaving him in a cloud of oily blue smoke.

"Ya mutie-loving son of a bitch," a coldheart snarled, coming out of nowhere and pulling the trigger on his blaster. "Faroot was my buddy!" But the hammer merely clicked on spent brass.

Just as the coldheart yanked out a machete, Doc squeezed the trigger on the LeMat, while fanning the hammer to quick-fire the single-action weapon. But it shot only once, the round merely grazing the cheek of the other man. As the furious coldheart slashed out with the machete, Doc deflected it with the LeMat, the sound of steel on steel ringing loudly. Incredibly, the low-grade steel of the homemade machete actually bent around the barrel of the twentieth century reproduction.

As the startled coldheart gasped at the dented blade,

Doc fired from the hip, the .44 round coming out the back of the coldheart in a hot red geyser. Shooting at two more coldhearts heading his way, Doc cursed himself for a fool. This new model was obviously double-action. He had almost died because of having superior firepower. The irony of the situation wasn't wasted on him, but the Vermont scholar banished such considerations from his mind and concentrated on simply putting his next four rounds where they would do the most good.

Spotting a coldheart on a sandhog coming his way, Jak emptied his M-16 at the driver of the sandhog. As the coldheart fell off, stitched from waist to shoulder, the three-wheeler raced away to plow into the side of a wag. Still working, the pinned vehicle stayed in place, the spinning tires throwing out volumes of dirty grass.

Racing over to the corpse, Jak was surprised to discover that the coldheart wasn't carrying an AK-47, but a Galil. The two weapons looked remarkably similar, but the Galil used 5.56 mm rounds, the same as an M-16! Quickly checking the man's pockets for any loose brass, he found nothing. However, the leather bag hanging over the shoulder of the corpse was packed with loaded magazines, plus some plastic jars of loose brass. What a find! He had to be the only coldheart using this size ammo, and was carrying his whole supply!

Wiggling the heavy ammo bag free, Jak slung it across his shoulders, paused, then grabbed the Galil to yank out that magazine, too, when he heard a sound from behind. Shoving the magazine back in, he started to turn, until cold steel pressed against the back of his head.

"Too slow, Whitey," a coldheart snarled, knocking aside the Galil.

Raging internally, Jak cursed himself. His greed over the stash of brass had made him lower his guard for a split second, and now he was about to get chilled, or worse.

The coldheart grabbed Jak by the feathered collar of his camou jacket.

Instantly, Jak threw himself forward, and the coldheart shrieked as his severed fingers fell off, the spurting blood from the stumps briefly revealing the layers of razor blades hidden among the feathers.

Blind with pain, the coldheart fired twice, but Jak had already moved to the side. Swinging in a crouch, the albino teen grabbed the Galil to knock aside the booming handblaster and send a burst into the man's belly. The halo of perfectly imbalanced 5.56 mm tumblers ended his life in splattering glory.

Starting to leave, Jak noticed the fallen handblaster was a S&W .357 Magnum, which used the same size ammo as his Colt Python. Snatching it off the ground, he stuffed it into his belt for later. Waste not, want not.

Just then, a piercing whistle sounded across the battlefield, and all eyes turned toward the skinny coldheart sitting astride a purring sandhog. "Red Roger!" he bellowed, revving the engine. "Red Roger!"

Instantly, every coldheart turned and started running for the trees, pausing only to snatch up blasters from their fallen comrades in passing.

"Thank Gaia, they're leaving!" Krysty said with a sigh, lowering her blaster.

"Not gone yet!" Ryan said, swinging up the Remington to ruthlessly shoot at the retreating figures.

As two of them fell, he saw the skinny leader again and put a round directly into his back. Pitching forward, the coldheart merely jerked at the impact, and they heard the distinct clang of metal hitting metal.

"Bastard has an iron shirt!" J.B. snarled, putting a burst of 9 mm Parabellum rounds into the escaping coldhearts.

"That won't protect his head," Ryan stated, levering in another round.

As the skinny coldheart began to fishtail the sand-hog, Ryan shifted his aim for the engine, but then the Remington seemed to explode as it was torn from his stinging hands. Smashed apart, the destroyed weapon sailed away, and they heard the echo of a high-powered longblaster.

"Snipers!" Ryan cursed, diving to the ground and rolling to the side. As he did, dirt exploded just in front of him, the impact geysers following along until he reached the safety of a chilled coldheart.

Firing both the M-16 and the Galil, Jak sprayed the trees and bushes until the other companions reached the safety of a wag. Then he also scrambled for refuge as they cut loose with their own blasters.

Crawling behind an aced horse, Mildred pulled a battered set of minibinoculars from her med kit to try to find the enemy marksman. There was no sign of him anywhere on the floor of the hollow, so she switched to the crest. If it had been her, she would have placed an empty blaster prominently sticking out of the grass several yards from her actual position, to draw incoming fire. Sure enough, she found a longblaster sticking out of the brambles, and swept upwind to detect a subtle movement in a patch of juniper bushes.

Grimly, Mildred began to swing the barrel of her Winchester in that direction, when a BAR longblaster rose from the bushes to shoot several times straight up into the air. What the hell? Then she saw the face of the sniper and felt her blood run cold. It had been about three years, but there was no denying that strong profile and curly black Cawdor hair.

"Dean," she whispered, then her voice came back strong. "Don't shoot! The sniper is Dean!"

"What did you say, madam?" Doc demanded, twisting his head about to stare in open confusion.

"Dean! It's Dean! I swear to God!"

"Mutie shit," Ryan said, pulling out his Navy telescope.

Sweeping the crest of the slope, he soon found the sniper, crawling quickly through brambles. But as he broke cover for a split second, Ryan inhaled sharply as he looked directly into the face of his son. Then Dean was behind a maple tree and gone from sight.

"Dean," Ryan whispered, the full weight of a father's emotions compressed into the single word.

"Told you we find again!" Jak said, grinning. Then he frowned. "If prisoner, why shoot at us?"

Without comment, Ryan dropped the telescope and pulled the SIG-Sauer, to charge forward at a full run. A moment later, the rest of the companions followed close behind, their weapons at the ready.

Chapter Twelve

"Nuking shit storm, they saw me," Dean muttered, working the bolt on the BAR to shove in another magazine.

Now what was he supposed to do? Seeing his father and the companions charge over that slope and into the fight had been one of the most glorious sights in his life. Then the reality of the situation came crashing down, and he cursed whatever bizarre chain of events that had led his former companions to this place. If he joined them, he would be safe at last, the masquerade finally over. But then he thought about what Camarillo would do to Althea if he did. If captured, deserters were sold to the cannies in the north, but even worse, their women were used as gaudy sluts by the coldhearts until they eventually died. He felt physically ill at the idea of Althea reduced to merely a thing for the pleasure of the other coldhearts.

There were only seconds in which to act, but Dean couldn't decide what to do, torn between the only family he had ever known and the woman he loved. The unexpected use of that word startled the teenager. Love? When had that happened? But now he could see that his attachment to the beauty had slowly been deepening over the past few days. It was more than friends having sex, or even fellow prisoners combined against a common foe. Althea was a part of his soul, making him stronger, more alive.

The idea of trying to reach the camp first briefly flashed into his mind, but not even a horse could outpace a sandhog on level ground. The attempt at a rescue could have disastrous results. His father and the others would never understand the complex matter without a lot of explaining, and there simply was no time for that. Dean had to leave with the other coldhearts right now, or else Althea would soon be praying to be chilled. Somehow, he had to stop the companions from following him, to buy some time, get a chance to think of a way to save both himself and Althea. Only one solution came to mind, and try as he might, he couldn't come up with another plan. He didn't like the idea, hated it in fact, but it would work, that much was certain. So be it, then.

Working the arming bolt of the longblaster, Dean aimed for his father's stomach, adjusted for the wind and droppage, then moved to the left and fired. Blood erupted as Ryan spun away into the bushes and fell out of sight.

Resisting the urge to vomit, Dean turned and ran down the opposite slope to rejoin the coldhearts gathering around a railroad car chained to the rear of the *Atomsmasher*. Most of them were rolling sandhogs into the open doors of the car, only a few coldhearts standing guard with rapidfires and crossbows, waiting for pursuit to arrive over the slope.

Hannigan and several more coldhearts were on the roof, feeding belts of linked ammo in a brace of squat and ugly .50-caliber machine guns. With a fiendish grin, Hannigan sat down behind the deadly rapidfire and began to swivel the vented barrel back and forth along the crest of the slope, eagerly waiting for targets to present themselves for chilling.

"Where have you been, Tiger?" Camarillo demanded from inside the grilled cabin of the huffing steam truck.

"Chilled their leader," Dean replied, climbing into the tinder carriage. Keeping his face neutral, he sat on a split of cordwood, the BAR oddly feeling heavier than ever before.

Dully, the chained slaves took wood from another pile and continued to feed the blazing heart of the great machine.

"Nice work!" Camarillo growled. "We'll get the rest of them next time!" Throwing a lever, he started the massive war wag forward with an earsplitting blast from the steam whistle.

To Dean the noise sounded like the end of the world, but he said nothing, and routinely began to clean and reload the dirty longblaster, his mind filled with swirling chaos.

GRUNTING SOFTLY, Ryan peeled off the blood-soaked shirt. Tossing it aside, he sat on a tree stump, the slight motion opening wide the score along his rib cage, making fresh blood trickle down his side.

"I've seen worse, but not on anybody who lived," Mildred muttered, starting to wipe the area with a clean rag and some raw shine. "You were lucky. A half inch deeper, and right now we'd be going through your pockets for loose brass."

"Lucky," Ryan said, as if he'd never heard the word before.

Just then the bushes rustled and the rest of the companions stepped into view, their clothing decorated with hastily broken pieces of leafy tree branches as crude camouflage.

"Gone," Jak announced, resting the M-16 on a shoulder. "Got locomotive. Pulled out fast."

"There's a railroad track in the next hollow?" Ryan demanded, raising his left arm high, then inhaling sharply at the application of the stringent antiseptic.

"Dried riverbed," J.B. said, resting a boot on a rock and tilting back his fedora. "They have the damn steam engine of a railroad locomotive mounted on truck tires. Sort of a steam truck. Got a troop carriage, too. Modified an old Mack truck trailer."

"Always go with the Bulldog."

"Nothing wrong with a Peterbuilt," J.B. said, kicking at the grass. "Good thing the ground here is too soft for that nuking big engine, and they had to send in the sandhogs. Or else they could have simply smashed through those wooden wags with the locomotive and then gone through the pieces, picking out what they wanted."

Ryan grimaced. "Like getting the meat out of walnuts."

"Yon dastardly Visigoths also possess a plethora of heavy ordnance," Doc added lugubriously, holstering the LeMat. "Several .50-caliber machine guns, and I believe there was a bazooka or three ensconced inside the car."

"LAW rocket launchers," Krysty stated, her hair curling around her face. "Those are much more deadly than a bazooka."

Doc bowed. "I stand corrected, madam."

"If we had gone over the slope, we'd all be on…well, on the last train west," J.B. said. "You catching some lead saved our asses, and that's a fact."

"So it would seem," Ryan said, his eye narrowing. "Any sign of Dea… Did you see my longblaster?"

"The Remington is busted, lover," Krysty said, squatting on her heels. "The BAR fires a .308 round, but it hits like a sledgehammer. Would have done the same to you if Dean had used a triburst."

"Good shot. He miss on purpose," Jak stated, slinging the Galil rapidfire across his chest.

"Just wish I knew why he felt it was necessary," Ryan grumbled, then turned his head. "Is that an Israeli 5.56 mm Tavor?"

"Please stop moving until I have this stitched!" Mildred said, laying aside a needle and thread to mop the oozing wound clean again.

With a scowl, Ryan did as instructed.

"No, this Galil," Jak said, proffering the rapidfire. "Want? Prefer M-16."

"Just until I get some more 7.62 mm brass for the Steyr," Ryan said, looking at the ground.

"No prob," Jak replied, placing the rapidfire at that spot, along with a couple of magazines.

Her hands moving steadily, Mildred sutured the wound closed, the upholstery needle curving into the torn flesh and back up again, dragging along the blue nylon fishing line.

"Is there any more ammo in that bag, my dear Jak?"

Doc asked hopefully. "My M-16 is as empty as the pockets of a Union Army bummer."

"Sure, lots! Brass the same as M-16, but different mags. Gotta swap."

Doc smiled. "Yes, I know."

"Has anybody considered the possibility that it wasn't Dean?" J.B. asked, looking over the battlefield of the hollow. "You haven't exactly lived the life of a eunuch, old buddy, and we've encountered clones before, too. Could be either of those."

"Not to mention that palliardic rapscallion Delphi," Doc added with a dark scowl. "The bedamned cyborg could remove his face and put on another easier than changing his shoes!"

"We ace," Jak reminded him.

"True. But where there was one cyborg, there could easily be two."

Chewing his lip, Jak frowned at the unpleasant idea. It had taken everything they had, plus some help from friends, to put Delphi into the dirt. They might not be so fortunate next time.

"What do you think, lover?" Ryan asked, without looking up.

"It was Dean," Krysty replied, taking a couple of spare magazines for herself. "Just for an instant, I could sense his presence. It was uncanny."

"From that distance?"

"He was a caldron of powerful emotions…pretty much the same as you are now." She rested a hand on his good arm. "I'm sure he didn't want to shoot you, and we both know that Dean is a good enough shot to have blown your head off if that was his intention."

"He is a Cawdor," Ryan said, almost managing a smile, but failing. A wild mixture of emotions filled him, betrayal, hope, fear, and others too complex to name.

A series of hard thumps echoed across the hollow, and several thick wooden doors opened in the wags. Armed people stepped down, their muskets and flint-lock handblasters sweeping the area for any possible dangers.

"My guess would be that the coldhearts have Sharona a prisoner," Mildred said, snipping off the fishing line and tying the end in a neat knot. "He obeys, or they ace her."

"If that is true, it would mean that we now have two people to rescue," Doc said, resting the butt of the M-16 on a hip. "If not more."

"How do you figure that?" J.B. asked.

Placing the soiled items into a plastic salad bowl, Mildred washed and dried her hands, then did the same to Ryan's chest, removing as much of the dried blood as possible to stem off any infections.

"It has been a few years since Dean was among us. The boy is now a young man. Ergo, he may have a family of his own. A wife."

At that last word, Ryan went very still and said nothing as Mildred started to wrap his chest with a clean white cloth in lieu of a proper bandage.

"When find coldheart camp, we ask," Jak stated confidently.

"Bet your ass we will," Ryan said softly, a smile briefly flickering into existence before vanishing just as fast.

Briskly snapping off orders, two men began directing the rest of the travelers. Soon a band of heavily armed scouts dashed off to set up a sentry line on the crest of the two slopes, and some large men wearing leather aprons freed the aced horses, to then drag away the bodies, hang them from a tree branch and begin gutting them and cleaning the meat.

Meanwhile, women carrying toolboxes began hasty repairs on the damaged wooden slats of the wags, while some older people scavenged among the aced coldhearts for anything useful. Boots, brass, blasters, gun belts—everything went into wicker baskets to be hauled away by the children. Teenagers equipped with shovels gathered the chilled travelers and started to dig shallow graves. Completely ignored, the naked coldhearts were left on the cold ground.

"Okay, you're done," Mildred said, critically inspecting the battlefield dressing. "Just no sudden moves or heavy lifting for a few days, or those stitches will pop, and I'll have to start all over again. This time with a dull needle."

"I'll do my best," Ryan said, getting his spare shirt from his backpack. "Jak and Doc, get the horses. Unless the leader of this convoy is a feeb, they're going to be moving again in double-quick time. We don't want to be left behind."

Nodding, the two companions dashed off through the crowd of busy people. The children shied away from the armed strangers, but the sentries gave casual salutes in passing.

"Okay, let's go talk with our new employers," Ryan said, tucking in the shirt and flaring the collar.

"Employers?" J.B. frowned, rising to his feet. "We hiring on as mercies? Ah, to wait for the next attack by the coldhearts!"

"There's no chance they're not going to come back for another try," Ryan stated, slinging the Galil over his good shoulder and stuffing the spare magazines into his pants pockets.

"This convoy has way too much of their iron to let it pass unmolested," Krysty said in somber agreement.

"Not to mention the little matter of twenty or so dead coldhearts to avenge," Mildred added, closing her med kit. "Think you can get us the job as outriders?"

"That shouldn't be much of a problem," Ryan said, massaging the bandage over his ribs and starting forward. "Since I already cut a deal with them."

As the companions approached the two leaders of the bustling throng of travelers, the people turned from inspecting a sandhog. The man nodded in greeting, while the woman did her best not to openly scowl.

"Nice to see you folks still sucking air," he said, stroking his beard. "We didn't have time for any names before. The name is Crane, Alan Crane. They call me Big Al, but never to my face, and I'm the leader of this caravan."

Why the man had that moniker was clearly obvious. He towered over any of the other travelers by nearly a foot, his massive body more reminiscent of a grizzly bear than a man. Long golden hair seemed to merge with his mustache and beard, almost making him appear to be a barb, but his clothes were clean, and the rawhide gun belt around his waist was in good condition, the pouches heavy with powder and shot, the flintlocks shiny with oil. A knife jutted from his left boot, a plain wooden 'rang was tucked behind his belt buckle and the curved handle of what looked like a Japanese samurai sword rose from behind his right shoulder.

"I'm Cordelia Johnson, the sec boss," the woman stated with a noted mark of pride. "Della to my friends, which you ain't yet."

She was of average height, bustier than Krysty and with even darker skin than Mildred. Her curly hair was closely cropped, and there was a scar across her cheek marring her handsome features. The tiny row of double circles clearly showed where a stickie had gotten hold, and she had managed to get the chilling hand to release it before it removed her face. The sec woman was covered with blasters, with a .63 flintlock on each hip, two more in crude shoulder holsters, a flare gun tucked behind a bronze belt buckle and a .78 musket draped across her back.

Briefly, Ryan made introductions.

"How are the unconscious folks doing?" Mildred asked, hefting her med kit.

"Don't know yet," Cordelia stated. "We can't get inside without chopping a hole in the armor." She squinted. "They're only asleep, not aced?"

"That's very likely, given the ventilation of those blasterports," Mildred replied, studying the closest wag. "I'm a healer. Those jugs were most likely filled with something called ether. When I have some, I use it in surgery so that the patient doesn't go crazy from the pain. Ether knocks you out quickly, but only lasts as long as there's a constant supply. As soon as you stop applying it to the patient, or the fumes dissipate—"

A door creaked open on one of the silent wags, and a blinking man staggered to the threshold, only to drunkenly stumble and fall to the ground. Quickly, people rushed over to help, one woman sticking her head into the wag. She came right back out again. Gasping for breath, she limply dropped onto her rear end and clutched her head in both hands.

"Holy skydark, they look like jolt addicts on a bender," Alan muttered with a frown. "Anything we can do for them?"

"Fresh air will do fine," Mildred stated. "Although some strong coffee sub wouldn't hurt if you have any."

"Nope, they'll have to make do with air," Cordelia replied curtly. Then she added, "Willow bark tea any good?"

"Even better! That's a natural analgesic…a natural painkiller, similar to aspirin," Mildred finished lamely.

"Yeah, she's a healer, all right. Half of what she says don't mean squat to regular folk." Alan chuckled, giving a crooked smile. "You and Dewitt are going to get along just fine."

"Dewitt. Is that your healer?"

"Good one, too. A real artist with a knife." He glanced over at a bald man kneeling in the mud, slitting the throat of a coldheart, then taking his boots.

"That ether stuff, that what she use on you?" Cordelia asked, indicating the fresh bandages.

"Just shine and fishing line," Ryan said, inadvertently rhyming.

"Yeah, got some of that in me, too," Cordelia muttered, rubbing her leg.

"You could have a couple of people fan the blasterports with blankets," Krysty suggested. "That should rouse the rest of your people quick enough."

"That so?" Cordelia asked suspiciously.

"Brass in your blaster, friend."

"Well, I'm old enough to know the spring water from piss," Alan drawled. "So I reckon that's pure quill. Take care of it, will ya, Della?"

"Yes, Alan. Be right back," she replied, slowly walking away, as if unwilling to let the companions out of her sight.

"That woman doesn't trust her own shadow," Alan said, watching her leave.

"That just makes her a good sec chief," J.B. stated. "Why does she carry so many blasters?"

"Ask her sometime. It's a real good story," Alan said, turning again. "Well, I see you've already started gathering your share of the blasters. Fair enough, a deal is a deal." He frowned. "Don't think you're gonna get any working sandhogs, though. You folks were kind of rough on the previous owners."

"Not a problem. We have horses," Ryan said with a shrug. He immediately regretted the motion as a sharp pain stabbed his side. "Which way are you folks heading?"

"Nor'east, toward Centralia," Alan said, squinting. "Why do you want to know?"

"We'd like to ride along some, if you don't mind."

"Safety in numbers," Krysty added sagely.

"Not always," Alan countered with a grimace, looking

at the grave diggers. "We got a dozen wags and a hundred folks, most of them with working blasters, and those damn coldhearts shoved us into a nuking meat grinder. Must have lost fifteen. All of them friends, and kin."

The companions said nothing, letting the man make up his mind. The trickiest part of any negotiation was knowing when to speak and when to shut up.

Crossing his huge arms, Alan frowned. "You folks any good with blasters, or did those rapidfires just throw so much lead at the coldhearts that they caught some by accident?"

"Better than most," Ryan said honestly.

"Della, think they'll do as outriders?"

"Well, they helped out," Cordelia sniffed, ambling back. "I saw some of you shoot. Can all of you people shoot good?"

"Just ask," Krysty countered, jerking her chin.

Turning, Alan and Cordelia looked up the western slope to see two men riding over the crest, leading four more horses.

Studying them, Cordelia noted with satisfaction that they both looked tougher than a boiled Army tank, and carried their longblasters with the calm assurance of seasoned chillers. There was something odd about the younger man, and she couldn't quite figure out what it was, until she realized that he had to be hiding something up his sleeves. Probably knives. Yeah, he had the look of a blade master. Hmm, good-looking and lethal. That was a nice combination.

"They'll do," Cordelia said, hitching up her gun belt.

"Then it's settled," Alan declared, spreading his

arms. "You're hired. We can offer hot food for the journey, shine if you want, plus a slice of anything we find along the way. But you sleep outside. Nobody goes inside a wag but my people."

"We look like spring water," J.B. translated, "but might still be piss."

"Close enough," Alan said, tugging on his mustache to hide a grin. "Now, there are six of you, so loot six bodies. Everything else goes into the war chest. We'll be going past Cobalt Lake, and that's bad mutie country."

"I'll send you a note when I get frightened," Ryan said, deadpan.

"You're a card, One-eye, sure enough." Alan laughed, then stopped, suddenly noticing the odd motion of Krysty's hair. He started to say something, then obviously changed his mind. "Anyway, just don't take too long. We bury our friends, then we leave."

Somewhere in the far distance, a steam whistle loudly keened, the strident noise echoing through the multiple hollows until it seemed to be coming from every direction.

"Agreed. Just stay on soft ground and away from any bedrock or dried riverbeds," Ryan advised. "The cold-hearts have a monster war wag along with those sand-hogs, but it's too heavy to roll on soft dirt."

"Good to know," Cordelia replied, resting a hand on a flintlock. "The sooner we're out of this half-ass valley and in some open countryside, the better."

"You got that right," Alan grunted, kicking his horse into a gentle trot. "Better get busy. We move in thirty!"

"Ten would have made me happier," J.B. said, pulling out a knife and testing the edge on the ball of his thumb.

"Okay, everybody knows the drill," Ryan added, drawing the panga and heading toward a corpse. "Let's go looking for supplies!"

DEAD LEAVES sprinkled down from the withering trees as the howler moved through the forest glen. As the glowing cloud touched them in passing, birds and other small animals tumbled from the branches to land on the crispy earth, feebly twitching, and then going horribly still.

In the far distance, a wolf howled loudly, sounding the alarm to the rest of the pack that death was approaching. Oddly, that made the howler pause for a long moment for some unknown reason. Then it continued on once more, never flagging in its hunt for the hated two-legs. The prey had switched from their not-live-thing to horses, but their spoor was unmistakable, even when mixed with the smell of the other two-legs, and then the dried blood of the four-legs-that-were-not-wolves.

Feeling a vibration on the surface, an underground feeder lashed out blindly with a dozen tentacles, the spiked limbs attempting to sink their hooks into the tender flesh of a two-leg, or even better, a bear. That was food for a week!

But at the first contact, agonizing pain surged through the feeder, and it quickly tried to release the unseen food. However, its tentacles wouldn't come off, and the feeder felt itself being bodily hauled up through the loose dirt toward the surface.

In blind terror, the mutie fought back, thrashing wildly, but it was useless, and soon the subterranean dweller was out of its burrow and being dragged helpless across the ground.

At the sight of the glowing green cloud, the feeder redoubled its attacks, then threw itself toward the unknown thing, wrapping every tentacle tight, trying to squeeze the life out of this new enemy. The ghastly pain steadily increased, but the feeder never ceased to struggle, and wrapped two of its smaller tentacles around a nearby tree as an anchor.

However, the bark crumbled away from its touch, and the plant visibly withered as the cloud expanded to fill the quiet forest glen. With a splintering noise, the tree broke apart, and the startled feeder was bodily hauled into the searing mist.

Even as its skin began to blister and bubble, the feeder raged once more at its enemy, whipping about the smaller tentacles in an effort to remove the eyes of its tormentor.

Then something obscene rammed into the feeder, splitting it wide open and exposing its brain to the all-destroying cloud. Convulsing with unimaginable pain, the vivisected feeder insanely tightened every tentacle and attempted to bite the other thing. Its iron beak shattered at the contact. Then the howler flowed inside the writhing mutie and began to feed.

The wailing death scream of the feeder rang across the landscape and seemed to last in inordinate length of time.

Chapter Thirteen

With a strangled cry, sec chief Abigail Ralhoun sat bolt upright in the darkness, clawing for a blaster on her hip. However, her fingers found only blankets and a bedroll. Frantically looking around, she saw the gun belt and her longblaster lying neatly coiled on top of her horse saddle, safe from the morning dew.

Confused a she was by the surroundings, it took her a few moments to realize that she was among her troops, and no longer being horribly tortured. *Camarillo, the name of coldheart will be Camarillo.*

Grabbing the handblaster, she thumbed back the hammer, taking great comfort in the weight of the weapon in her fist. Fighting to control her pounding heart, Ralhoun listened to the familiar sounds of the night, the gentle snoring of the sleeping sec men mixing with the eternal song of the cicadas. Silently, a huge owl flew by overhead, the shape briefly blotting out the moonlight. Nearby, a campfire softly crackled, the dancing flames illuminating a ring of sleeping bags and bedrolls. Heavy blankets covered the still forms of the sec men, their saddles positioned close at hand, their sweaty boots perched on top to air out in the cool night.

With a longblaster resting on his lap, a guard sat on a fallen log slowly sipping a tin cup of coffee sub, while another man was facing the bushes, whistling to cover the gentle sound of splashing. Off to the side, the horses stood with heads bowed in sleep, only the occasional swishing motions of their tails showing that they were still alive.

Slowly, Ralhoun allowed herself to relax. Black dust, it had just been a bad dream, only a dream. However, the ghastly images remained crystal clear in her mind, and she slowly had to accept the fact that it hadn't been a dream, but a vision of the future.

Her doomie father had been amazingly accurate in his predictions, but her powers were as unreliable as brass taken from a stranger. Numerous times she had seen doom and death looming fast, only to have something unexpectedly change the course of events. At a very early age she had learned that the visions weren't carved in stone, but merely the most likely future. It seemed that time was in a constant state of flux, forever changing. The most minor decision this day could invoke major alterations for the next, some good, some bad, while others were completely pointless.

Once, she had a vision of the local potter getting aced by his cousin over a game of dice. Then the cousin fell ill with the yellow cough and died. However, the very next day the potter got eaten by a mutie while burying the man. He still died, just not in the way she had foreseen. Mebbe that meant some things could be changed, while others couldn't? She had no idea, and deeply hated the uncertainty of the gift, but had learned to grudgingly accept that aspect of it. Life was pain. Only the dead felt nothing.

Pulling on a shirt, she strapped on a gun belt and padded barefoot over to a stream. Kneeling in the grass, she splashed some cold water on her face, then rinsed her mouth and spit into the reeds. An unfamiliar taste filled her mouth, sickeningly salty, and her mind was filled with the images of an underground chamber, her sec men chained to the stone-block walls. Most of them were missing their fingers. Although gutted like a spring buck, one of them was horribly twitching with life. It was John Cordova, her best tracker. Dimly, she remembered that he had discovered the hidden base of the coldhearts, and against her direct orders, had charged in, screaming and shooting, determined to avenge the death of his friend Hohner. His were the actions that led the rest of her sec men to this horrible fate.

In the middle of the dungeon was a tanning board covered with the tightly stretched skin of the outlander called Ryan Cawdor, his missing eye only one of many holes in the leathery hide. It was peppered with bulletholes, along with several knife cuts. Clearly, he had been aced very hard.

Hanging from a scaffold was the skinless body of a teenager, his white teeth fully exposed, the lidless eyes staring into eternity. The word *tiger* came unbidden into her mind, then faded away like a whisper in the wind.

Shivering, she remembered being stark naked on a cold stone table, spread-eagled and helpless, heavy metal chains clamped to her wrists and ankles. Laughing coldhearts surrounded the table, and some big man named Camarillo was thrusting between her legs. Pain filled her inside, but even worse was the sense of helplessness and utter humiliation. There was blood smeared on her breasts, on her stomach. Vomit rose in her throat at the memory.

Desperately needing some coffee sub, she shuffled back to the campfire and poured herself a mug from the softly bubbling pot. The black brew had been heated all night and tasted bitterly strong. The flavor was overpowering, and that was a blessed relief. Draining the mug, she had a second, and then a third.

"Something wrong, Chief?" a sec man asked in concern, putting aside his cup. "You have a vision or something?"

Looking at the man, she recognized him as one of the corpses on the wall. "Corporal Latimer, take over for a minute," she commanded, getting to her feet. "Sergeant Cordova and I have some ville biz to discuss."

"Not a prob, Chief," Latimer said, ambling over to pour out the cold dregs from his tin cup, then get some fresh coffee. With a pleased smile, he sat down on the log and pulled out some jerky to start gnawing contently.

"I swear he eats his own bodyweight in chow every couple of hours," Cordova muttered in disgust. "How is that possible? Think he's a mutie, Chief?"

"No talking," she directed sternly, trying to think of what to say to the him.

In an awkward silence, Ralhoun and Cordova walked out of the camp and into the night. She angled away from the creek, toward the south. Soon they were moving along on a rocky cliff overlooking a sylvan valley of pine trees and rocky tors. The full moon was so low in the sky it almost looked like it was about to crash into the valley, and the light was incredibly bright.

Stopping on a jagged escarpment, they stood looking down upon the cold forest, listening to the sounds of the night.

"Okay, we're far enough away," she stated, crossing her arms. "Now, listen sharp, this is important."

"What's up, Chief?" Cordova asked, swinging around his longblaster to work the arming bolt. "Somebody trying a nightcreep?"

"No, nothing like that," she said tolerantly. "Look, I had a vision, and it was a bad one. A real nuke storm. We got our arses kicked in a fight and everybody was aced."

"Shitfire," he replied, giving the word several syllables. "So what's the plan? We gonna hit them first, or swing wide and strike from the rear?"

She grunted at that, pleased that he never even mentioned the possibility of running away. "I want you to ride back to the ville—"

"And come back with fresh troops," he interrupted, slinging the longblaster. "I won't let you down, Chief. We'll chill the bastards! Was it the outlanders or somebody new?"

"Stop firing from the hip and listen to me," she growled, staring at the man in annoyance. "I want you to go back to the ville and stay there. No rescue attempts, no fresh troops. Just keep the gates closed and wait for me to come back. That's it. Nothing else. Understand?"

"Hell, no." He frowned. "I ain't gonna leave you, Chief. There's no yellow in my belly. I'm with you till the end!"

Which was exactly what was going to happen to all of them unless she could somehow alter the future.

Mebbe having him leave wouldn't change the outcome of the fight, but it was all that she could think of doing, aside from shooting herself in the head to avoid the rape.

"This is a direct order," she said, poking the man in the chest with a stiff finger. "You must leave right now, and don't come back."

"Not going to happen…Chief."

"This is a direct order, Sergeant! Disobedience means a hundred lashes, and expulsion from the ville!"

"Aw, fuck your vision. Some of them have been wrong before," he said stubbornly. "I won't go, Chief, not ever. You can count on me to the grave!"

Suddenly, she saw his face in a new way, the passion and deep concern clearly evident, and knew the truth. "You love me, don't ya?" she asked softly, hoping for a denial.

"Since the day we met." He exhaled, as if he had been holding his breath forever. "Yeah, yeah, I know, you're the baron, and the sec chief, but hellfire, Abigail, everybody needs somebody."

"Shit," she muttered, flexing her fingers.

"I'll never leave your side, Chief," he stated adamantly. "You can count on me!"

"So be it, then." She sighed. "Sorry about this, old friend. But I'm never going onto the stone table."

Puzzled, he squinted. "What stone table?"

"Don't worry about it," she said, pulling a Beretta and firing.

The soft lead 9 mm slugs slammed hard into the sec man, blowing away chunks of flesh and driving him backward off the cliff. As silent as a snowflake, he plummeted into the darkness, to vanish from sight.

She remained quiet until hearing a meaty impact far below.

Holstering the smoking blaster, she turned away and started back to the camp, meeting a dozen sec men in various stages of undress, their hands full of weapons.

"What happened, Chief?" one asked, his blaster sweeping the night for targets.

"Cordova and I were talking some ville biz when a mutie condor grabbed him," she lied, turning to pretend to stare hatefully into the night. "We both fired, but it took him over the cliff."

"Well, nuke me running," a sec woman whispered, stepping to the edge and peering below. "Any chance he's still alive down there?"

"Not after having his throat removed," she said, trying to sound grim.

"Did ya get the mutie, at least?" another sec man asked.

His chest was completely covered with tattoos, and for some reason that reminded her of the tanning rack in her vision. Already it was becoming hard to recall the details, the currents of time swirling away in new directions.

"Yes, I aced the danger. We're safe now," she said, starting back to the camp. "Davidson, you're captain of the guard for the rest of the night. Double the sentries and chill anything that comes in sight."

"Got'ya, Chief," he grunted, thumbing back both hammers on his double-barrel scattergun. "Take no chances. I got your six!"

"Me, too," she replied cryptically. It was been a hard

price to pay, but she had done what was required to save the rest of her troops, and herself.

As well as those accursed outlanders, she added privately, taking off the gun belt and coiling it neatly on top of her saddle. I only hope this new future was worth such a sacrifice.

Getting under the blanket, she wiggled into a comfortable position. At the very least, she now knew the name of her real enemy, Camarillo. And that he couldn't be trusted under any circumstances.

Then again, neither can I, she thought, drifting off to a peaceful and dreamless sleep.

JUST BEFORE DAWN, Alan got the convoy under way through the twisting maze of hollows. Ryan, Mildred and Krysty took the job of outriders, keeping their horses ahead of the rattling convoy. J.B., Jak and Doc brought up the rear. Always on the move, Cordelia rode with both groups, switching back and forth every couple miles. Meanwhile, Alan stayed in the lead wag, constantly watching the crest of the slopes with a pair of binoculars, a loaded musket lying across his lap and a softly ticking rad counter on the floor near his boots.

There had been no sign of the coldhearts since the attack in the hallows, and some of the travelers had started to relax and chat among themselves, but Alan made that nonsense stop fast.

"Just because you can't hear quicksand don't mean it won't chill you," he declared gruffly. "Until we're out of these damn valleys, keep your yaps shut and iron in your fist!"

The previous evening had been awkward for the

companions, with the travelers watching them for any
sign of betrayal. Their help in the fight notwithstand-
ing, outlanders always meant trouble. Then Ryan and
J.B. had offered to help Alan and Cordelia make some
bombs with the oddball rounds they had recovered from
the aced coldhearts. Mildred joined forces with Ben-
jamin Dewitt, and the two healers checked on every
wounded member of the convoy, stitching bulletholes,
setting bones and changing bandages. Krysty and Jak
helped make repairs on the wags, never going inside,
of course, while Doc entertained the children with tall
tales of Atlantis, King Arthur, Robin Hood and Zorro,
although he used the more conventional terms of baron,
sec men and mutie.

Slowly, the tense atmosphere warmed, and dinner
had been a pleasant affair of horse meat. There had been
a few wild turnips and some acorns tossed into the stew,
but mostly it was just horse, some of the chunks roasted,
while others got fried, to try to change the flavor a little.
Without refrigeration, or a significant amount of salt as
a preservative, the raw meat would soon go bad, so it
had to be eaten fast. A tiny blonde woman called Library wanted to halt long enough to jerk the meat, but
Alan flatly refused. A sitting convoy already had one
boot in the grave. Distance was their best armor against
the coldhearts. That, plus ground too soft for the bedamned steam truck to traverse. Nobody had seen the
colossal war wag in action, but from the description, it
was clearly something best to avoid entirely.

Riding at the back of the convoy, Doc and J.B. did
their best to keep straight faces while Cordelia flirted
outrageously with Jak. Intent on watching for the

coldhearts, Jak didn't seem to notice. But Doc and J.B. knew that he'd tweaked to her intentions quite a while ago, and now was just teasing her by playing dumb.

"So, how many knives you carry?" Cordelia asked, rocking gently in the saddle to the motion of her horse. As the morning became warm, she had unbuttoned her shirt to reveal an amazing amount of cleavage.

"Enough," Jak said, pretending to misunderstand the question. "How many blasters you got?"

"Never enough," she answered. "Think I should start carrying some blades?"

"Some steel in right place do you good," he replied, riding closer until they were side by side. Ebony and ivory.

"I hear N'Orleans steel is the best," Cordelia said suggestively.

"Is!" Jak grinned, then he smiled and added, "We camp, I show."

Realizing that she was being joshed, Cordelia frowned, then grinned, and bumped her mare into his stallion. Then, leaning sideways, she grabbed Jak by the shirt and pulled him in close for a hard kiss. It was fast, but fierce.

"Now, that's just a horse-diver, as they say," she murmured. "A sample of the main meal tonight."

"Damn good cook!" Jak chuckled, reaching out to pat her thigh. He could feel her warmth under the faded denim and gave a gentle squeeze. She patted his hand in return, then whispered something in his ear that made him blush fiercely.

"Never do before," he murmured. "Is fun?"

"Hell, yes."

"That another horse-diver?" he asked, shifting his palm a little higher.

"You better believe it," she replied, removing his hand. "But keep that blaster holstered! I don't want it going off early and spoiling our fun tonight because you're outta brass."

"Never been that tired," Jak boasted, giving her a wink.

"Do Millie and I ever get like this?" J.B. asked out of the corner of his mouth, his hands resting on the pommel of the saddle.

"Never, my friend, and we all deeply appreciate that," Doc answered, then softly added, "And the word is hors d'oeuvre, not horse-divers."

"Don't think they care." J.B. chuckled softly.

Scratching his horse behind the ear, Doc sighed. "As it should be, John Barrymore. And in truth, they do make a good pair, eh?"

"Seems so."

Just then, a stingwing rose from some muddy weeds. Instantly, both Jak and Cordelia drew and fired their blasters. Gushing blood, bits of the mutie tumbled back into the water.

"Damn near a perfect match," J.B. stated, releasing the safety on the Uzi rapidfire.

"Indeed," Doc agreed. The LeMat was only halfway out of its holster, and he tucked the weapon back into position.

Entering a forest, the convoy traveled for a few miles under a leafy canopy of interlocking branches. Even though it was approaching noon, there was only a dappled scattering of sunlight, the shadows as thick as flies on a corpse.

With a hand resting on his longblaster, Ryan reacted violently, and almost fired when something plummeted from the branches above to land on the dirt with a wet splat. Backtracking the trajectory, he easily found an opossum scurrying through the boughs. He grunted, and lowered the Galil. It wasn't an attack, just piss from an animal. He debated chilling it, but the convoy already had more horse meat than they could eat in a month. There was no sense wasting brass.

Then it happened again from another opossum, the juicy deluge almost hitting Mildred.

"Gardyloo!" she called out with a chuckle, removing her finger from the trigger of the Winchester.

"What did you say?" Krysty asked, her M-16 combo sweeping the trees overhead.

"That's what people used to call out in the Middle Ages to warn pedestrians in the streets that they were about to toss their night soil out the window," Mildred glibly explained.

"Out the window onto the ville street?" Ryan asked, clearly shocked. "Were these feebs, or barbs?"

"Oh, no, just ordinary folks." Mildred grinned sheepishly. "It was a simpler time, I assure you."

"Simpler than now?"

"I concede the point," she said. "But still—"

"Is that why a shitter's called a loo?" Krysty asked, moving away from the next aerial bombardment. Whatever the possum had eaten reeked worse than a chem storm.

"I think it comes from the word *lavatory*," Mildred said hesitantly. "But I do recall that the word *crap* comes from Thomas Crapper, the man who popularized the flush toilet."

"Are you serious?" Krysty said.

"Sure! Take my word for it."

Coming out the forest, the companions started across a rolling hillside of smooth green grass that was dotted with large sunflowers. In the distance, an aircraft carrier rose up from the ground like a surrealistic skyscraper. The bow was buried into the earth all the way to the command island, and at the stern the three propellers spun listlessly in the wind, clearly showing that they were was no longer connected to the engines. The entire hull was heavily corroded with rust, and the shadow of the carrier extended across the landscape like the pointed gnomon of a sundial, indicating that it was just before noon. Oddly, nothing was growing on the vessel, and the nearby ground was bare of plant life.

Even as Ryan started to check his rad counter, the device began clicking steadily. "It's hot," he announced, veering sharply away from the wreckage.

Driving the lead wag over the hill, Alan stared at the huge military craft, then immediately angled after the companions to head due north. A moment later, his rad counter started to click wildly.

"The nuke must have gone off underwater, and blew it so fragging high that it came straight down like an arrow," Krysty said, her hair flexing and curling in amusement. "Then again, we're pretty far inland. Think it's one of those mil sats orbiting the moon?"

"No, it's just a ship," Ryan countered, watching the sunflowers to make sure the plants weren't turning to track their progress. This close to a rad pit, he suspected even the bastard rocks of being muties.

Waving gently in the breeze, the plants did nothing unusual, but Ryan still kept a close watch on them until they were far behind.

Several hours later, something large began to appear on the horizon. At first Ryan thought it was a mountain, but as the haze of distance cleared, he grunted at the sight of a predark city. Pulling out the Navy telescope, he extended it completely and swept the array of crumbling buildings. Most of the homes in the suburbs were gone, only crumbling piles of bricks remaining to mark their former locations. However, the downtown structures seemed relatively intact, with reflected light from the skyscrapers telling of windows still being present.

"Don't recall any large cities in this section of Georgia," Mildred said, digging out her binoculars. "Then again, I've really only been to Atlanta for a few medical conferences." She sighed. "My God, it was a beautiful city."

"Well, these ruins look good to me," Ryan stated, lowering the telescope. "There's no sign of any blast craters or spiderwebs. Some minor damage possibly from the carrier, and what looks like a meteor strike, but nothing serious."

"Just as long as there's no ivy," Krysty muttered, referring to an incident where she'd almost lost her life to an infestation of the mutie plants. Tiny vines burrowed inside a person, infesting every part of the body, seizing complete control until the poor bastard was nothing more than a puppet, yet horribly alive. She clearly recalled the expressions in the eyes of the victims. It was an image that would never leave her.

"No ivy in sight," Mildred said, adjusting the focus on her mini-binoculars. "I'd say it was well worth a quick recce to see if there's anything to salvage. Just one untouched bomb shelter, and we're fully stocked on ammo again."

"Or just one robotic tank, and we're a stain on the pavement," Ryan countered, tucking away the telescope. "Those big guns have a hell of a range."

She shrugged. "True enough."

"Then again," Ryan continued, his voice taking on a new tone, "these ruins would be a good location for a gang of coldhearts to hide, and waylay convoys avoiding the carrier."

"You've been expecting something like this," Mildred stated, shifting the strap of her med kit to a more comfortable position.

"Be a fool not to," Ryan replied, patting a pocket to count the number of magazines it held for the Galil.

Thoughtfully scratching her chin, Krysty started to ask a question, but then the horses whinnied in fear. Suddenly alert, she caught a faint stink on the wind, a tangy rotten-egg smell that burned her nose.

"Acid rain!" she yelled, tightening the reins to try to control the mare. "Acid rain is coming!" Dancing with terror, the animal desperately wanted to bolt, to try to escape from the melting death from above.

At the cry, every driver in the convoy jerked up his or her head to study the sky. In dark harmony, a soft rumble of thunder sounded, and sheet lightning flashed among the purple-and-orange clouds.

"Nuking hellfire, head for the ruins!" Alan shouted, lashing his team into motion. "We'll try to take cover under a bridge!"

Cursing, the rest of the drivers did the same to their horses, and soon a ragged line of wags was jouncing and rattling across the grassy field, heading toward the crumbling ruins.

"Shitfire, there are no intact bridges!" Mildred yelled, heading toward the suburbs. "Follow me! I know where to go!"

"Parking garage?" Ryan asked, leaning into the wind to help his stallion run faster.

"No, over there!" Mildred pointed. "See those hourglass shapes?"

"Are you a feeb?" Alan demanded hotly, nearly losing his seat as his wag bounced over a cracked piece of highway pavement hidden in the grass. "Those be nuke towers! We'll fry for sure!"

Among the weeds, all the flowers were quickly closing their petals to try to survive the coming assault.

"No, they're steam towers!" Mildred lied. "Trust me! There is no safer place in a rainstorm than an electrical power station!"

"You sure?" Alan demanded, not looking in her direction, his full attention on trying to control the team. The animals were wide-eyed with terror, the blind instinct to run from the storm nearly overwhelming their years of training.

"It's my ass, too, you know!" Mildred countered.

A minute passed, then another. On the hillside, a single drop of rain fell, and a clump of grass began to wilt and turn brown.

"Follow Mildred!" Alan bellowed, the words almost lost in a deafening crash of thunder and lightning.

Chapter Fourteen

Galloping madly through the decaying suburbs, the rest of the companions joined Ryan and the others as they tried to find the smoothest path for the wags along the ancient streets. But after a century of neglect the pavement had buckled in numerous areas, cracking wide to expose the bed of loose gravel underneath. Potholes were everywhere, many of them with trees growing inside, and the rusting remains of wags blocked entire intersections.

"A power plant, madam?" Doc demanded, banking his horse around an open sewer drain, the manhole cover nowhere in sight. "Pray tell, what was the logic behind that choice, if any?"

"If rain ever got inside the place everybody would die, right?" Mildred said quickly, briefly slowing her mount to trot through a low hedge. Birds erupted into flight at the stomping of the horse hooves, and a two-headed snaked wiggled away, loudly hissing in stereo.

"So?" Jak demanded, reins in one fist, the Colt Python in the other.

"So a power plant has to be absolutely waterproof! It's mandatory!"

"Sounds good to me!" J.B. growled.

"And what if the roof was damaged from falling debris?" Doc demanded.

Mildred grinned. "Then it's been nice knowing you!"

"Dr. Weyth, you are the most genuinely annoying person I have ever meet in my entire life!"

"Thanks, Doc! I like you, too!"

Barreling around a corner, Alan came into view wildly lashing the horses into a frenzy. Their hooves pounded the pavement so hard that sparks flew from the iron shoes. In tight formation came the other eleven wags. Some of the travelers were staring at the rows of destroyed homes and strip malls in obvious fright, but nobody said a word. Survival was paramount. Everything else, including terror, was only a secondary concern.

Weaving around the larger potholes, the wags hit a lot of the smaller ones. Incredibly, the patched tires held, and while the wooden axles bent alarmingly, none of them actually broke.

Careening around another corner, the wags encountered rush hour, perfectly preserved, and plowed on through, smashing aside the piles of rust, and shiny fiberglass sedans. A few of the delivery trucks still had windows, but those noisily shattered at the violent collisions. Several of the repaired wooden slats on the wags had cracked open again, and the occasional loose item went sailing away, a leather boot, a wooden bowl. And then a swaddled infant went flying off, to land squalling in a patch of the weeds.

"Adrian!" the mother screamed. "Lawrence, stop the wag!"

Still bringing up the rear of the convoy, Cordelia never slowed as she swung low in her saddle and snatched the living bundle off the ground.

"Keep those wags moving!" she bellowed, tucking the wailing baby under an arm.

More and more often, fat yellow drops fell, smacking into the ground and cracked sidewalks. Visibly, plants withered. The pungent reek of sulfur was becoming strong, and everybody was braced for the inevitable shreaks as living flesh was touched by the hellish rain.

"There it is!" Ryan bellowed, trying to make his horse run even faster. "Move with a purpose, people!"

Covering a city block, the power station rose above the sprawling ruins to dominate the landscape. Once there had been a ten-foot-tall fence to keep out the curious, rampant ecologists, media reporters and terrorists. But that had fallen long ago, and now only galvanized steel posts and loose strands of rusty wire stuck out randomly. Beyond that was an extensive parking lot, without vehicles, the pavement cracked into a gray-and-black mosaic. Several of the outer structures had fallen down, including the guard kiosk. However, the main building seemed completely intact.

"Thank you, Lord," Mildred whispered, her heart starting to beat once more.

Destroyed by implacable time itself, the front gate was completely missing, and the companions charged up the front drive, only to ride past the barred front doors and circle around to the rear.

Lightning flashed brightly overhead as the companions reached the loading dock. As expected, there was a concrete ramp for the larger deliveries, and at the top was a double set of doors, closed with a heavy steel chain.

"Give me a minute," J.B. said, reining in his mount and pulling out a package of tools.

"No time!" Ryan countered, drawing the 9 mm SIG-Sauer, but then holstering the blaster. This task needed brute force, not accuracy. "Doc, open the bastard door!"

"With pleasure!" Doc declared, firing from the saddle. The big bore .44 LeMat boomed louder than the thunder, and the padlock exploded into pieces, the chains sliding away with a rattle.

Riding up the ramp, Ryan and the others reined to a fast halt and scrambled off their horses. It took all six of them to push open the squealing doors, flakes of rust sprinkling to the floor from the stubborn hinges, and then they were forced to retreat for a precious minute to allow any trapped air to properly vent. Sealed tight for more than a century, many predark buildings were rich with organic poisons and deadly molds from decaying matter, most of it former people.

A visible cloud of grayish fumes swept across the loading dock just as the first of the wags rolled into view, the horses whinnying in terror.

Igniting a road flare, J.B. led the way inside, dragging along his reluctant horse. Ryan and Krysty were next, their blasters searching for any possible dangers.

Only a few yards into the building, a second set of doors blocked the way, but those were easily opened. Now the companions walked into a huge room filled with hulking generators set into the terrazzo floor. A complex maze of catwalks lined the walls, and the ceiling was lost in dim shadows. A thick layer of dust lay over everything, and as they watched, a couple of skeletons in bright orange uniforms crumbled away.

"Millie?" J.B. asked anxiously, slapping a hand over his mouth and nose.

Warily, she took a tiny sniff, then gratefully exhaled. "Just stale air, John, nothing harmful." Actually, the air wasn't that dusty. She found the fact rather curious.

"There's no place else to go even if it was," Ryan said, then turned and shouted, "All clear! Get those people inside!"

As the wags began to clatter up the ramp, Jak looked around and tapped Mildred on the shoulder.

"This not coal plant, it nuke!" he whispered.

"I know that," she answered quickly. "But I had to get those people moving. Besides, the core would have converted back into lead by now. The elements only had a half-life of fifty years."

"You sure?" Jak demanded.

"Of course!" she replied, crossing her fingers.

Taking down some coats from pegs set into the cinder-block wall, Ryan and Krysty used their knives to slash the material into rags, then set the strips on fire to direct the wags deeper into the power plant.

"Move to the rear!" Ryan shouted, guiding a pale driver around a massive generator. "Make space for the next wag!"

In spite of the size of the room, it was a tight squeeze for the wags and their uneasy teams of horses. But finally Cordelia rode in through the double doors and holstered her flintlock.

"Seen better," she drawled, releasing a white-knuckled grip on the reins. "But then, seen worse, too."

"Is that everybody?" Alan demanded, rushing from the gloom. "Are we all inside?"

"Seem to be," Cordelia said, sliding off her horse.

He sighed. "Good. Then let's shut those doors!"

Eagerly, a score of people rushed to obey, and quickly closed the outer doors, dragging over several large pieces of equipment to help hold them in place. Then they did it again for the inner doors, using a desk and a forklift.

"That'll do for now," Alan declared, brushing back his long hair. With a start, he saw a fresh burn mark on the back of his hand where the rain had hit. When had that happened? He had to have been just too bastard busy to notice the pain.

A moment later, thunder and lightning heralded the gentle patter of rain.

"See, we had plenty of time," Cordelia said casually. "The rain missed us by a good two or three seconds."

Laughing weakly, Alan slapped the woman on the arm, then ambled away to check over the rest of his people.

"Wash that hand!" Mildred directed.

Waving backward over a shoulder, he merely nodded.

"Ben?" Mildred asked with a scowl.

"I'll take care of him, my sister," Dewitt replied, grabbing his fishing tackle box of medical supplies.

"'Sister'?" Ryan asked, resting the Galil on a shoulder.

"Just professional courtesy. Brothers-in-arms, that sort of thing."

"Like J.B. and me." Ryan nodded. "Gotcha."

Just then, the burning rags died out, and there was only the sputtering flame of the road flare.

"God's balls, those things smell bad," Alan said with a cough, waving away the magnesium fumes. Then he loudly clapped his hands. "Listen up, people! Time to break out the alcohol lanterns! This is what we have been saving them for all these years!"

"'Malt does more than Milton can…'" Library said, using a butane lighter to ignite the wick on a hurricane lantern. The glass reservoir sloshed with raw shine.

"'…to justify God's ways to man,'" Doc finished, breaking into a smile. "Great Scott, madam, you know the works of A. E. Housman?"

"Just the one," she admitted, as a clear blue light began to infuse the area. "When I was a child, I found a book called *Bartlett's,* and have been studying it ever since."

"You have memorized *Bartlett's Familiar Quotations?*" Doc gasped in delight. "Both volumes?"

"'In all things be mighty.'" Library grinned, holding the lantern high. "Marcus Cicero, 63 B.C."

"Ahem. 'For death is nothing, comfort less,'" Doc started, then paused in a friendly test.

"'Valor is all in all,'" Library continued.

"'Base nations who depart from it…'"

"'Shall sure, and justly, fall!'"

"General George S. Patton," Doc stated.

The old man and Library grinned like idiots, then bowed to each other.

"Nuking hell, now there's two of them," Cordelia muttered, massaging a temple.

"I vote for immediate sterilization," Mildred said.

Unexpectedly, light began to infuse the shadows. Everybody looked up to see the deadly rain washing away decades of dirty, grime and dried bird droppings from a series of decorative skylights in the curved roof.

"Dark night, I sure hope the glass in those is strong if it's a hard acid rain," J.B. declared, shifting his fedora.

"Well, we'll find out soon enough," Krysty said.

Among the travelers, several made a gesture of protection.

Outside the building, something screamed in unimaginable agony, the sound continuing for an incredibly long time before finally stopping. Then there was only the soft patter of rain on the roof.

"Was that a norm?" a child asked, struggling to cock back the hammer on a longblaster twice her size.

"Just possum," Jak said, relaxing his grip on the M-16 rapidfire. "Come help get saddle off horse. Be here while. You like horses?"

"Sure!" She grinned, cradling the weapon. "Who doesn't?"

"Well, once knew trader named Fat Stephen…" Jak began, and chatting away, they walked over to start tethering the nervous animals.

"Okay, listen up, people!" Ryan commanded, working the arming bolt on the Galil. "I want a perimeter sweep of these offices, storerooms and catwalks!

"Two by two!" Alan continued, removing a small cork from the end of the barrel of his black powder longblaster. "Nobody goes anywhere alone, until we know for certain this place is clear! If you need the shitter, then find a friend, or tie it in a knot! No exceptions!"

A ragged chuckle coursed through the group of travelers they hauled out their newly acquired weaponry from the coldhearts. There were of lot of small caliber zip guns and homemade scatterguns, but also a fair number of handblasters, and a smattering of bolt-action longblasters. It was evident that until their recent defeat in the hollows, the coldhearts had been extremely successful in their chosen field of work.

"Know a good hunting poem, Lib'ary?" a man asked, hoisting a Browning .22 bolt-action longblaster.

"Lie-brar-ee," she replied, exasperated. "Why is that so hard for folks to say?"

Dramatically clearing his throat, Doc started to respond, but then a low growl came from the flickering shadows deep within a maze of steam pipes, electrical conduits and pressure valves.

Everybody turned fast just as a grizzly bear lumbered into view, twice the height of a human. The dark fur of the colossal beast was speckled with tiny white areas, patches of wrinkled gray skin showing where the acid rain had singed the animal.

"Light it up!" Ryan ordered, cutting loose with the Galil rapidfire. The 5.56 mm rounds stitched the huge animal across the chest, but the bear only seemed enraged by the attack. It raised both clawed paws to start forward, roaring defiantly.

Shooting from the hip, J.B. put a burst of 9 mm rounds into the bear, just as Alan pulled back the heavy hammer on his flintlock longblaster, aimed and fired. Smoke and flame vomited from the blaster's muzzle, the booming discharge rattling the office doors.

Screaming in rage, the bear was slammed backward by the trip-hammer arrival of the .78 miniball, crimson flowing freely from its wounds front and back.

The travelers unleashed a flurry of arrows, the shafts

feathering the bear's chest. Sneezing blood, the animal turned to try to escape. A boomerang spun past it, only to return and slam into its head. With a grunt, the bear dropped.

"Cordelia, slit its throat!" Alan bellowed, already busy tamping a fresh charge into his longblaster. "Davies, Jacamor, find out how that thing got inside!"

Brandishing blasters and lanterns, a dozen travelers started to spread out from the wags, the nimbus of blue light diverging as they went to check the cinderblock walls for any cracks or missing doors. Then a woman screamed, and her lantern crashed to floor. As the glass reservoir shattered, the shine ignited and a pool of flames formed to rise high, exposing the back of a man holding the woman by the face.

The stranger was wearing only tattered rags, and every inch of exposed skin was covered with tiny suckers that opened and closed with moist sucking sounds. Then he turned to hoot softly at the travelers, his inhuman face streaked with fresh blood.

Everybody instantly cut loose with a wild barrage of blasterfire and arrows. Torn to pieces, the stickie tumbled away, releasing the woman's twitching corpse, most of her face and throat gone.

"Nuking hellfire, what is this place?" Alan demanded, dropping the longblaster to draw both his flintlock pistols.

"A safe zone where everything in the area goes to hide when the rain comes!" Krysty snarled, her M-16 combo jerking about at every flickering shadow.

"But the doors were locked…." a man began, then

flew backward into the gloom. He shrieked briefly in pain, which was followed by ghastly tearing noises.

Sending a chattering volley of 9 mm rounds into the darkness, J.B. cursed as the muzzle-flashes revealed several more stickies, their hands and faces shiny with fresh blood.

Once more the two groups unleashed assorted weapons, and some of the stickies fell, but the rest stayed in the shadows. Igniting one of his remaining Molotovs, J.B. smashed the vinegar bottle on a maze of steel pipes and liquid fire rained down upon the creeping muties. Their anguished hoots were quickly terminated by a brief rattle of blasters. But then, on the other side of the power plant, a horse whinnied and rose defiantly as a second grizzly bear came forward to rake the animal with its sharp claws.

Swinging up her longblaster, the little girl fired, the booming weapon sending a miniball humming past the bear to smack into the ceiling only inches away from the skylight.

Snarling a curse, Jak fired a volley into the bear, the stream of 5.56 mm rounds doing scant damage. But the sheer volume of lead held the animal at bay until the child could race back to the safety of the wag.

As the rapidfire emptied, Jak dived aside and Doc triggered the LeMat. The face of the bear exploded in a horrid spray at the arrival of the .44 Magnum bone shredder. But as the decapitated body collapsed, another bear was revealed, along with a snarling cougar, and then a shambling crowd of softly hooting stickies. A lot more of them.

"Blessed Buddha save us!" a traveler whimpered, dropping his longblaster and backing away in terror.

"Ace them all!" Ryan and Alan shouted in unison.

Chapter Fifteen

On the top of a rocky hill, a laurel bush quivered slightly, and a pair of blue eyes peered from within the branches. Soon it was joined by more eyes, brown, green and black. The faces of the Alton ville sec men were streaked with dry mud, their clothing covered with twigs and leaves. One of them even had an aced bird tied to a shoulder as additional camouflage. But more importantly, everybody was heavily armed, and not smiling.

"Now, who are these assholes?" a sec men whispered, squinting at the norms below. "There's no sign of Ryan and his gang."

"Trust me, they're here somewhere," Chief Ralhoun muttered, trying to extend her powers down into the valley, and failing completely.

"Shah tracked these folks from that fight in the hollows," she continued, "and he's never wrong. Never!" She scratched the old pit bull behind the ears. Shah wagged his tail in pleasure but didn't make a sound.

A crude wall of railroad cars encircled a large campsite situated inside a box canyon. The predark containers were made of corrugated iron, and a small crack here and there showed that they were filled with dirt. Stacked two deep, and reinforced by hundreds of black iron rails, the cars made a formidable barrier, even without the thicket of punji sticks along the perimeter, or the coils of razor wire on top.

The front gate was merely another railroad car, the wheels set sideways. It was braced from behind by a sheaf of railroad ties set deep in the ground, and four massive ties served as locking bars. There were no hinges; the gate had to be pushed open from the inside. Pulling it out would be damn near impossible.

The fortified camp was very well defended with numerous guard towers, armed sentries walking along the top of the wall, and what looked like a pack of cougars running about inside an enclosure made of punji sticks. There was a second enclosure that was empty for some reason, another filled with horses, and a fourth filled with barefoot people dressed in rags, wearing collars and chains.

"Nuke me, but that's a slave pen," a sec men said with a dark scowl. "Don't like those much."

"Nobody does," Chief Ralhoun answered gruffly, easing the safety off a Beretta.

Most of the slaves were hard at work, drawing water from a well, mucking out the shitters or chopping wood.

Surrounding the pen was a double row of low buildings made of wooden railroad ties notched together like the tree trunks in a log cabin. The slanted roofs were also made of railroad ties, and thickly coated with what looked like tar as protection from the acid rain. Each structure had its own private shitter with a half-moon on the door, and there were dozens of sandbag nests scattered about in strategic locations so that the coldhearts could use them as fallback positions in case the camp was invaded.

Which, considering their wall, was highly unlikely, Ralhoun thought dourly. She was very proud of her home, but this military hard site made Alton look like the pitched tent of a Sippy barb.

Off to the side of the camp were a couple empty gallows, and a lashing post with a rotting corpse nailed in place. And smack in the middle of the camp was a brick roundhouse with a domed roof made out of some green metal.

"Is...is that copper?" Latimer whispered.

"Gotta be," Ralhoun answered, trying hard not to be impressed. A metal roof. She had never heard of such a thing before! There was enough copper showing to make a million rounds of brass, which meant that either the coldhearts didn't know how to make brass, or they had a monumental supply of ammo.

The banded doors of the roundhouse were large enough for a mil wag to roll through, and smoke rose from three separate stone chimneys. Another sandbag wall surrounded the roundhouse, with chained cougars and armed sec men stationed along the length. A smooth stretch of brick road extended from the front gate in the wall directly to the largest door in the roundhouse, which was garishly painted with a skull and crossbones.

"That must be where their baron keeps his war wag," a sec woman stated, hefting a heavy crossbow. "Holy shit! What a stronghold! I don't think even ol' Bessy here could breech that wall!" A half stick of dynamite was attached to the arrow in her crossbow, the outside of the cylinder covered with rusty nails held in place by a thick layer of candle wax.

"I can take it out," Latimer boasted, patting the pocket of his nylon windbreaker. It bulged ominously.

"Only if ya don't miss," the sec woman said.

"Have I ever?"

"Not yet," Ralhoun replied. "How many of those grens you got left?"

"Just the one," he replied grimly. "But it'll do."

"Damn, there's a lot of them," a young sec woman muttered uneasily, twisting her hands on an Enfield longblaster. "Must be fifty coldhearts, mebbe more!"

Deep in thought, Ralhoun merely grunted in reply.

"That's too many of them for us to risk a night-creep, Chief," a sec man stated, lowering a Thompson rapidfire. "I want them bad, the same as you, but trying to get inside that camp would be suicide."

In the distance, lightning flashed, and thunder rumbled softly.

"Yeah, agreed," Ralhoun growled, easing deeper into the bushes. "So we'll hide in those caves we found in the foothills. Sooner or later, something will happen and we'll get our chance for revenge. A rival gang of coldhearts will attack to get their hands on the big-ass wag, or some barbs will raid the place for the horses, or mebbe the slaves will revolt. That would be perfect."

"And if nothing happens?" Latimer asked, crawling through the morass of greenery.

"Then we make it happen," Ralhoun said softly, grinning without any trace of humor.

As the sec men snaked through the thick foliage, lightning flashed again in the distant mountains, the storm heading swiftly in their direction.

SHAMBLING OUT of the shadows inside the power plant, a stickie came forward, waving both sucker-covered hands in the air as if greeting an old friend. Shooting from the hip, Ryan put a single round into the mutie's forehead, and the back of the misshapen head exploding in a pinkish geyser.

"Get up the bastard stairs!" Ryan shouted, putting a long burst of the 5.56 mm rounds from the Galil into a cougar creeping through the maze of pipes and conduits. In these tight confines, that was the real danger.

Cornered by some stickies, a terrified horse was torn apart, the still-beating organs stuffed into the inhuman mouths with happy gobbling sounds.

"You heard the man, up those stairs!" Alan bellowed, shooting one blaster, then the other. "They can't reach us on the catwalk!"

However, a score of travelers scrambled into their wags and slammed the doors, locking them tight.

"Stupes," Cordelia growled, blowing the head off a stickie just as it reached for her face. "Never again, ya rad sucking feebs! Never again!"

Waving his arms, a man ran out of the shadows, the upper half of his body covered with a gelatinous mass that pulsed red with every beat of his dying heart.

"Flapjacks!" Mildred snarled, and swung up her rapidfire to put a mercy round through the head of the dying norm.

Crawling along the ceiling were more of the translucent muties, and as she watched, one of them let go, to plummet straight down onto a horse. The animal reared, its hooves pawing the air, as the pulsating flapjack began to darken in color.

Pausing for only a second, Mildred put a single round into the horse's head, and as it dropped, the flapjack burst under the weight, sticky fluids spraying outward in every direction.

"Stairs! Now!" Ryan commanded, slapping a fresh magazine into the Galil.

Moving fast, the companions formed a tight cluster around the base of the nearest set of iron steps, and began to lay down suppressing fire, using only short bursts to keep the growing horde of animals and muties at bay.

"Follow me!" Cordelia ordered, pounding up the stairs, her boots loudly clanging on every step. As she reached the landing, she cursed and fired at a movement in the darkness. Half masked by flickering shadows, the rabbit was torn in two by the impact of the .63 miniball.

Clutching weapons, the travelers hastily charged onto the catwalk until the metal began to groan from their weight.

"Disperse!" Mildred shouted over the blasting Winchester.

Nobody moved, unsure what to do.

"Scatter, ya stupes! Stop bunching up!" Library yelled, and her friends quickly spread out along the network of walkways, their boots scraping free decades of dust.

The last one up the stairs, Ryan poured hot lead into the growing crowd of animals, waiting until the very last second in an effort to build a wall of fallen bodies. But there didn't seem to be an end to the invasion. Squirrels, rats, opossums, and now even birds were streaming into the power plant. Most of the woodland creatures were harmless, but the sheer mass of them seriously hindered the efforts of the people to ace the more dangerous species.

Then from out of the darkness four bears waddled closer, their fangs bared for battle.

Shooting the first one in the throat, Ryan dropped the animal at the foot of the stairs. As the others started climbing over, he paused, then chilled them both. Snarling in rage, the last bear tried to reach Ryan from the side railing, the claws missing him by the thickness of a prayer.

Spinning through the smoky air, a 'rang came from nowhere and slammed into the animal's open mouth, shattering several teeth. Howling in pain, the bear quickly retreated, blood dribbling from its snout. But as it departed, several stickies converged upon the makeshift barrier of corpses, hooting wildly as they started to feast.

Walking up the stairs backward, Ryan chilled the muties with carefully placed head shots as several more boomerangs flashed by, closely followed by some arrows and then a hatchet. As Ryan reached the catwalk, a tall mound of corpses blocked the staircase.

"That'll do!" he shouted, inserting a fresh magazine into the Galil rapidfire. "But everybody check the other stairs! Block them with whatever is available—bodies, barrels, boxes! Just keep them off the catwalks!"

"Move with a purpose, people!" Alan shouted, running away into the shadows.

"Dark night, how are they getting inside?" J.B. demanded, shoving a fresh shell into the hot scattergun and immediately firing. Then he did the same thing again, and again.

"No bastard idea!" Ryan snarled, firing directly into the eye of a stickie. The inhuman head jerked back, and the body dropped, but the hand stayed anchored to the railing by the sucker-covered fingers.

"No spoor litters the floor, so they have never been in here before!" Doc yelled, triggering the M-16 combo.

Down on the ground level, a wounded bear stumbled backward to trip over a cougar. Instantly, the two animals began to roll about, snarling and biting, sharp claws ripping away great hunks of flesh and fur.

"So why are they here now?" Krysty demanded, using both the M-16 and her hand blaster.

"Survival instinct!" Mildred told her, hastily shoving fresh rounds into the side of the Winchester. "They followed the sound of our horses!" She had seen something like this on a nature program once, on cable TV. During a forest fire, the first animals to take flight suddenly became the leaders of everything else alive. Usually, they went in the correct direction, reaching a river, or lake, where all the animals could wait out the blaze, but sometimes they took a wrong turn, and everything ended up going off a cliff.

"We lead in here?" Jak demanded, leaning over the railing to trigger single rounds from the M-16. The 5.56 mm rounds weren't powerful enough to chill most of the creatures below, so he was concentrating on shooting out their eyes, and then letting blind rage do the rest as the frantic beasts attacked the first thing they encountered. The trick worked well on the bears and cougars, but there were no visible eyes on a flapjack, and with their misshapen faces, it was difficult to tell where the eyes were located on the stickies in the dim light.

"Look out!" Library cried, pointing her crossbow directly at Doc.

Dropping low, he saw the arrow flick by to slam into something furry with a lot of sharp, white teeth, which had been crawling along an overhead girder.

"My thanks, dear lady!" Doc shouted, sending a burst of perfectly imbalanced tumblers into a bear pounding on the side of a wag on the floor below. The animal convulsed at the arrival of the 5.56 mm rounds, but otherwise seemed undamaged. Drawing his .44 handblaster, Doc fired a fast four times, and the bear eased to the floor with a low groan as if going to sleep.

"Anytime, Doc!" Library answered, unleashing another arrow into the back of a stickie ripping off strips of hide from a team of screaming horses.

"Volley fire, on my command!" Dewitt commanded, ramming a fresh charge into a musket. Cocking back the stone-tipped hammer, he aimed over the railing. "Three…two…one…fire!"

Along the catwalk, a dozen of the travelers cut loose with an orchestrated barrage from their longblasters. The thundering discharge rivaled the storm overhead in sheer volume, but billowing gun smoke masked any results in the sea of animals below.

Jerking open the cylinder of the LeMat, Doc dumped out the spent brass and began shoving in fresh rounds, when a stickie grabbed the railing and starting climbing over the barrier. Snapping the partially loaded blaster shut, Doc pulled the trigger three times before finding a live round. The muzzle-flash illuminated the hideous mutie in crystal clarity as it sailed away from the catwalk to land on top of a generator housing. It stayed there, stuck to the dusty metal by the rows of moist suckers.

Overly excited by the sound of blasters, a swarm of stickies converged around the generator, hooting wildly and waving their arms in the air.

"By the three Kennedys, we have got to locate that entrance and seal it shut!" Doc shouted over the blaster-fire and growls, removing the single exhausted cartridge to quickly shove in nine more brass.

Kneeling, some travelers fired their crossbows directly through the perforated flooring of the catwalk, impaling a pinkish flapjack that was gorging on the fallen body of a still-living horse. Both mutie and horse were chilled.

"Well, there's no way we're going to find it up here!" Krysty countered, slapping her last magazine into the M-16 rapidfire. "Not in this weak light!"

"John, we need some more road flares!" Mildred declared, ramming the stock of her Winchester into the face of a hooting stickie climbing up the smooth cinder-block wall. The stunned mutie fell away, taking along the weapon stuck to its suckers.

"All out!" J.B. replied, firing his scattergun downward. Crouched on top of a wag, amid a sea of punji sticks, a cougar leaped upward for the catwalk. In mid-air, the animal was torn apart by the hellstorm of double aught buckshot.

Grabbing the Navy flare gun in her belt, Cordelia looked up at the skylights in the ceiling awash with acid rain, then tucked the blaster away again. With a grin, she lifted an alcohol lantern high and threw it over the railing to smash onto the floor near where the first bear had been seen. If there was a breech in the wall, it had to be close to that area. A fireball erupted, the bluish light revealing a set of tattered plastic curtains.

"What the fuck are those?" Cordelia demanded as several deer walked through the shredded partitions, closely followed by a mutie spider almost a foot tall.

"That how get in!" Jak snarled, emptying his M-16 into the spider. The 5.56 mm rounds tore ragged holes on the soft body. With a high-pitched wail, the huge mutie dropped to the floor, the serrated mandibles snapping closed. Then a dozen much smaller spiders scurried out from underneath the gory form and began to feed upon their deceased parent.

"But how do they get in from the outside?" Alan demanded, kicking a wolf in the throat, his hands busy reloading a blaster.

Working the arming bolt of the Galil to free a jam, Ryan grunted at the sight of the thick plastic sheets—a bastard sound curtain, a room divider used by the whitecoats working here to hold down the noise of the generators. Possibly there was a cafeteria on the other side, or at least a break room with vending machines. However, neither of those should have any access to the outside.

"Let's take a look!" Quickly aiming her crossbow, Library let a shaft fly and neatly pinned back the plastic curtain. But there was only darkness beyond. Then a swarm of squirrels poured into view, several with splotches of discolored fur, or patches missing entirely.

"Can't see dreck from up here," Ryan growled,

switching the Galil from single-shot to full-auto. "We gotta do a hard recce!"

"No prob. I'll do that!" a traveler offered, frantically ramming a fresh charge of black powder into his musket. However, his haste proved fatal when the overpacked weapon discharged, sending both it and most of the man's fingers spraying upward. With a scream, he fell, hugging the ragged end of his arm to his chest.

Unable to pause in the battle, Mildred kept shooting and tried to ignore the cries of pain. However, Dewitt rushed to the aid of the fallen man, clubbing a stickie out of the way with his fishing tackle box. The mutie staggered away from the minor blow, its face gushing blood with a score of small punctures.

Pivoting at the hip to shoot the stickie in the throat, Mildred felt a rush of professional pride. Dewitt had spiked his tackle box so that it could be used as a weapon. She almost laughed at the bitter irony of death by medical kit. Welcome to the Deathlands!

Suddenly, a flaming arrow shot from a wag lanced past the plastic curtains. As it disappeared into the darkness, more arrows came from the convoy. Slowly, the gloom was brightened by the accumulating firebrands, the flickering light revealing the lobby of the building, the sagging ruin of a reception desk, a jumbled pile of plastic chairs and a row of dreck-splattered vending machines. More importantly, there was a large crack in the floor, with small animals climbing out of the jagged opening to look around in confusion.

"Cover me!" Ryan shouted, hopping over the railing and dropping onto a wide steam pipe. He almost lost his balance as his combat boots slipped, from the layers of rust and dust sprinkling away. But grabbing a fluorescent light fixture, he moved onward, carefully shuffling along the pipe to jump down to a feeder pipe, and then to the top of a generator.

A score of small animals ran away at the clang of his landing, but several stickies eagerly moved closer, hooting at the arrival of the tasty two-legs. However, their hands couldn't reach Ryan at his present location, so he ignored them and waved for another flight of firebrands.

As arrows flew into the darkness once more, Ryan cursed at the sight of a curved brick wall inside the crack. That was a bastard storm drain…and suddenly he realized the truth. The local animals had to have been taking refuge inside the power plant for years, mebbe more, using the predark sewer system to gain entry into the lobby and offices. But they had never gone inside the main section of the building because of the plastic curtains. Designed to baffle the noise of the generators, they also held back the foul air of the decomposing people. However, when the companions smashed open the loading doors and vented the place, the wind had ripped the curtains loose, allowing the creatures full access.

Nuking hellfire, we did this to ourselves! Ryan fumed privately, then out loud shouted, "There's a bastard storm drain we have to close! Toss me down a pipe bomb!"

"No good, old buddy!" J.B. answered. "I don't have anything powerful enough for that big a job!"

"Used all!" Jak yelled, shooting a flapjack wiggling along the ceiling. Undamaged by the passage of the bullets, it continued onward, to disappear into the shadows.

Without a word, Alan sailed over the railing to land

on top of a wag. Dodging tentacles and claws, he raced along the punji sticks and barbed wire to jump to the next wag, and then another. Kneeling, he gave a complicated knock, and a split second later a roof hatch jerked open and he scrambled inside.

Nothing happened for a moment, then the rear door to a wag was slammed aside and a wooden plank extended to crash onto the floor, accompanied by five travelers with their blasters blowing hellfire and death. Standing in the middle of the group was Alan, pushing a large wooden barrel along the sloping plank. There was a short fuse jutting from a bunghole set into the top.

As the group started across the floor, a stickie raced toward them, only to be cut down by a burst of blasterfire from Ryan on top of the generator. "We got your back!" he shouted, slapping in his last magazine.

The air was thick with the smoke from the black powder weapons, and carried the strong taste of salt. More stickies came forward, and the companions tore them apart with short bursts, then the travelers on the catwalk feathered the corpses to make sure nothing was playing possum.

Moving around a complex set of pipes, Alan and his men stayed in a tight formation, the travelers shooting at anything that got close, and kicking aside any corpses, or grisly debris, that might impede the progress of the heavy barrel. Passing a team of screaming horses, Alan slipped in some fresh crap on the floor, and as he landed sprawling, a wolf darted out of nowhere. As it leaped, Alan desperately swung up a machete, then cried out as the wooden barrel rolled backward over his boot.

Landing on top of him, the wolf tried for his exposed

throat, but Alan managed to block the attack with the machete. Swinging around their muskets, his men took aim, then realized it was impossible to chill the wolf with their longblasters without the .78 miniballs coming out the other side of the animal and also acing their leader.

Raising their weapons like clubs, they started forward as another hooting stickie appeared. Turning fast, they blew it away, just as Ryan jumped off the generator to land on the back of the wolf, his combat boots centered on the spine. There was an audible crack of bone as the wolf went flat on top of his intended victim, who then slashed it across the throat.

"Th-thanks," Alan gasped, shoving the corpse aside.

"No prob," Ryan grunted, passing over the Galil and putting both hands on the barrel to start shoving it forward. It was a lot heavier than he expected, and he really needed put some serious muscle into the job to keep the thing rolling along. As he proceeded across the floor there came a soft, whispery sound from within, and he guessed the contents. This was probably the main supply for the whole bastard convoy!

Using the rapidfire to lever himself off the floor, Alan briefly checked over the weapon, then began limping after Ryan. The pain was tremendous, but he said nothing, merely dragging his left foot along behind, the hem of his pants already turning dark with blood.

More animals and muties attacked, but now the people on the catwalk renewed the defense, and the little group on the ground soon reached the plastic curtains, wounded, but very much alive, and still moving.

It was an effort to get over the jamb in the floor, but

Ryan put his full strength to the task, and finally got across the threshold. Once past the curtains, he cursed as the barrel started to roll forward all by itself. Fireblast, the bastard floor was tilted! he realized.

Brandishing a longblaster, one of the guards stepped forward, but paused, unsure what to do. Then Alan triggered a burst from the Galil, angled high. A fluorescent light fixture on the ceiling danced from the arrival of the 5.56 mm rounds, then came smashing down onto the floor, spraying out white shards of curved glass. Crashing into the wreckage, the barrel stopped just short of the crack, less than a foot away from the blackness.

"Bastard good shot," Ryan declared, pulling out a butane lighter and flicking it alive.

"This ain't my first fandango," Alan grunted, then swung around the rapidfire to shoot directly at the one-eyed man.

Ryan flinched as the muzzle-flash stung his cheek, then he heard something scream with pain and scamper away. He started to nod thanks, but saw a motion on the ceiling, and instead brutally shoved Alan aside. With a wet plop, a large flapjack landed exactly where he had just been standing.

Both men cut loose with their blasters at the monstrous thing, the Galil and SIG-Sauer tearing away gelatinous hunks of the translucent body until the mutie ceased to move, and began to turn a solid white.

"Everybody start running!" Ryan ordered, kneeling to light the stubby fuse. "A few more of these things get inside, and we're all on the last train west!"

With a pyrotechnic sputter, the black length of twine

soaked in black powder ignited, to start sizzling toward the huge barrel.

"Haul ass, people!" Alan bellowed, hobbling away at his best speed.

Dropping their longblasters, two of the guards grabbed their leader under the arms and lifted him off the floor, to start running away.

"Fire in the hole!" Ryan shouted, sprinting past the plastic curtains. At the rate that fuse was burning, it was going to be close. Too damn close.

High on the catwalk, everybody burst into frantic motion at the clarion call of the ancient battlefield warning, the companions and travelers dashing away from the area toward the blocked staircase.

Down on the floor, Ryan, Alan and the guards barely got behind the housing of a generator when the universe seemed to explode. The power plant rocked as a hot wind slapped their faces, and hellish tongues of writhing flame completely filled the shuddering building, accompanied by the gut-wrenching sound of breaking glass.

As the acid rain fell, the howler found itself irresistibly drawn to the north, then quickened its progress at the sight of the crashed aircraft carrier sticking out of the ground.

The glow of its cloud intensified as the mutie maneuvered through a slim crack in the hull to reach the dark interior. Traversing the sideways corridors and decks, the howler proceeded mindlessly to the nuclear generator as if compelled by forces beyond its comprehension, concentrating on reaping the rich harvest of uranium-238 from the core of the reactor.

Several of the oval hatchways set into the bulkheads were seriously warped by the crash, and the mutie had to make complex detours throughout the vessel, switching from one deck to another, removing crumpled doors and burrowing through access panels, before finally reaching the main power station.

As it entered, a 9 mm Colt auto-sentry bolted to the ceiling gave a single loud click, then went still forever, the brief microsecond surge of activity completely exhausting the very last spark of the weapon systems emergency reserve power.

Pushing aside piles of skeletons, chairs and assorted equipment, the howler unearthed the primary fuel port. Incredibly, the radiation-proof shielding was undamaged and still sealed tight. But guided by something deep inside, the howler wisely attacked the much weaker steam pipes going from the reactor to the turbines of the huge electric generators. Those pipes were only made of a four-inch-thick titanium-steel alloy, and the glowing cloud soon weakened them enough that the howler could smash them into jagged metallic splinters.

Snaking a jointed limb along the interior of a pipe, the mutie bypassed numerous valves and relays to eventually reach the uranium core at the heart of the reactor, only to find it cold and inert. Over the centuries, the unstable isotope had reverted into a more base form of inert matter.

Furious over the betrayal, the howler wildly attacked the machinery, ripping out control boards and servo-mechanisms.

Unexpectedly, a section of the wall disengaged to
slide away, and out stepped a black metal droid. The
machine possessed a globular body and six telescoping
legs, making it resemble a spider. The eyes were small
black dots set into curved recesses of the face, barely
distinguishable in the glowing green light of the howler,
and bolted to the bottom of the curved belly was the fer-
ruled rod of a compact Bedlow laser.

With a low pneumatic hiss, the tarantula swiveled its
head and its Bedlow laser in opposite directions, then
locked both on to the howler across the room.

Instantly recognizing danger, the mutie immediately
expanded the glowing cloud to its maximum size, then
turned to flee. However, the fresh piles of destruction
hindered a rapid escape, and the howler promptly found
itself trapped amid the endless coils of cables and loose
wiring.

Audibly throbbing into operation, the Bedlow laser
sent out a scintillating rainbow beam of hellish inten-
sity that burned through the glowing fog and the mutie
inside. Cut in two, the howler wailed as it fell apart, the
cloud dissipating to fully reveal the segmented horror
within.

Unaffected by the esthetics of the living nightmare,
the tarantula advanced through the topsy-turvy room,
its slim ebony legs finding purchase on the walls, floor
and ceiling. As it had been programmed to do, the built-
in comp of the droid swept the polychromatic energy
beam steadily back and forth across the howler until
there was nothing remaining of the creature except for
a bubbling pool of molten steel on what had once been
the wall.

Calmly waiting a few minutes for the steel to begin to solidify, the tarantula then proceeded to the nearest exit, only to find the hatchways serious distorted and completely useless. With no other recourse, the droid chose the shortest distance to the outside, and began burning a series of holes through the bulkheads.

Carving an opening through a particularly thick one, the tarantula paused at the sight of an armorial wall. The material was colored a soft green, with horizontal stripes of gold.

Backing away, the droid choose a new direction, and several hours later emerged from the side of the battleship. Bathed in the rain, the tarantula perched on the hull and attempted to contact the Pentagon for fresh instructions, but there was no reply. Switching frequencies, the droid then tried for the NORAD High Command, then for the Situation Room of the White House. Nothing. Puzzled, the tarantula switched to the civilian airwaves, then finally the internet. But the result was always the same—only the soft crackle of background solar radiation, as if radio had never been invented. Even the brand-new GPS network wasn't functioning.

Boosting its transponder to full power, the tarantula swept the skies for any telecommunications satellite in orbit—military, governmental, civilian or even foreign. Instantly, it connected with several machines of unknown origin, but as they started relaying garbled information about a worldwide thermonuclear war, the tarantula promptly dismissed them as malfunctioning. If there had been such a conflict, the droid would have been properly notified via official channels.

Locked in a subelectronic dilemma, it paused for a long second, then, automatically falling back on preestablished protocols, walked down the side of the hull to the ground, and patiently waited for the rain to stop. It knew that the stars would emerge eventually, and after orientating itself by stellar cartography, the tarantula would proceed directly to the nearest redoubt, and wait in the antechamber for somebody with the proper B12 authority to come and issue new instructions.

Until those orders arrived, the tarantula would do the same thing as always: stand, wait and terminate with extreme prejudice any unauthorized personnel on sight. Especially any life-forms not genetically pure humans.

Chapter Sixteen

With a start, Althea awoke to the gentle patter of falling rain, and a palm firmly pressed to her mouth. Raw terror filled her, and she clawed for the knife hidden beneath her pillow. But just as she grabbed the weapon, she suddenly recognized the hand and relaxed slightly.

"Take a sniff," Dean whispered, removing his hand. "Sniff hard."

After a moment she did, and smelled nothing. "Thank Gaia, the acid rain is over." She sighed. "This is just water."

"Which means we have to leave right now," he stated forcibly, walking over to a small window. Holding on to the wooden bars, he studied the coldheart campsite. Runoff from the pitch roofs was still trickling along the bamboo gutters and pouring into wooden barrels. But mixing with the clean water, the acid rain was thinning to a pale yellow now. Soon it would begin to flow clear, then coldhearts would rouse, to switch barrels and keep the drinkable water from polluting the precious acid rain.

Converting the acid rain into sulfur to make black powder had been one of the first tricks Dean had taught the coldhearts in order to increase his worth. The process was easy once you knew how, but they had acted as if he were pulling live brass out of his arse. Then he showed them how to use a diluted form of the acid rain to toughen boot leather, and Camarillo had made him a corporal. However, the promotion hadn't lasted very long, because he'd accidentally on purpose shot a slave sentenced to the lashing post. But now he was a lieutenant, the second in command of the whole camp!

Dean moved to a wooden shelf. Opening a locked metal chest, he extracted a bulky sack.

"Are fifteen enough?" Althea asked, climbing out of their bed and stepping into a plain cotton dress with a deerskin bodice.

"It'll have to do," Dean answered, setting aside the sack to tuck a brace of flintlocks into his belt. "Took me a bastard long time to steal this many machetes!"

"Then they will suffice," Althea said, slipping a knife into her bodice before lacing it closed.

Incredibly, the bodice was another contribution by Dean. Usually, the coldhearts allowed the slaves to wear only rags, rain or shine, summer and winter. But now they demanded the female slaves wear the thing because it plumped up their breasts like a gaudy shut on parade. The fact that it also kept them from freezing to death in the snow seemed to go completely unnoticed by the coldhearts, but not by the slaves.

With this one act of kindness, Dean soon established a covert network of thankful spies in the camp that constantly fed him information on where supplies were stashed, which coldhearts liked to get drunk on sentry duty, and so on. Over time, he had slowly treated each bodice until it was now as tough as boot leather and able to stop the blade of a machete, or the lash of a bullwhip. Blasters could still ace the slaves, but some protection was better than none.

A knife in the hand was better than a blaster in the bushes, as Doc always liked to say. Just for a moment, Dean thought about all of the good times he had had with the man, discussing philosophy, women, war, and women again. Then he shook his head to dispel the memories, and concentrated on the bloody task at hand.

"We're not going to have much time to find your cousin," Dean said, stuffing a length of rope into a pocket. "If he gets stubborn about leaving his friends behind, I'll have to knock him out, and we'll drape him over a horse. But we'll have no time for friends, or friends of friends." He turned, looking worried. "You have no other family here, right? Bill is your only blood kin?"

"Just my cousin…and you," Althea replied, sliding another knife up her sleeve.

Smiling gently, Dean stepped closer to cup her face and kiss her lightly. As always, the touch ignited a fire of passion within him, but he broke away to place a small-caliber revolver into her hand.

"That's for emergencies only," he said, looking her straight in the eyes. "Whatever happens to me, don't let them take you alive. That's paramount. Now swear it!"

"I will not be taken alive," Althea promised, opening the cylinder to check the load, as he had taught her to do during the long nights. There were four live .22 rounds nestled inside the Ruger revolver, each one carefully cut into what Dean called a dumdum. They were supposed to go into a person like a pinkie, but come out the back bigger than a closed fist. Chilling was guaranteed.

How that was possible she had no idea, but Dean was an endless river of knowledge, and she trusted him completely. Even more so than ever after last night. It had been their first time.

"Where do we meet again?" Dean asked, peeking through the window shutters. On patrol, a coldheart was sloshing through the rain, a hand-rolled cigarette smoking safely under the wide brim of his straw hat. From this distance, he appeared to have no arms, but that was due to the plastic poncho he was wearing. Under it, the sentry was carrying a brace of blasters and a 9 mm Uzi rapidfire.

"We meet at the second gallows," Althea answered, slipping the tiny blaster into a pocket.

"Remember the ABC code?"

"Alfred, Brian, Charles. Yes, I do."

A second guard strolled past the little cabin, this time leading a cougar on a rope harness. The big cat was drenched to the skin and appeared very unhappy. Dean smiled at that. The brick streets were edged with gutters, but the lingering traces of acid rain would still completely ace the animal's sense of smell. Another small point in their favor.

"If grabbed from behind, what do you do?" Dean asked, patting his clothing in a military ritual. His father had taught him this trick. It saved vital seconds in a fight to know exactly where every weapon was located without having to pause and search, or even look.

"Stab with my knife over my left shoulder, going for the face," she repeated dutifully. "Then around my right hip, going for the groin. When he lets go, I turn and slash the throat."

"If we lose each other afterward, where do you go?"

"My cousin and I," she corrected, "both go to Front Royal, just east of the Sorrow River, in North Virginny. The local baron is Nathan Cawdor, your cousin. The sec boss is Clem Turpin. I'm to remind him of the battle on Rolling Rock Hill to prove that I know you."

"Good. Now, there are how many rounds in your blaster?"

"Four," Althea replied. "One for a coldheart, one for my cousin and two for me. Into the temple if possible, or the throat if necessary."

"Don't take a chance on chilling anybody else," Dean ordered in a hard voice, watching a distant coldheart walking along the top of the camp wall. "If they come for you, eat the barrel, and keep pulling the trigger for as long as you can."

"I've seen the lashing post, Dean," Althea said simply, tying the laces of the bodice with a bow. "Forget about me, and concentrate on getting the sandhog. I'll meet you at the gallows with my cousin."

Overhead, thunder rumbled as Dean opened the door to the cabin. He paused to look at Althea, unable to speak for a moment. There were just too many words in his head, and too much feeling in his heart. Stepping in close, he kissed her, long and hard. It wasn't a goodbye, but a promise of survival, and better times to come. Letting go, he inhaled deeply, and she stroked his face with her fingertips, saying more with the simple gesture than with a thousand words.

Stepping away, he went to the worktable in the corner, pulling aside a ragged piece of cloth. There was a pile of tools on the table, along with a disassembled rapidfire. Warily lifting a screwdriver, he revealed a small nubbin of fuse stuck in the table. Using a butane lighter, he got it sizzling, then piled the tools over the hole again.

"Here we go, my love," Dean said, sliding on a poncho and straw hat.

Lifting the sack, Althea slung it over a shoulder, then also donned a hat and poncho.

Now resembling the guards, the couple stepped outside and glanced about to see if anyone was watching. But there was nobody in sight, only the rain, the low gurgle in the gutters mixing with the steady patter of the easing downpour.

Locking the door, Dean dropped the key into a puddle. Then he shared one last look with Althea, and they separated to their assigned tasks.

Back in the cabin, the fuse continued to burn along the bottom of the worktable, heading directly toward a small wooden keg.

With her heart pounding, Althea strolled along the rainy street, and casually nodded in passing to a guard sitting under an woven bamboo awning eating a sandwich.

"Want some coffee?" he asked, proffering a steaming mug.

Waving off the offer, she immediately changed direction and headed toward the nearest outhouse. Turning the corner, Althea waited a minute to make sure the guard didn't follow, then she relaxed her grip on the .22 blaster hidden under the poncho, and started toward the slave pen.

She heard the soft snoring of the sleeping horses in

the corral long before she could see them, and again nodded in greeting at a guard stationed among the animals, an ugly sawed-off scattergun cradled in his wet hands.

The gurgling water in the brick gutters edging the paved street got steadily louder as she approached the slave pen. The surrounding cluster of punji sticks and barbed wire were almost invisible in the downpour, and she had to navigate purely by the sound of the gutters.

Passing a cabin, she heard the unmistakable noises of a man and woman having sex. Consensual sex it would seem, from the cries of pleasure. Unbidden, that brought to her mind last night with Dean, but she shoved that pleasant memory aside. If they survived this night, they would have the rest of their lives to enjoy such wonderful things again.

Deliberately sloshing through a puddle to herald her approach, Althea walked toward the guard stationed at the entrance to the slave pen. Past the punji sticks, she could see the chained people huddling in tight clusters under a very small sheet of plastic, the middle bowed from an accumulation of acid rain. They were visibly shivering.

"That you, Bob?" the guard asked as a greeting, peering through the misty rain.

Without a word, Althea stepped in close and rammed her knife up into the man's jaw, pinning his mouth closed. As he mumbled a scream, she buried her second knife into the middle of his chest. Dean had made her practice the move a hundred times, ramming the knife into a wooden table to get her arm strong enough to drive the blade past the ribs of the guard and reach his heart in a single stroke.

His eyes going wide, the coldheart rocked backward, then kept on going and landed in a puddle with a splash.

Standing there breathing hard, her hands empty, blood spreading across the damp bricks, Althea listened with her entire body for any reaction from the wall guards, or some unnoticed coldheart. But there was only the sound of the soft rain.

Hurrying to the corpse, she got the key from under his poncho and took back her knives, along with his gun belt and blaster. The man was also had a wooden cudgel with nails embedded in the top. Dean called it a morningstar. This was a weapon meant merely to wound slaves, not ace them, and drive them back into the pen. Pain to the chains, as the coldhearts joked. A surge of visceral hatred rose from deep inside her, and Althea fought the urge to scream. Instead, she unlocked the iron gate to the pen and walked to the first group of shivering slaves.

"I'm looking for Bill Stone," she said in a deep growl, trying to disguise her voice.

"Over there, master, by the piss bucket," a scrawny woman answered, indicating the direction with a dripping finger.

In a flash of recognition, Althea realized that she knew the woman. It was Lee-Ann RunningHawk, the ville healer. She was covered with bruises, and had several teeth missing

Kneeling, Althea unlocked the chains, easing it through a thick metal loop embedded into the bricks. "There, you're free," she said, pressing a heavy iron key into the palm of the woman. "Now do the same for the next chain. Then have one of them do the next group, and so on."

"Is…this a dream?" Lee-Ann murmured, closing her fist around the key, but otherwise not daring to move.

"Very much real, old friend," Althea said, removing the sack from under her poncho and passing it over. "Give these only to the strongest, but make damn sure that none of them has ever willingly helped the cold-hearts. Chill those bastards immediately, but do it quietly! This is a nightcreep, not another nuke war. Got it?"

In silent amazement, Lee-Ann took the heavy sack and looked inside. She gasped at the sight of the machetes, pulling one out in slow motion. "Now I know this is a dream," she whispered, turning the blade about to watch the rain dance off the oily steel.

Grabbing the woman's hair, Althea tightened her fingers into a hard fist. Grunting at that, Lee-Ann looked up angrily, the machete in her hand starting a deadly swing that immediately stopped. "Black dust, it is you!" she gasped. "But…but you're aced! I saw a coldheart drag you away!"

"I'm far from chilled," Althea countered, releasing her grip. "Now get sharp, or we're all buying the farm tonight!"

"Sure, sure, whatever you say," Lee-Ann gushed, looking at the key and machete. Slowly, she closed her hand into a hard fist over the former and looked directly at Althea. "What's the plan?" she demanded, hefting the blade to check the balance.

"Be quiet, and free the other prisoners," Althea commanded once more, using small words as if dealing with a drunk. Hellfire, the woman *was* drunk. Drunk on freedom. "Stay low, move fast and chill your way into the roundhouse. That's the coldheart armory. Get blasters, and come out shooting. Ace anybody not wearing rags."

"What about those mutie cats?" Lee-Ann asked in a worried tone.

In the distance, they heard a gasoline engine sputtering into life.

"Already got somebody working on that," Althea replied with a confident grin, starting to turn away.

"A coldheart named Hannigan wanted to know where the ville hides its cache of predark cans," Lee-Ann said quickly. "Bill tried to make a deal, barter the food for our release. But they…he…he's been to the post."

That single word crystallized the universe around Althea into immobility. Mutely, she nodded in understanding and headed toward the plastic bucket the coldhearts let the slaves use as a communal toilet.

Even with the rain still coming down, she could smell the contents of the bucket from yards away. Lying on the bricks nearby, a shivering man was chained to a post, his head bowed as if in prayer.

"Billy?" she asked, kneeling on the wet pavement.

As if it weighed a thousand tons, Bill Stone sluggishly raised his head to reveal the pair of scarred holes where blue eyes had once been located.

"No more, please," he whimpered, lifting a three-fingered hand wrapped in dirty bandages. "Please, don't cut off any more of me! I told you where the food is hidden. Under the rock, near the ville gate. It's there, I swear! Please, I'll do whatever you want! Just no more cutting…."

Dragging the chain, he tried to scuttle away, the end of his left leg scarred and blistered, the foot missing entirely. When he broke into wild sobbing, Althea also started to weep, as she leveled the stolen Ruger and pulled back the slide. In this wretched condition, there was no way he could climb over the wall with her and Dean. She desperately wished there was something else to do, but there were only two hard choices. She either abandoned him here to be taken apart like a blaster in need of oil, or set him free forever.

"Hush now, cousin," Althea whispered, pressing the barrel to his temple. "Time to sleep."

"Al…Althea?" William asked in a startled whisper.

"Goodbye," she said, and squeezed the trigger.

The 9 mm blaster sharply cracked, rocking back his head, and he toppled over limply. In spite of the downpour, the noise oddly seemed to echo across the entire camp dozens of times, rapidly building in volume and power until it rivaled the thundering storm.

What was that? she wondered, hunching her shoulders. Dean had rigged a firebomb in their cabin, not a keg of plas-ex!

Unexpectedly, a bright white light banished the night, and a column of flame rose from a distant section of the wall, the gate lifting off the railroad tracks to tumble away and violently crash into the base of a guard tower. In a splintery explosion, the wooden support legs were smashed and the cupola on top came hurtling down. The armed coldhearts trapped inside briefly screamed, until it reached the brick-lined street, and then they went mercifully silent.

Holstering the blaster, Althea sprinted from the slave pen, leaving the puzzled prisoners behind. She had set them loose and given them some blades. The rest was up to them. She wished them well, but they were little more than a diversion to keep the coldhearts busy while the three of them… Her heart stopped beating for a moment at the horrible memory of what she had done.

Window shutters were slamming open all over the campsite, the cold bluish light of shine lanterns spilling into the rainy streets. An alarm bell began to ring softly, then she heard the rattle of a rapidfire, followed by the dull boom of a black powder weapon.

Silently boiling out of the slave pen, the prisoners charged along the wet streets, waving the machetes. Coming out of an outhouse, a yawning coldheart fell under the onslaught, hacked to pieces. His blaster was taken and the mob raced onward, spreading across the camp, acing anybody they found.

Throwing open the shutters of a cabin, a coldheart cut loose with a rapidfire, the withering hail of hot lead sending a dozen of the former slaves tumbling to the unforgiving street. Then a man rose alongside the cabin and hacked off the coldheart's arm. Torrents of red blood gushed from the hideous wound as the coldheart bellowed in agony.

Snatching up the rapidfire, the man sprinted away, chilling two more coldhearts before the magazine ran dry. Then he was aced by a coldheart with a booming handblaster.

"The gate is down!" another man screamed, waving

a machete as if attacking the rain. "Follow me to freedom!"

"Forget that!" Lee-Ann countered. "Head for the roundhouse! We need blasters!"

Suddenly, a figure appeared on the roof of a cabin. "Red alert! It's the slaves!" a coldheart bellowed, firing a scattergun.

Caught in the chest, Lee-Ann seemed to exploded from within, bloody gobbets of steaming flesh smacking into the cabin wall. But as she fell, the ville bartender snatched up the machete and expertly flipped it forward. The long blade slammed into the belly of the coldheart, the sharp end coming out of his back. Groaning into death, he fell off the roof and hit the paved street with a hard crunch.

Moving fast, the slaves poured over the corpse like ants, snatching away the scattergun, his belt knife and the machete. Laughing insanely, a gaudy slut chopped the aced man into pieces before continuing onward, leaving bloody footprints in her wake.

Just then, an arrow arched down from the clouds to impale a running coldheart through the leg. Even as he stumbled, the half stick of dynamite exploded, sending out a hissing corona of shrapnel. Torn into pieces, a dozen other coldhearts fell, their tattered clothing soaked with blood.

Hearing the sound of running boots, Althea ducked behind an outhouse just as a squad of coldhearts appeared, their hands full of death. But as they took aim at the mob of howling slaves, the muffled report of a powerful longblaster sounded, and on the corner a water barrel burst apart, releasing its contents of acid rain. As the yellow fluid sloshed over their boots, the leather partly dissolved, and they frantically tried to hop out of the way. But the distant longblaster spoke again, and a second barrel exploded. Even though the acid rain was slightly diluted, the living flesh fell off their bones, and the coldhearts went sprawling, only to rise once more with most of their faces burned.

Scrambling onto the roof of the rickety outhouse, Althea could only wait until the downpour of rainwater washed the streets clean. Then she climbed down and streaked pell-mell toward the gallows.

Throughout the camp, she could hear the growing chaos of explosions, blasters, screaming, and the high-pitched shrieking of coldhearts encountering more acid rain barrels. Boomerangs spun out of the darkness, as silent as death itself, only to arch back again even faster than before.

More arrows descended, exploding like predark bombs across the camp. Several bounced off the copper roof of the roundhouse, to ignite harmlessly in the air, the shrapnel only sloshing the water in a couple of wooden barrels and chilling a cougar.

Althea heard the joyful cries of her fellow ville folk, and she almost smiled. Somebody was invading the camp, just as they were trying to get out. With all her heart, she wished both groups the best of luck. Lead hummed by her constantly, to musically ricochet off the brick streets, or wetly slap into the side of a cabin.

Running past the lashing post, she was grateful to see that the rain had washed away the lingering residue of its former occupant, her cousin, Bill.

A low puttering noise lead her straight to Dean, sitting astride a sandhog. The noose from the gallows was already lashed firmly to the frame of the odd little three-wheeler. His BAR longblaster was gone, and he was bleeding from several minor injuries, but he greeted her with a wide smile.

"Relieved that you made it!" he said, holstering the Browning Hi-Power. "Where is your..." He stopped talking at the sight of her grim expression.

"Get on," he commanded. "We'll need the extra weight to make this work!"

Wordlessly, she climbed on the seat, then hugged him tightly. Dean felt her shake and heard a muffled sob, but wisely said nothing. Mildred had taught him that tears were a natural release and helped a person stay sane.

"Here we go!" he growled, revving the engine and releasing the hand brake.

In a surge of power, the sandhog darted forward, and the rope snapped tight, creaking tightly, as the wooden gallows groaned. Then the base snapped and it came hurtling down, smashing onto the top of the railroad carriage wall.

"It worked!" Althea whispered.

"Not yet," Dean countered, climbing off the machine to cut away the noose and lash it tightly around the hand controls.

Aiming the sandhog back toward the heart of the camp, Dean saw that several of the cabins were in flames, and the flashes of red light in the streets told of blasters being used. Then the firebomb in his cabin detonated, and the roof was blown off, a column of flame reaching high into the stormy sky.

"Never saw black powder so strong before," Althea said in surprise.

"That was something else—a plas-ex called C-4," Dean replied, releasing the brake. Instantly, the sandhog streaked away to disappear into the night.

"But that's mil stuff!" she gasped. "Where did you find that much?"

"Didn't, I made it. An old friend named J.B. taught me how when I was a little," he replied, taking her hand and running back to the gallows.

"Why didn't we use that on the wall?"

"This batch was too unstable to risk moving. I had to cook it in the dark, you know!"

"Fair enough!" She smiled. "Is there anything you can't do, my love?"

"Don't know how to fly yet!" he replied, grabbing hold of the notches carved into the stout wooden beam used by the coldhearts, and starting up the gallows.

The wood was slippery with the rain, but the angle helped, and soon he reached the top of the wall. Staying low, he swung around the Browning Hi-Power and swept the darkness for any dangers. He couldn't really see much because of the downpour, then lightning flashed and he spotted a coldheart fifty yards away. Taking aim, he fired once, and the man fell backward into eternity.

"All clear!" he announced, working the bolt to chamber around round.

A moment later, Althea was by his side, her knife and blaster at the ready.

Going to the first coil of barbed wire, Dean pulled out a knife to start cutting, and was startled to find the wire already pushed aside. A grappling hook was set into the roof, and a knotted length of rope trailed over the side. This had to be how the invaders got in. What a stroke of luck!

Just then, Althea fired the Ruger.

Spinning low and fast, Dean saw a coldheart fall off the wall, his throat squirting out a geyser of blood.

Grunting at the sight, he sheathed the knife and drew the Browning Hi-Power. "You first," he commanded.

Nodding, Althea took hold of the rope and climbed out of sight.

"All clear, Adam!" she whispered from the darkness, using the code.

Holstering the blaster, Dean did the same, landing on the soggy ground in a splash.

"Where now?" Althea asked quietly.

Holding up a finger for silence, Dean tried to recall every trick Jak had ever taught him about following footprints through muddy water. The trail seemed to meander aimlessly into the bushes, and he began to think he was lost when he heard the low snort of a horse.

Sure enough, just past a bend in the canyon wall was a line of horses tethered to some juniper trees. He checked, but there were no guards, which was understandable. The invaders would need every blaster they had to take on the Stone Angels.

Choosing the best two horses, Dean and Althea quickly checked the saddlebags for supplies, and found dried meat, grens and brass. Climbing onto their new mounts, they then cut the reins of the rest of the horses and got them all moving as they rode out of the box canyon and along the muddy banks of the swollen river.

Traveling past the front gate of the camp, they saw the wreckage of the railroad, and the fighting inside. Murky figures on sandhogs were zooming about, while the cougars roared and the slaves screamed obscenities, hacking to pieces anything they could reach. Blasters were firing constantly, grens boomed, 'rangs and flights of arrows filled the air, then the piercing steam whistle of the *Atomsmasher* sounded.

"Time to run," Dean said through clenched teeth, kicking his stallion into a fast trot.

With Althea close behind, he broke away from the scattering horses, and together they charged along the bank of the river. There was little moonlight at the bottom of the canyon, and given the rain, visibility was almost nonexistent. Speed could ace them, but the couple didn't dare delay. Staying close to the murmuring river, they rode blindly onward until the noise of battle faded.

Gradually, the irregular canyon walls fell away and they were riding across open countryside brightly illuminated by the moon. In heartfelt relief, they both broke into a gallop, their horses pounding across the scrub grass.

"Where now, lover?" Althea called, bent low in the saddle, her long hair fanned out in the wind.

"We're gonna try and find some old friends," he replied grimly, moving to the motion of the stallion.

She glanced sideways. "How?"

"Working on it!" he replied, using his knees to urge the horse to a greater speed.

Chapter Seventeen

Punching, kicking, biting and cursing, Latimer and Hannigan fought like animals in the gentle rain.

Ducking under a fist, Latimer kicked the coldheart in the stomach. Hannigan grunted from the brutal impact, and butted the sec man in the face, breaking his nose. Snarling obscenities, Latimer reached for his blaster and found Hannigan's hand already there. Both men grabbed the weapon and struggled for control, the Colt .45 firing several times into the air before the hammer merely clicked on spent brass.

Releasing the blaster, Latimer drew his knife and slashed Hannigan across the throat, but the coldheart jerked back just enough so that the razor-sharp steel only left a shallow cut that oozed droplets of blood instead of a gushing torrent of hot life.

Kneeing the sec man in the groin in retribution, Hannigan felt his knee crack as it hit something as hard as rock. Clever son of a bitch had a wooden bowl in his crotch as protection! he realized.

Wrapping both hands around the throat of his enemy, Hannigan now tried to squeeze the life out of the invader, his thumbs going deep into the muscles. Unable to dislodge the insane coldheart, Latimer frantically looked about for help, but the entire camp was filled with sec men, slaves and coldhearts locked in bitter combat, illuminated by the flickering glow of the burning cabins.

"Hear that whistle, outlander?" Hannigan growled, spittle flying from his mouth. "That's the last train coming for you!"

Saving his breath, Latimer said nothing in reply. He tried to raise his knife again, but the berserker rage of the coldheart had given the man fantastic strength. The sec man knew it wouldn't last for long, but by the time it faded away, he would be meat in the street.

Lurching sideways, Latimer forced them both to the ground and they rolled along the bricks, but Hannigan never relinquished his hold. The sec man's world was starting to grow dim, his laboring lungs feeling as if they were on fire.

Flailing about for a loose brick to use, Latimer accidentally touched a small puddle of diluted acid rain, his hand convulsing from the pain. Instantly, he reached up to wipe his palm on the coldheart's face, deliberately going for his adversary's left eye.

Shrieking in pain, Hannigan released the sec man to race over to a covered rainwater barrel. He jerked off the lid and plunged his head into the cool, clear water, then jerked it right back out again, and jumped backward. A split second later, a knife thudded into the wooden barrel exactly where he had just been standing.

Crouching like feral beasts, the two men circled each other, panting for breath, their hands splayed, their faces full of raw hatred.

Unexpectedly, a pair of men riding horses raced down the street.

"Stop that right now!" Camarillo shouted, triggering a short burst from his AK-47, the 7.62 mm rounds throwing off red chips as they hammered across the street between the two combatants.

"Fuck that. I'm never going into a collar!" Latimer sneered, diving to the side to recover his knife and thrust it toward Hannigan's throat.

But a shot rang out from the second rider, and the blade was violently torn from his grip, to spin away into the misty night.

Looking up in surprise, Latimer saw Chief Ralhoun riding closer, a smoking blaster in her grip.

"Chief?" he asked in confusion, cradling his wounded hand.

"We were tricked, Latimer!" Ralhoun growled, holstering the Beretta. "Ryan Cawdor was never part of the Stone Angels!"

"Ryan…Cawdor?" Hannigan asked in a low growl, stressing the last name. "You mean Dean, right?"

"You heard correct the first time," Camarillo growled. "And from the way Chief Ralhoun describes the mutie-lover, I'd guess this Ryan was the older brother, or mebbe even the father of Tiger Cawdor. A father and son team out to set us onto each other, so that those fragging travelers can scav. Tried your ville and failed. Set their eyes on our camp!"

"This was about jacking supplies?" Latimer muttered, flexing his stinging fingers. The accuracy of the chief had been amazing. His hand was undamaged, but hurting worse than the one that found the acid rain pool.

"Got another reason?" Ralhoun inquired, sliding off her horse.

"You mean that Tiger Cawdor was a spy?" Hannigan asked. "But he was with us for quite a while!"

"So what? I'll bet this Ryan fellow has a whole army of bastard sons living in villes across the Deathlands, and when Daddy arrives, they ace the baron, open the front gate and turn the place over to him!"

"Shitfire, that be a good plan," Latimer muttered, glaring at Hannigan. The entire left side of the cold-heart's face was blazing red, and his eye was horribly bloodshot, but he still seemed able to see.

Taking a step forward, Latimer thrust out his wounded hand. "What do ya say, coldheart? Allies until we ace these rad suckers?"

After curling a lip as if about to spit, Hannigan took his hand and shook. "You dig the grave and I'll toss them in," he declared. "Deal?"

"Done and done," Latimer said, releasing his grip and fighting the urge to wipe his hand clean.

"Glad you both agree." Ralhoun snorted. "Now go find some horses and grab anything that throws lead! We're leaving immediately to hunt down Tiger and force him to take us to where Ryan and his people are hiding."

"They're probably both with the convoy," Latimer said, going over to retrieve his own dropped blaster.

"Only if he's a feeb," Camarillo snorted. "Travelers can't fight worth a damn."

"Hunt down," Hannigan said slowly, repeating the phrase. "Then Tiger isn't in the camp?"

Ralhoun scowled. "Nope. Must have left during the fight."

"Bastard coward." Hannigan sneered, a hand going

to his empty holster. "Anybody loan me some iron? I damaged mine beating a slave to death."

"Here you go…Lieutenant," Camarillo said, pulling a massive revolver from his belt and tossing it over.

Grinning coldly, Lieutenant Hannigan checked the handblaster before tucking it away. "Thanks. I promise to put it to good use."

THE SUN WAS JUST RISING over the distant mountains when the doors to the loading dock were forced aside and the companions emerged, leading their horses, followed by what remained of the convoy. The previous day there'd been a dozen Conestogas, each with a team of six. The convoy of travelers had been reduced to a mere ten wags, with a team of four horses, several of which were covered with bandages. However, they were still mobile.

"Della, what's the count?" Alan asked, shifting uncomfortably in the saddle. Hanging alongside the stirrup, his broken ankle was tightly wrapped in a thick cocoon of wooden sticks, furry pelts and leather belts.

"That still hurt?" Cordelia asked in concern.

"Damn, woman, of course it does," he growled, resisting the urge to scratch under the wrappings. "Now what's the nuking count!"

"Fifteen horses aced and nine people," Cordelia reported gruffly. "And we have two folks missing, presumed eaten." One of her four flintlock handblasters was gone, replaced with a 9 mm Mauser recovered from the coldhearts. It was a weird blaster, with the magazine in front of the grip, not inside where it should be located. But the weapon worked well enough, now that it had been thoroughly cleaned of the former owner's brains.

"Bastard muties," Alan growled, his voice thick with hate. His precious Japanese war sword was gone, buried in the back of a stickie that had somehow lived long enough to run away. Now, aside from the pair of flintlock handblasters tucked into his gun belt, he had a bolt-action longblaster recovered from one of the aced coldhearts slung across his back. The weapon, called a Springfield, was supposed to be from the First War, what some of the wrinklies called World War I. He had never heard of the weapon before, and the action was a little stiff. However, the heavy 30.06 longblaster was made of honest steel and wood, not with a plastic stock like an M-16, and it felt more than capable of beating a mutie onto the last train west.

Past the parking lot, the ruins stood in stark relief, every trace of softening greenery gone. The few homes that still had shingles were relatively undamaged. The rest were merely shells, brick walls surrounding a soggy mess of partially dissolved drywall, furniture and drapes. The sodden material was sprinkled with brightly colored plastic tufts from wall-to-wall carpeting, the canvas backing gone, but the carpet fibers themselves never more colorful.

"Rainbow in a dung heap." J.B. snorted, warily eyeing the fiberglass car chassis parked along the street. A neon-blue sports sedan seemed to be filled with bees, and the intact windows of a Toyota Starlet were so dirty it was impossible to tell what was inside without first opening the doors. No verbal commands were needed for everybody to ride on the extreme far side of the road, and keep a safe distance from any possible inhabitant of the little Japanese coupe.

"Better keep those wags on the main road," Ryan directed, ruffling the tuft of hair between the ears of his stallion. "That'll be the least bumpy, and Mildred says we have a couple of folks hanging onto life by their fingernails."

"Doc and Jak will stay in front as a vanguard," Krysty added, checking the flint in a borrowed handblaster, "while the rest of us sweep along the sides, and scout for anything we can scav."

The oddball blaster was a collection of twelve small barrels that fired all at once. Sailors in the South Pacific had called such a weapon a pepperbox; she could only assume because the discharge peppered you with a dozen .18-gauge miniballs. It took forever to load, but at close range it should chill anything.

"There's nothing here but dirt and dreams," Library muttered with a scowl, hunching her shoulders to adjust the crossbow slung across her back to a more comfortable position. Her left arm was in a sling, a knife lashed to her wrist, the blade extending just past her busted knuckles.

"That may be true, dear lady," Doc said, loosening the LeMat in his holster, "but that dire combination is perfect cover for muties and coldhearts alike." His M-16 combo rapidfire was down to its last magazine, so he had a spare .78 musket tucked into the gun boot alongside his saddle. The ammo pouches in his canvas gun belt bulged with powder, miniballs and spare flints. The familiar weight was an oddly reassuring sensation.

"Want me to ride with you some?" Library asked, glancing sideways. "Two weapons are better than one."

"How true. Are we assembling a new edition of *Bartlett's,* madam?" Doc asked, clearly pleased.

"Life goes on," she answered with a shrug, then winced and massaged her wounded hand.

"You two take front," Jak said, reining around his new horse. "I take rear with Cordelia." His former mount had been chilled by a flapjack, the corpse unfit even to eat. However, this mare was a killer, and had aced a stickie all by herself, caving in its head with both hooves and then pounding the body into mush. Generally dumber than rocks, the other stickies got the message and wisely stayed away from the deadly mare, and the horses she had been protecting.

"After last night, call me Della," Cordelia stated, clicking off the safety of the Mauser in her gun belt. There had been a movement in the second-story window of a shop, and she could have sworn she'd heard a soft hoot. With a flutter of wings, an owl took wing into the sky, and she released the blaster, easing down the hammer.

"Can't do that," Jak said.

"And why is that?" she asked in a dangerous tone.

He grinned. "Was gonna call on you tonight."

Snorting a laugh, Cordelia shook her head. "Whitey, you tie me into all sorts of knots."

"Not yet," Jak replied, kneeing his mount into a gentle trot. "Need to wash first!"

"Della, you better ride him soon, or I will," a woman said, removing the dirty scarf from around her neck to expose a wealth of cleavage.

"Don't even think about it," Cordelia muttered, riding off to join Jak at the rear of the convoy.

Trying not to openly laugh at the suggestive comments, Ryan and the other companions moved away from the convoy and onto a secondary street. In silence, the four of them rode for a while until they could no longer hear Doc's booming voice quoting a long poem about love, lust, lubricant and a woman named Nell.

"Okay, we're out of listening range," Mildred said, brushing back her beaded plaits. "Now, what are we really looking for?"

"Dean," Ryan replied. "If the coldhearts are hidden in the ruins somewhere, he would have left us a marker to warn us away."

"You mean, now that he knows we're nearby," Mildred corrected. "So, what exactly are we looking for? The acid rain would have washed everything clean."

"Not on the inside of a window," J.B. replied. "Trader taught us this trick. Draw a six-point star, then rub out the section that points where you want others to go."

"Saved my ass more than once," Ryan admitted grimly, scanning some windblown debris in a yard. The timbers almost resembled a star, but not quite.

Farther down the street, the companions found a stretch limo. The undamaged windows were tinted dark green, and clearly reflected their somber faces.

"Airtight," J.B. said, rapping a window with a knuckle.

Experimentally, Ryan rammed the stock of the Galil into the glass, but it didn't break or even crack. Flipping the rapidfire, he discharged a single round, and the lead deflected off the bulletproof hard plastic.

"Dark night, we're not getting inside that without plas-ex," J.B. stated, pulling a pipe bomb from his munitions bag. "Only got three of these, so I don't want to waste one recovering nothing better than a pair of shoes. See anything good inside?"

"Let me check." Pressing her face against the window, Mildred could vaguely see a skeleton slumped in the rear seat. The man was wearing a pinstripe business suit, with a neatly combed toupee still perched on top of his skull. A diamond stickpin glittered from his collar, and a gold watch was on his wrist. Nearby lay an open briefcase full of papers, documents and stacks of cash.

"Nothing in here but Jimmy Hoffa," Mildred stated, tossing off a two-finger salute to the deceased passenger.

"How could you possibly know his name?" Krysty asked, puzzled.

"I don't, but where's the fun in that?" she admitted with a wide grin.

"Sometimes your sense of humor makes no damn sense at all," J.B. stated with conviction.

"Sometimes?" Ryan asked, stressing the word.

Climbing back on their horses, the companions followed the road to a traffic circle and rode around it twice, looking into shops and burned-out office buildings. Small purple lizards darted in and out of rusty storm drains. A condor flew by overhead, its shadow skimming along the debris-filled street, and from far away came the sound of Doc belting out a song about marching through Georgia.

"He making that up?" Ryan asked curiously.

"No, it's a real song from the Civil War," Mildred

answered with a grimace. "But it seems kind of rude to be actually singing it in the state of Georgia."

"Who knows this is Georgia anymore?"

"Good point."

"Hey, there's a police car over there," Krysty announced, pointing into an alley. "Might be some weapons we can scav."

"That's not a police car, but a county sheriff's patrol car," Mildred said, veering her horse toward the vehicle. "They use a star for their badge!"

After galloping over, the companions left their horses at the mouth of the alley, then proceed deeper into the shadows.

The patrol car was parked alongside a cinder-block wall, the tires long gone to the insect population, but the windows were closed and intact. Apparently it had remained airtight over the long decades, because there was a skeleton dressed in rags sitting behind the steering wheel, the regulation mirrored sunglasses still balanced precariously on the bony bridge of where there had once been a nose.

"Crap, that's a five-point star, not a six," Mildred said, pointing at a badge hanging from the tattered uniform.

"I see a 9 mm Glock in the holster," Krysty said excitedly, then scowled. "Along with an open can of soda in the cup holder."

"Useless then," J.B. stated, turning to walk away. From bitter experience, he knew the sugary fumes of the carbonated beverage would have severely corroded the inner workings of the weapon, especially the springs, rendering it useless.

"Mebbe the spare ammo is okay," Ryan said, going to the trunk and using the panga to pop the lid. Inside, safe from the evaporating soda pop, was a host of items: nylon rope, a fireproof blanket, a first-aid kit, road flares and a plastic rifle box containing a Remington pump-action shotgun, an M-16/M-203 combination and a dozen mixed boxes of ammo, including a couple boxes of standard 9 mm brass for the Glock. Plus, there were a dozen 40 mm grens for the M-203. Even better, everything was in the original airtight plastic wrapping.

"Jackpot!" J.B. cried, and began happily distributing the wealth.

"God bless the sheriff's department," Mildred said, slinging the Winchester over a shoulder and tearing into the first-aid kit.

Most of the medicine inside was simply too old to risk using, even in an emergency, such as the ampoule of adrenaline and the antihistamine pen. But there were a lot of clean bandages, and a myriad of small Mylar packets containing aspirin, muscle relaxants, and some of the old-fashioned silver-based antiseptics. Those would still be good in another hundred years! There was an assortment of surgical instruments, medium forceps, scissors, two scalpels as sharp as the day they had been forged, and three packs of dissolving sutures with needles already attached. There was even a stethoscope, and an untouched box of latex gloves. No more barehanded surgery!

"We're back in biz." J.B. smiled, filling the loops of the strap for the scattergun. Along with the double aught buckshot, there were a few deer slugs, and two bright red-orange cartridges that he knew contained steel slivers. They were designed to blast open a wooden door, and the damage they did to a norm, or a mutie, had to be seen to be believed.

"Save a couple of those twelves for Doc," Ryan directed, stuffing the fireproof blanket into his saddlebag, along with the nylon rope.

"Already did," Krysty said, patting a bulging shirt pocket. Then she added, "You know, if this wag was missed by other scavengers, do you think we should check on their headquarters?"

"Good a place as any for Dean to leave us a message," Ryan said, returning to the horses.

Easily locating what had once been the ville common, the companions found city hall, and discovered the sheriff department right alongside the main courthouse. There was no mistaking the stout brick building with iron bars covering the small windows.

Unfortunately, there were no other patrol cars parked near the structure, so they went inside. It was readily evident that the place had been gutted to the walls ages ago, and nothing usable remained. Even the wooden gun racks were missing, probably now the prized decoration in some baron's bedroom.

"What do you think, lover, wall or floor?" Krysty asked, resting her M-16 combo on a shoulder. The rapid-fire felt a lot heavier with a full magazine and a 40 mm gren in the launcher.

"Wall," Ryan stated, easing his finger off the trigger of the Galil. "That's where I'd stash a spare blaster…or a message."

Going into the office of the sheriff, Ryan swung aside a portrait of General Robert E. Lee on the wall to reveal a built-in safe. He wasn't surprised in the least. Nearly every police station had a small safe to store important documents, critical evidence and an emergency weapon or two.

Eagerly, Mildred loaned J.B. her new stethoscope, and he expertly twirled the dial, listening for the clicks. In only a few minutes, he had it open. The steel box was empty, aside from a black metal keypad.

"No way," J.B. whispered, hesitating a second before tapping the access code to a redoubt onto the alphanumeric pad.

For a long moment nothing happened, then there came the muffled sound of hydraulic pumps building pressure, and the office wall broke apart, the thick veneer of plaster crumbling away as the blast door of a redoubt slid aside to reveal the standard entrance.

"What is a redoubt doing in the middle of nowhere?" Mildred demanded, stepping over the threshold. As she did, the wall vents came to life, issuing a steady breeze of clean, warm air.

"Somebody important must have lived in town," Ryan theorized. "A retired general, or kin to the President. Something like that."

Since the entrance to the redoubt was hidden inside a brick building, the companions fully expected the garage level to be empty. But they were wrong. The entire space was stacked high with rows of wooden packing crates.

"Wonder what this ident number means," Ryan muttered, running a finger along the military code stenciled across one crate.

Going to a workbench, J.B. got a crowbar and pried

off a lid. Inside were mounds of fibrous packing material, and buried beneath was a smooth metallic dome, with two large red crystal eyes.

"Dark night, these are filled with spare parts for sec hunter droids!" he said, pushing aside the cushioning to find the steel torso of the armored machine, then the arms, wheels, a buzzsaw, and finally, the pneumatic hammer that could smash through any civilian-made door, dent the armor in an APC, or crush a person's head in a split second.

Squinting at the rows and stacks, Mildred did some fast calculations. "If there is one droid per crate, then these hold a total of…three…six…nine—four hundred and two sec hunter droids," she finished, her voice fading away at the end. That was a veritable army of the blasted machines!

"Just sec hunters?" Ryan asked, shifting the packing material with the barrel of the Galil. "No spider droids, or high-rollers?"

"Nope, only hunters," J.B. replied, working the pump on the scattergun to eject the buckshot cartridges and replace them with the ones containing the stainless-steel slivers, and his only deer slug. After those crazy red eyes were shattered, the machines were relatively easy to avoid. As long as you didn't move, cough or breath too hard. Their hearing was extremely acute.

"At least we're ready if there's a working droid in the place," Krysty said confidently, cradling the M-16 combo. "This 40 mm gren should blow the damn thing to pieces."

"Just make sure you're far enough away for the warhead to arm," J.B. advised, studying the floor for any sign of scoring from the treads of a droid. "Or else the gren will only bounce off and do about as much damage as a well-thrown rock."

"Eighty feet?"

"Make it a hundred, just to be safe."

"Fair enough."

Doing a fast recce of the garage level, they then worked their way down to the armory. As expected, it was completely devoid of weaponry, like most redoubts. However, this one was packed solid with nuke batteries. Roughly the same size as a conventional car battery, a nuke battery delivered a lot more power and never became drained. None of the companions had any idea how they worked. But it was primarily because of nuke batteries that the companions ever got a predark civilian, or mil, wag running again after a century of neglect.

"Do these go inside a sec hunter?" Mildred asked.

"Never noticed any there before," J.B. answered truthfully. "But then, I never really looked. Just aced the tin bastard and ran away, in case another was coming."

Going to the cafeteria-style kitchen, the companions found a large whiteboard prominently on display to announce whatever was the special for the day. Hoping against hope for a message from Dean, Ryan grunted in disappointment that there was no note, but then admitted it only made sense. There were just two ways into this particular redoubt, and they had been the first through the disguised entrance in the sheriff's office since the blast doors had been plastered over. What had he been thinking?

Briefly checking the pantry and walk-in freezers, Krysty found them barren. Even the saltshakers were empty. It was as if the redoubt had been built purely to store the spare parts for the droids, then been forgotten.

As the companions continued their recce, it was soon apparent no one else was present, norm or machine.

"Okay, enough stalling," Ryan stated. "Time for the real reason we're here."

Summoning the elevator, the companions piled inside and ascended to the middle level. As they rose, the silence among them become more and more pronounced, until it was almost a tangible presence.

"Lover, have you given any idea to what we're going to do if this mat-trans is also deactivated?" Krysty finally asked, her animated hair tightening into fiery ringlets.

"Stay with the convoy until the travelers reach their destination," Ryan replied gruffly. "Then barter a deal with Alan for a couple of the wags."

"We going to become traders, like the Trader?" J.B. asked, a smile slowly forming. "Dark night, I like that idea!"

"We could always go to Front Royal," Mildred suggested hesitantly. "Your nephew would be delighted to have us stay."

Ryan scowled. "And work as his sec man? No, thanks. He's the baron. I'd just be in the way."

With a musical ding, the elevator reached the floor, and the doors opened wide with a soft sigh.

"If this mat-trans is off-line, then we check one more before hitting the road," he stated. "Just one more. Then it looks like we choose a redoubt to use as a base, one that has enough equipment, tools and fuel to build some proper wags for a trader: a hundred feet long, twenty tires, lots of steel armor, bathroom, kitchen, blasters, rockets, flamethrowers, radar, radio, the works."

"We sure as nuking hell know how to do that," J.B. said, grinning as they walked along the corridor.

"That redoubt down in New Mex, the one that Jak likes to call Blaster Base One, had a ton of blasters and brass," Krysty stated, her hair starting to loosen again and gently move. "Plus, the local baron loved us. Make a great place to start our circuit of the Deathlands."

"Doc might leave us," Mildred said simply. "He wants to get back home more than anything else. That is what is keeping him sane. If we're not traveling through the mat-trans system, he'll keep going from redoubt to redoubt until he finds one that is working and lets him go back in time, or until he dies of old age."

"That'll be his decision," Ryan said, pushing open the door to the comp room. Then he softly added, "But I'll miss Doc, sure enough."

The dozen comp stations seemed to be functioning normally, a low hum filling the room. A spectrum of lights blinked on the bank of control boards, with the rows of meters flickering in the safe zone. Only a single monitor was active, the monotone screen scrolling an endless deluge of binary code.

"This seems to be working," Mildred said hopefully.

"So did the last one," Krysty retorted harshly.

Grabbing a wheeled chair from in front of a control board, Ryan pushed it through the anteroom and over to the gateway door. Working the access lever, J.B. opened the portal, and the one-eyed man shoved the chair into the mat-trans unit. He stepped back and waited while J.B. closed the door firmly.

A minute passed, then another. Nothing happened. The great machine didn't initiate a jump. It remained as still as a stone in the dirt.

Silently, the companions turned and walked away.

Two redoubts down, one to go.

Chapter Eighteen

Leaving the redoubt, the companions stopped in the armory to take a couple nuke batteries, then left through the sheriff's department and reclaimed their horses.

"Not sure what Alan and his people are going to do with these," J.B. said, easing the heavy battery into a saddlebag.

"They can always sell them to a ville," Ryan replied with a shrug. "Walls need lights."

"Wish we could have hit the showers," Krysty said. "But there wouldn't be any way to explain to the others how we happened to come back freshly scrubbed and wearing clean clothes."

"Yeah, me, too," Ryan replied, climbing into the saddle and starting along the road at an easy trot.

Spotting the remains of a firehouse across the ville common, Mildred rode her horse in through the smashed doors, hoping for some medical supplies. But the trucks were gone and the shelves clear. However, perched on top of a locker, where it couldn't be seen from the ground, was a slim aluminum cylinder. Thoroughly repulsed, she almost left it there, then felt guilty, and tucked it into a pocket.

"Find anything good?" Krysty asked hopefully.

"Something for John, anyway." Mildred sighed, proffering the tube.

Accepting it, J.B. curiously glanced at the tube and burst into a wide grin. "A cigar! A predark cigar!" He chuckled. "I'll bet something like this has been buying blasters, horses and gaudy sluts for a dozen owners since skydark!"

Popping off the cap, he tilted the tube, and out slid four slim homemade cigarettes.

"Wolfweed." J.B. snarled in disgust, casting the drug into a puddle on the pavement. "I'd rather smoke my own socks than that shit!"

"Sorry," Mildred murmured, even though she was secretly pleased. Ever since they first met she had been encouraging him to stop smoking, with some success.

"Well, I appreciate the effort." J.B. sighed, pocketing the tube. "At least this'll still be good for protecting the next cigar I find. Or I can always pack it with plas-ex to make one hell of a anti-pers!"

"Don't you have one of those already?" Ryan asked, guiding his mount around a pothole filled with murky yellow water.

"Never hurts to have a spare," J.B. said with a chuckle, kicking his horse into an easy gallop.

As THE NOISE of the horse hooves rang across the acid-washed ruins, a low growl came from the direction of city hall. Broken granite pillars lay askew around the collapsed marble dome, and from the darkness underneath, two sets of red eyes glared hatefully at the departing two-legs and their beasts.

Loose rocks shifted, and pillars loudly cracked as the thing trapped beneath the dome attempted once more to get free. But the ancient steel beams set inside the granite columns had been driven into the hard ground like the bars of a cage, and the colossal mutie could only silently rage against its inadvertent prison.

Then a section of the terrazzo floor settled, exposing the basement level. Sensing a possible route to liberty, the mutie began to claw aside the mounds of moldy furniture, stained marble walls and concrete flooring. Soon it was tunneling into the compacted earth, angling slowly back up toward the sun and the rapidly escaping meat....

STOPPING HIS HORSE near the skeleton of a two-headed cow lying on the sidewalk, Jak unscrewed the cap off a U.S. Army canteen and took a long drink.

"Hi, Adam," a familiar voice whispered from the dark interior of a crumbling store.

Caught in the middle of a swallow, Jak almost choked on the water, and needed a moment to catch his breath. "The name's Alvin," he replied, screwing back on the cap. "Nice know you alive."

"Hard to chill a Cawdor," Dean said, stepping into view from the shadows inside a crumbling ice cream parlor. "Thanks for leaving such an easy trail for me to follow."

"Well, you came up with broken star idea."

"You twist those twigs into a star while riding?"

"Sure, easy do," Jak said, shrugging.

"Where's my father?" Dean asked, looking at the line of big wooden wags and horses trundling along the ancient road.

"Hunt for you," the albino teen replied, slinging the

canteen over the pommel of his saddle. "Where Sharona?"

"Don't know. We got separated in a flood a few months ago," Dean replied stiffly. "I've been living with the Angels since then."

"Willingly?" Jak asked with a scowl. In truth, he barely recognized this young giant for the child who had traveled with the companions. Then it occurred to him that Dean was now almost sixteen, older than Jak had been when he first joined the companions.

Dean grimaced. "Hell, no!"

"Why not leave?"

"Hostages," Dean replied. "If I left, I know Camarillo, the gang leader, would have sent a dozen slaves to the lashing post."

Somberly, Jak nodded in understanding. "So you set free first?"

"Yes, we did," Althea said, appearing behind Dean, the reins of a limping stallion in her hand.

Studying the young beauty, Jak started to ask a question, then saw that it wasn't necessary. From the way they looked at each other, it was clear the two were a couple. "Jak Lauren," he said simply.

"Althea Stone."

"What happen horse?"

"The first got aced by a flapjack," Dean said with a scowl.

"Then this one caught a hoof in a gopher hole and sprained a muscle," Althea added, patting the stallion's neck. Softly, the animal nickered in reply.

"Any chance of getting another?" Dean asked, hitching up his gun belt. "We can trade for it."

"Nope," Jak stated bluntly. "Lost about half last night in fight during storm."

"What attacked this big a group?" Althea asked, glancing at the rattling convoy of wooden wags and horses.

"Everything." Jak heaved a sigh.

Dean grinned. "Found the local safe place, eh?"

"And so did every mutie in the valley," Cordelia declared, riding her horse closer. She held the reins loosely in one hand and cradled a flintlock longblaster across her lap. The hammer was cocked, but her finger wasn't resting on the trigger. "So, are these the two that Ryan and the others really went searching for?"

"Dean, Althea," Jak said as an introduction, jerking a thumb.

After a moment, Cordelia tilted her head in greeting, then shouted over a shoulder. "Hey, Dewitt! We got a lame horse here!"

Instantly, the rear doors of a wag slammed open, and Dewitt jumped to the cracked pavement, his fishing tackle box in hand. But before he got halfway there, something powerful exploded in the distance, the concussion making ripples in every puddle in the road.

Pulling out blasters and crossbows, everybody looked around for the source of the detonation, but nothing was in sight except for decaying ruins. Then it happened again and again, the dull thumps coming ever faster until they sounded like the beating of a human heart, or—

"Nuking hell, they found us!" Dean snarled, drawing the Browning Hi-Power.

Only a half-second slower, Althea pulled out the

Ruger and jerked back the slide on top. Trained in combat, the lame horse backed deeper into the shadowy interior of the ancient structure.

A moment later, the brick wall of a movie theater exploded into the street and the *Atomsmasher* rolled into view with the steam whistle screaming. Close behind was a boiling mob of coldhearts on horses and sandhogs, as well as a dozen people in matching uniforms, riding horseback in a tight formation.

"Alton ville sec men!" Jak shouted in recognition, even as his M-16 started chattering at the better-armed sec force. Only the best shots got the good weapons, so he always aced those first.

The spray of 5.56 mm rounds stitched several of them across the chest, but the coldhearts only flinched as tufts of splinters erupted from their bulky canvas jackets. Damn, he had forgotten about the bastard body armor!

"Aim for their heads!" Cordelia yelled, triggering her longblaster. Smoke and flame vomited from the pitted muzzle of the black-powder weapon, and a hundred yards away, a coldheart flew backward off a sandhog with most of his face removed.

A flurry of blasters answered back, the bullets humming past the woman as thick as summer flies. As if she didn't have a care in the world, Cordelia coolly reloaded, directing her horse to move backward with some knee jabs.

"Blue Thunder!" Camarillo yelled from within the tiny control room of the pounding steam truck. "Blue Thunder!"

At the code phrase, the coldhearts promptly spread

out in a skirmish line to flank the massive war wag, leaving the middle avenue wide open for the *Atomsmasher* to charge through, coming up behind the convoy of wooden wags.

"Scatter!" Alan bellowed, discharging both his blasters at the colossal machine. The .63 miniballs slammed against the iron bars covering the windows, but ricocheted off harmlessly.

As if in reply, Camarillo released a long blast from the steam whistle, the unnatural sound terrifying people and horses alike.

Rapidly increasing in speed, the *Atomsmasher* headed for its target. Frantically whipping their horses, the drivers attempted to get out of the way of the machine, a handful of the wags arching into the ruins. The rest of the convoy foolishly tried to outrun the steam truck.

Looming like the armored fist of God, the modified locomotive rammed into the rear wag. The wooden slats disintegrated into splinters and the broken wheels went flying, people and horses vanishing under the armored bulk of the *Atomsmasher*.

Angling sharply away, the second wag received only a glancing blow. But it burst apart anyway, and boxes and barrels went tumbling, along with the hapless passengers. However, the galloping horses escaped intact. Still harnessed together, they pelted away, dragging along the driver. Cursing wildly, he was scraped along the cracked pavement until reaching a pothole. Then he was gone, a severed arm still holding on to the flapping reins for a few seconds before finally coming off yards away.

The next three wags were even less fortunate, with travelers and horses ruthlessly slaughtered by the rampaging iron juggernaught. Laughing triumphantly, Camarillo careened off into the ruins, only to start circling back toward the convoy for another chilling pass.

Ignoring everybody else, Hannigan headed directly for Dean, only to be cut off by the sec men on sandhogs.

Firing in every direction, the travelers let loose with their assortment of blasters. Several of the coldhearts and sec men jerked as the miniballs hummed past them, but nobody fell, wounded or aced. Then the dense cloud of dark gun smoke rolled toward the invaders, and they were forced to slow their advance, or risk going into a pothole and breaking their necks.

"Ryan! I want Ryan Cawdor!" Chief Ralhoun bellowed from a sandhog, firing a Beretta steadily into the mob of travelers and horses. Her white scarf billowed in the wind as she drove over the dead and the dying in her mad search for revenge.

Suddenly, a flurry of boomerangs darted from the wags. The coldhearts ducked low. The sec men didn't, and two of them fell, their faces crushed into jelly. Blindly, the dying sec men continued to shoot, the rounds mostly hitting empty air, or shattering a pre-dark window.

Pausing to chill a big black dog that started coming his way, Jak slapped a spare magazine into the M-16, then kicked his horse into a full gallop.

Drawing her Navy flare gun, Cordelia stayed right alongside, sending the fat magnesium charges sizzling into the invaders. Screaming, a sec man fell with a flare buried in his chest, the brilliant vermilion flame extending outward for almost a yard.

Crouched on a sandhog, a coldheart aced a traveler with his sawed-off scattergun, then triggered the second barrel toward Cordelia. She loudly grunted as the spray of broken glass and bent nails peppered her side, starting a red stain spreading across her shirt. Then she fired back, the flare punching through the sandhog's gas tank. The vehicle erupted into flame, the coldheart falling out of the saddle a human torch.

"Fix!" Jak commanded, tossing her a clean cloth. "I cover!"

"No time, Jak!" she bellowed in reply, grinning like a madwoman as she threw away the flare gun. Coughing blood, she sagged a little in the saddle, then sat straight and began to calmly fire the Mauser at the scattering enemy.

Discharging the LeMat as fast as possible, Doc took out a cougar and a coldheart, then stumbled backward as an arrow slammed into his thigh. Reaching down, he snapped off the wooden shaft at skin level, then dumped the spent brass from his blaster. He'd started to reload when a sec man came pounding toward him, waving an ax and grinning widely.

Quickly, Doc switched to the second barrel, and waited until the rider was almost on him before discharging the miniature shotgun. The 12-gauge cartridge tore open the throat of the horse in a bloody geyser, and the animal veered sharply. Caught off balance, the sec man sailed out of the saddle to land on the sidewalk with an audible crack. Incredibly, the panting man tried to rise once more, and Library sent an arrow straight down his gullet, the barbed tip coming out his neck.

With a snarl, a coldheart cut loose with a short burst from a MAC-10 rapidfire. Dropping the crossbow, Library clutched her stomach and doubled over in pain.

His face ablaze with anger, Doc snapped shut the cylinder of the LeMat and sent two booming rounds into the coldheart. Spinning away, the man lost his life and his blaster at the exact same time.

Shooting her stolen blaster nonstop, Althea darted into the fray to grab the MAC-10, then rummage in the pockets of the corpse for any spare magazines. A coldheart aimed a longblaster at her, and Dean stroked the trigger of the Browning Hi-Power. The .38 dumdum round hit the coldheart in the shoulder and exploded out his back like a cannonball, blood squirting from a severed artery. The man was fumbling to staunch the flow when Althea sent a burst across his chest, then continued onward, cutting down two more coldhearts, and a sec man working the arming lever of a longblaster.

"Short bursts!" Dean yelled while firing twice, hitting the coldheart in the chest and wounding his horse.

Starting to laugh in disdain at the miss, the coldheart abruptly stopped when the horse charged away. As the animal tripped over the crushed remains of a destroyed wag, its rider took a nosedive and landed on a wrought-iron fence surrounding a burned-down synagogue. Impaled, he could only make gurgling noises and flail about helplessly as his life trickled down the rusty iron spikes. Then the front lawn of the synagogue stirred, and a horde of tiny beetles raced up the fence to begin feasting upon the unexpected bounty of fresh meat.

"Tiger, ace me!" the coldheart shrieked, as the insects crawled into his oozing wounds. "Please, in the name of friendship... Ace me!"

Turning away from the neutralized enemy, Dean checked to make sure Althea was undamaged, and then they marched deeper into the fight, chilling everybody in sight, their blasters steadily dealing hot, unforgiving justice.

Completing its turn in the remnants of a kindergarten school yard, the *Atomsmasher* crashed through a rusty jungle gym to start back toward the travelers once more. Baring his teeth in rage, Camarillo tried to find Dean in the chaos of explosions and billowing smoke. He didn't want to run over his own people, but if a few of the sec men got aced in the fight, well, that would only save them from going to the post afterward. In his opinion, anybody who walked a ville wall was never to be fully trusted.

Unexpectedly, a dull thump sounded, and Camarillo was slammed across the control room as the front of the steam truck was rocked by a powerful explosion. The ancient headlight vanished in the blast, and the front bumper broke loose to fall under the spinning wheels. Two of the tires blew off their rims, but the rest easily carried the weight, and the modified locomotive neither slowed nor swerved in its collision course toward the milling wooden wags.

"Hit it again!" Ryan snarled, sliding off his horse to send a long burst from the Galil toward the coldhearts in a classic sideways figure-eight pattern. Stitched from knees to throat, the coldhearts staggered, but none fell, given the splintery blocks of wood clearly revealed under their lumpy clothing.

Smacking her horse on the rump to get it out of the way, Krysty opened the gren launcher underneath the M-16 combo and dumped the spent shell.

Taking cover behind the rusty chassis of a Buick, a grim Mildred shot the Winchester as fast as she could work the lever, to cover the other woman. But the soft-lead .38 rounds only drove the coldhearts back. When she stopped to reload, they surged forward once more, shouting in delight. Oddly, they were all heading toward Ryan, not her or the others.

Stepping out from behind a pile of loose bricks, J.B. unleashed the full fury of the Uzi, sweeping the mob with a withering hail of 9 mm Parabellum rounds. Then the rapidfire jammed. Ducking behind the bricks again, he struggled to clear the blaster, and cursed himself for ever trusting the old police bullets.

Shooting a traveler in the back, Natters then dropped low and crawled over to the corpse to rip off the bloody shirt. Quickly, he removed his own canvas jacket, then donned the stolen shirt. These outlanders were just too nuking good with their blasters. But now, if the battle went badly for the Stone Angels, he could pretend to be aced, and sneak away when the travelers weren't looking. Natters didn't consider himself a coward, merely sensible. Fuck the rest of gang, he thought. His own survival was the most important thing in the world. No matter what the cost.

Closing the breech of the M-203 gren launcher with a hard snap, Krysty aimed at the onrushing steam truck just as it began to angle away and turn sideways.

Suspecting the ugly truth, she quickly switched targets and fired in a single smooth motion.

The 40 mm shell slammed into the tinder carriage behind the steam truck just as a brace of blasterports opened and the familiar barrels of AK-47 rapidfires were thrust through. The strident blast brutally ripped the weapons from the grasp of the coldhearts inside, taking along most of their fingers. As the coldhearts howled in agony, two fresh rapidfires were thrust through the charred blasterports and began spitting lead.

Putting a burst into the front opening, Ryan heard a man scream, and the rapidfire fell back inside. Doing the same thing to the rear port, J.B. fired until the Uzi cycled empty. With no more loaded magazines, he released the weapon to swing behind him on its strap, and unlimbered the S&W M-4000 scattergun.

Resting the barrel of the Winchester on the hood of the sedan, Mildred began to snipe at the coldhearts and sec men, blowing out the tires on the sandhogs or crippling their horses. Then she saw a cougar leap on Dewitt from behind. Instantly, she put lead in the head on the beast. As the healer shoved aside the twitching body, he looked about for his unknown benefactor. Spotting her, he nodded in thanks, then slit the throat of the cougar and rejoined the battle.

Unexpectedly, there was a tug in Mildred's hair and something incredibly hot brushed along her scalp. Diving to the side, she rolled away to take refuge behind a telephone pole, and came up with the longblaster firing. Across the street, a coldheart kneeling in a pothole jerked as the soft lead smacked into his throat. Gushing a crimson fountain, he dropped out of sight.

Taking cover inside a pothole larger than a bathtub, Ryan tried again for the coldheart driving the steam engine, but the bars were too close. Unless he fired directly into the window, his lead always ricocheted off harmlessly. Watching the titanic machine barreling into the parking lot of a small strip mall, smashing aside a fiberglass sign announcing the grand opening of a yogurt store, he suddenly got a wild idea.

"Krysty, shell!" Ryan commanded, holding out a hand.

Although she had no idea what he wanted it for, Krysty pulled a spare 40 mm shell from her pocket and tossed it over. Ryan made the catch, and immediately lobbed it high over the kinetic fighting to land squarely at the feet of a very startled Doc Tanner.

Chapter Nineteen

"Gren! Run for your lives!" Library yelled, throwing herself upon the shell.

Instantly, every coldheart and sec men in the area dived for cover. Rolling along the uneven ground, she went behind a cinder-block wall, and came up with her crossbow at the ready, the undamaged shell shining in the dark loam.

"Very clever, madam." Doc chuckled, joining her a moment later.

"The most dangerous thing in the world is the human brain," she muttered, releasing an arrow into fight. "Forget who said that!" The shaft slammed through the fiberglass door of a sleek civilian sedan. A sec man crouching inside screamed in pain, his rapidfire chewing up the roof, then he went silent.

"Anybody who ever met you!" Doc stated, snatching up the gren, and shoving it into the breech of the launcher attached underneath his M-16 rapidfire. "How's your belly?"

"Just a flesh wound," she grunted, notching in a fresh arrow.

Spotting a movement on top of a building across the street, Ryan fired twice, and a sec man fell off the roof of a ruined bank to land on a jagged slab of sidewalk. His spine audibly cracked from the impact, and the coldheart lay there, still alive, but unable to move or speak.

Another flight of arrows arched into the sky, then came down fast, acing several coldhearts and a couple of sec men. But then the rest responded in a volley, the hammering barrage ripping off the wooden slats of a wag to expose the people inside. As they scrambled for cover, the coldhearts fired again, wounding everybody.

"Sons of bitches are trying to take us prisoner!" Alan raged, working the arming bolt of the Springfield to eject a jammed round.

"Never gonna happen!" Cordelia snarled, the Mauser spitting high-velocity death. Throwing their arms high, two sec men cried out as they fell away, their blasters discharging impotently at the rumbling storm clouds.

"Try this, ya one-eyed bastard!" a coldheart snarled, pulling out a stick of dynamite covered with rusty nails and jagged pieces of broken glass.

Caught in the act of reloading the Galil, Ryan simply dropped the rapidfire to draw the SIG-Sauer, and fired twice.

The waxy stick jerked at the second bullet, and the coldheart vanished inside a cloud of black smoke and assorted body parts. A head shot past Ryan wearing an expression of total surprise. As the roiling fumes cleared, there was only a pair of tattered boots standing amid a field of steaming scraps of flesh and some tattered cloth.

Her twin blasters banging away steadily, Ralhoun blew a crimson path through the fight, slaying anybody who got in the way. Twice she caught glimpses of Ryan sniping at the coldhearts from behind some wreckage, only to reappear yards away to repeat the attack. In spite of her intense hatred of the outlander, she had to admit he was good at chilling.

"But then, so am I!" she shouted, shooting out a second-floor window. As the glass came down, a traveler covered with cuts staggered into view and she blew out his heart.

Tossing a pipe bomb, J.B. mentally counted to ten, then braced for the explosion. The blast thundered, then with a creaking groan a brick wall slowly eased away from an office building to fall on a group of coldhearts who had started to assemble an antique, hand-cranked Gatling gun.

Crawling under a wag whose horses had broken loose, a coldheart tried to sneak a peek inside through a blasterport when a knife was rammed into his eye, and another stabbed him in the throat. Gushing blood, the coldheart feebly struggled to get away, but the people within refused to relinquish their hold, while other hands reached out to snatch away the dying man's weapons. When the coldheart finally ceased moving, he was released, and the travelers burst out the rear door, firing their new weapons in every direction.

As his M-16 cycled dry, Jak tossed away the useless 5.56 mm rapidfire and drew the Colt Python. He targeted a nearby coldheart and fired. The heavy .357 Magnum round smacked into the wood armor with an explosion of splinters, then came out the man's back along with small pieces of major organs.

"Nuking hellfire, we're gonna beat these gleebs!" Cordelia shouted. Then an arrow took her in the chest, and she fell back, a crimson stain spreading fast across her shirt.

Quick-firing the Winchester, Mildred fought her way to the fallen woman and immediately started battlefield repairs on the ghastly wound.

Moving out from the safety of the wall, Doc easily located the steam truck as it plowed through a stand of withered trees, the ground beneath littered with the corpses of birds and squirrels. Unfortunately, the angle was wrong, so he took off in a run, hopping over a white picket fence that had somehow survived the thermonuclear doomsday.

Running up to a wag, a snarling Ralhoun shoved her weapons in through a blasterport and randomly shot around the interior. Travelers cried out in pain, and she promptly moved to the next wag. Her goal was to cripple these people, not chill them. Where was the profit in that? Ryan was the only person she wanted aced on sight. Seeking refuge behind a mailbox, she began reloading, until a coldheart appeared and fired a huge handblaster straight at her. She felt the wind of the ammo's passage, then heard a grunt of pain from behind. Turning, she saw a traveler fall to the cracked pavement, clutching his bleeding chest.

Nodding her thanks to the coldheart, Ralhoun moved onward.

Hannigan holstered the blaster to loot a Browning .32 and spare brass from the warm corpse.

Triggering the M-16 combo in short bursts to conserve ammo, Krysty then fired another 40 mm shell. It hit a sandhog, and the vehicle was blown backward to tumble madly along the street, crushing a dozen coldhearts on horses before coming to rest against a burned-out bookstore.

Darting across the ville commons, Doc finally caught up to the swiftly moving steam truck. Kneeling in the gravel to steady his aim, he fired a burst from the M-16 purely as a diversion, then triggered the gren launcher. The 40 mm warhead slammed into the coupling between the engine and the tinder carriage. The protective sandbags were blown clear, but the resilient steel linkage held firm, not even dented by the high-grade military explosive.

As it thundered by, Dean and Althea rose from a pothole to hammer the window with hot lead. When the MAC-10 cycled empty, he gave cover fire with the Enfield as she tossed aside the rapidfire and switched back to the Ruger.

Riding a wounded horse at breakneck speed, Alan moved in close to the steam truck, firing the Springfield. Using his good hand, a grinning Latimer shot him in the back.

Tumbling out of the saddle, Alan nearly went under the double row of spinning military tires. Uncaring of the pain it caused his broken ankle, he rolled away from the war wag, then threw a knife from the ground, winging the coldheart in the shoulder. But as Latimer recovered from the minor injury, a boomerang came out of nowhere to slam him in the side of the head, so hard that his eyeballs popped out of their sockets. Still connected, they dangled down his face at the end of glistening white ganglia.

Shrieking in agony, Latimer tried to find his eyes

with fumbling hands, and walked straight into a pothole filled with slightly diluted acid rain.

Crawling painfully erect, Alan looked at the thrashing coldheart for a long moment, then merely grunted and limped away to search for the dropped Springfield longblaster.

Revving the engine, a coldheart on a sandhog came barreling straight for Dean and Althea. Diving apart, they got out of the way just in time. Racing around a wag, the sandhog charged at Althea this time. Quickly, she fired the Ruger twice, but both rounds went wild and hit nothing. Forcing herself to remain calm, she took a deep breath, and instead of jerking the trigger, gently squeezed it as if she were trying to get juice out of a fruit. The Ruger smoothly fired, and the coldheart jerked back with a black hole in his forehead.

Streaking past her, the sandhog crashed into a brick wall and burst into flames. Shrapnel peppered her hard, but she moved on anyway, determined to regroup with Dean. Spotting an aced coldheart lying in the street, she hurried over and yanked off his lumpy canvas jacket, draping it across her shoulders for some added protection.

Standing up from behind a pile of rubble, Library sent an arrow into the fray and a sec man screamed, his hand pinned to the chest of a coldheart.

"Two with one shot," Doc muttered, taking them both out with the LeMat. "Well done, miss!"

"Needs must when the devil drives," she responded, clumsily notching in another arrow with her bandaged hand.

Shouting obscenities, a sec man charged around the

corner of a partially collapsed building to race straight at Krysty. Still shooting the M-16, she drew the pepperbox and fired at point-blank range. Black smoke and flame vomited from the multiple barrels to engulf her attacker's head. Thrown backward, the body landed in a sprawl, dark fluids gushing from the ragged neck stump.

While gunning down a sec man struggling to kick a stalled sandhog alive, Dean got hit by an arrow from behind. Staggering from the impact, he turned at the waist and shot back with the Browning Hi-Power. Standing behind a stripped SUV, a sec woman loading a crossbow took the .38 copper-jacketed round directly between her breasts. With a guttural sigh, she fell.

Just then a horn blared, and a flurry of crossbow arrows went straight up from the roof hatches of four different wags. Gracefully curving back down again, the arrows fell across the huffing steam truck, the wooden shafts harmlessly shattering upon the iron chassis.

"Ramming speed!" Camarillo roared, as the *Atomsmasher* pulped a team of galloping horses, then crashed through another wooden wag. Briefly, he could see the tumbling bodies of the family, their broken belongings a whirlwind of destruction hurtling past the stout iron bars of his window. Then the steam truck was back into the clear, entrails and red blood streaming off the hot exterior of the death machine.

Aiming carefully, Ryan sent a full magazine from the Galil into the window, but failed to achieve penetration. From across the street, Krysty put another 40 mm shell into the machine, but the explosion only cleared away the grisly human remains from the heavily armored chassis.

"All right, enough of this shit!" J.B. snarled, tilting back his fedora. Kneeling, he nimbly tied a length of fuse around the neck of the Molotov he held, then stood and swung it around faster and faster, building speed and momentum.

When the steam truck came into view, he waited a few precious seconds even as several coldhearts started shooting in his direction. An arrow grazed his cheek, and a bullet scored a bloody path along his side, but he stayed still, gauging the wind, then let go. Gracefully, the unlit firebomb sailed through the smoky air to loudly crash on the thick iron bars of the control room window.

Drenched with raw shine, Camarillo instinctively backed away from the window, wiping the stinging fluid from his eyes. Then he realized the horrible truth, a split second before the blazing hot door of the nearby hearth under the steam truck ignited the highly flammable alcohol. As his hands burst into flames, he cursed and tried to jam them into a bucket of damp sand kept in the control room for just this sort of emergency. But unable to see clearly yet, he only smashed his burning hands into the iron wall, shattering both wrists. As the hungry fire danced up his sleeves, he waved his arms about. But that only fanned the flames, and soon they went underneath his iron shirt, then upward to his face and alcohol-soaked hair.

Blind from the searing pain, Camarillo ran about the locked room of the *Atomsmasher,* crashing into the controls and metal walls. The AK-47 slung across his back discharged a single round, then violently detonated, the full magazine igniting from the heat of the flames. Now inhabited by only a smoldering corpse, the undamaged war wag continued on its last course, steaming down a side street and away from the ruins toward the distant jungle on the horizon.

At the sight of the *Atomsmasher* departing, the coldhearts and sec men slowed in their attack, defiance leaving their faces like windblown leaves. Reining their horses about, some headed after the chugging steam truck, while others simply took off randomly, to abandon the fight.

"Come back here, you filthy cowards!" Ralhoun bellowed, shooting several coldhearts in the back. But that only seemed to spur the rest on to greater speeds.

Noticing a sandhog with an aced sec man draped across the handlebars, Ralhoun started that way, then saw Ryan walking across the street. Even as she swung around her blasters, the one-eyed man spotted her and triggered the SIG-Sauer, firing from the hip.

The reports of the three blasters combined into a single noise, and both Ryan and Ralhoun buckled, almost toppling over. But after a moment, he slowly stood, clutching his bloody rib cage, while she continued on down to the pavement, blood pouring from the gaping hole in her throat.

As Ralhoun collapsed onto the ground, Ryan ruthlessly shot her in the temple just to make sure, then staggered off into the smoke-filled streets, looking for the other companions. Especially Mildred, or at the very least, that Dewitt fellow. Ryan had been in enough gunfights to know he was running presently on borrowed time. Ralhoun had come too bastard close to blowing him away, and he'd soon pass out from blood loss. Even with most of the coldhearts on the run, that would be tantamount to a death sentence.

WITH THE LOSS of the war wag, Natters realized defeat was coming to the Angels hard and fast, which meant it was time to make his move. Slapping his chest as if shot, he tumbled into the gutter, then rapidly crawled through the mud until reaching a storm drain. Glancing about to make sure nobody was watching, he wiggled into the drain and dropped out of sight.

DESPERATELY REACHING for the reins of a galloping horse, Hannigan cursed vehemently when he missed, so simply started running along a buckled sidewalk. But then his scowl converted into a wide grin as he saw Dean staggering along the smoke-filled street with an arrow jutting from his leg.

Quickly drawing his Webley revolver, Hannigan aimed the massive blaster in a two-handed grip to try to control the powerful recoil. "Goodbye, Mud Puppy," he said with a chuckle, thumbing back the hammer.

But before he could fire, Althea appeared, her Ruger spitting flame. "Dean, behind you!" she screamed.

Riddled with holes, Hannigan fell over and the Webley discharged into the street, blowing off a chunk of the cracked pavement.

Hearing somebody shout the name of his son, a galvanized Ryan glanced around and saw a woman running through the smoke. She was wearing the lumpy canvas jacket of a coldheart and carrying a Ruger. Then the gray clouds briefly parted, and Ryan saw that she was heading directly for a wounded Dean, who was facing in the wrong direction.

Cold adrenaline flooding his body, Ryan started to shout a warning, then realized he would never be heard from this far away, and quickly fired the SIG-Sauer from the hip.

Chapter Twenty

At the distant glimmer of light, Natters threw away the raw rat he had been gnawing, and eagerly scampered forward, almost giddy in relief. Sunlight! He had found the way out at last!

Crawling out of the storm drain, Natters saw that he was still in the ruins, near a collapsed building with a weird domed roof. Flicking a butane lighter alive, he stared into the darkness to see if there was anything useful he could scav to help him dig up the dead later. Travelers often buried their kin with their boots on, and such, sometimes even with knifes and blasters. He could use all that to help him reach a ville and start a new life. Barons always needed trained sec men, and he was one of the best.

A hot breath on the back of his neck was the first sign that he wasn't alone. Clawing for his blaster, he turned around fast, firing into the darkness. In the bright muzzle-flash, he briefly saw the mutie, one with too many eyes and way too many teeth. Then writhing tentacles wrapped tightly around his body, pinning his arms to his sides. He was stuffed into the mutie's flexible mouth and swallowed whole.

Natters held his breath for as long as possible, and was unfortunately still conscious when his compressed body reached the acid-rain-filled belly of the beast. Then searing pain filled his universe, and it seemed to last forever....

PLACING A SMALL BOUQUET of white daisies on the fresh mound of earth, Dean stiffly rose from his knees. His left arm throbbed inside a cloth sling, but he found the pain strangely reassuring. It said that he was still alive.

"Better fix the headstone," he growled, dusting off his pants. "The name is Cawdor."

"You sure about that?" Dewitt asked, leaning on a shovel. "I was told the name was Stone."

"Then you heard wrong," Dean stated, walking closer to press two live brass into the man's palm. "Her name was Althea Cawdor."

"Fair enough," Dewitt said, giving back the brass. "And there be no charge for such things. All part of my job as a healer for the convoy."

Nodding his thanks, Dean limped away from the long row of new graves. A lot of good folks had been aced in the fight the previous day, too many in his opinion, and the travelers had buried them all, including the sec men and coldhearts. Alan said it had to do with not wanting to give the local muties a taste for human flesh. But privately, Dean thought it might have something more to do with the travelers general regard for the sanctity of life. He disagreed, of course. If a person acted like a mad dog, then he or she should be treated like a mad dog. Shot in the head and forgotten. It was as simple as that.

The air was crisp that morning, cool and clear, with every trace of the acid rain gone. Softly, there came the sound of hammers and saws at work as the weary travelers doggedly salvaged whatever they could from the wreckage of the smashed Conestoga wags, to reinforce the remaining four. Each of them would have a full team of horses again, as well as a lot of fresh steak for dinner. Plus a lot of new blasters to replace their black-powder muskets.

After the destruction of their steam-powered war wag, the coldhearts and sec men had scattered far and wide, running for their lives. Alan and most of the companions had stayed with the travelers, while Ryan, Cordelia and a few others had promptly given chase. They came back several hours later with their horses laden with blasters, brass, boots and gun belts. The spoils of war. Nobody had bothered to ask what had been the outcome of the deadly manhunt.

Going to his horse, Dean checked to make sure the tether to the parking meter was still secure, then patted the animal affectionately. Dewitt had worked wonders. The stallion nickered softly in reply as Dean pulled out the Enfield longblaster to clumsily work the bolt with his wounded arm, and chamber a round. This had been an old weapon even before skydark, but it still worked perfectly and suited him fine. Accuracy was more important than firepower. His father had taught him that many years ago.

Angrily ramming the longblaster back into the gun boot, Dean dutifully performed the ritual of patting his weapons: the Browning Hi-Power on his hip, bowie knife at the small of his back, switchblade in his left boot. Then he slowly reached inside his coat to touch the Ruger riding in a repaired shoulder holster. The memory of his first night with Althea came unbidden to his mind, and he tenderly stroked the slightly raised flesh on his face, his thoughts deeply personal.

Boots crunched on loose gravel, signaling someone's approach. Lowering his good arm, Dean touched the cushioned grip of the Browning, his heart pounding wildly.

"Son, I—"

"Shut the fuck up," Dean said through gritted teeth, bending to tighten the saddle's belly strap.

The outburst completely startled Ryan, who felt a hot rush of anger at the response, but held it in check.

"Fireblast, I didn't know who she was," he said in a carefully measured tone. "All I saw was a coldheart with a blaster running toward you from behind!"

Turning his head, Dean looked at his father with a hard stare, his thoughts unreadable. With a jerk, he released the reins and climbed into the saddle.

"It was an accident," Ryan said, the words ringing oddly hollow. His chest felt tight, the layers of bandages wrapped around his ribs having nothing to do with the sensation.

"Goodbye," Dean said without emotion, nudging the stallion with his boot heels.

As the horse walked away, Ryan reached out a hand, but somebody took hold of his shoulder.

"Let him go, lover," Krysty said gently. "The last thing in the world he wants right now is to talk to you. Or anybody else, for that matter."

"Yeah, I know," Ryan replied, watching Dean disappear around a crumbling movie theater. "But still—"

"Think how you'd feel if I had accidentally chilled

Krysty," J.B. interrupted, removing his fedora to smooth down his thinning hair. Then he set the hat firmly back into place. "Or if some coldheart had aced me. Brother, you wouldn't be sane again until next winter."

"But she couldn't have been that bastard important," Ryan said hesitantly. "Althea wasn't blood kin, or…anything."

"There you are wrong, my dear friend," Doc rumbled, limping closer. His right leg was bandaged, and he was leaning heavily on his sword stick. "I briefly saw them right before the attack. It was obvious that they were a couple. Not merely friends, or bed partners."

"He's just a kid," Ryan said stubbornly, opening and closing his hands as if reaching for something that wasn't there anymore.

"I bury wife and daughter when same age," Jak said simply, resting the M-16 on a shoulder. "He not kid anymore. Man."

The noisy repair work on the wags stopped as Alan and Cordelia walked out of the crowd. Both of them looked exhausted and were covered with bandages. But new autofire blasters were tucked into their gun belts, along with a couple of grens recovered from the sec men.

Hefting his munitions bag, J.B. tried to hide a smile. They had only found the explosive grens, because he had already taken all the newer versions: thermite and white phosphorous.

"Well, we saw Dean leave," Alan said, hobbling over. There was fresh leather wrapped around his broken ankle. "Hope you don't mind, but Della and I agreed to give him some of the brass you had coming." He waited, as if expecting a rebuke.

"Anybody who fights should get a slice," Ryan said flatly.

Alan nodded. "Fair enough."

"So, are you folks still riding along?" Cordelia whispered, obviously trying not to speak any louder than necessary. Her throat was wrapped in several layers of bloody cloth.

"We have a deal," Ryan stated, using stiff fingers to brush back his long, curly hair. "We'll ride with the convoy until you reach the Green River in Kentuck, then we go our ways."

"You know, we're gonna build a ville," Cordelia whispered, studiously not looking at anybody in particular. "You could stay as sec men. Be glad to have you."

"Always good to have another healer," Alan added hopefully. "Not to mention a second Library."

"Indeed, your generous offer is greatly appreciated," Doc rumbled, casting a glance at Library, who was laughing with Dewitt while they cleaned his instruments together. "As for myself, I would be delighted to open a school. But, alas, we are not yet ready to settle down to hearth and home. Eh, my friends?"

"Miles go 'fore sleep," Jak misquoted with a shrug.

"Until Kentuck," Ryan repeated, stiffly walking away, his pensive face a somber study of reflection.

Epilogue

Five weeks later the convoy reached the Green River, which snaked along the wild border of southern Kentuck. There were no tearful goodbyes at the parting of ways, but nobody seemed very pleased at the separation, either.

Waiting until the travelers were over the horizon, the companions now headed northeast for several more weeks before locating the next redoubt, hidden inside a cave at the foot of a dormant volcano.

The exterior access tunnel of cooled lava reeked of sulfur fumes, and a forest of stalactites hung from the irregular ceiling. Watching those very closely, the companions finally reached the end of the tunnel, to find a set of blast doors. The area before them was unnaturally cool, as if the redoubt was siphoning away the awful heat to keep the entrance clear.

With the other companions on guard, Ryan tapped in the access code, and everybody braced as the huge doors rumbled aside to thankfully reveal an empty access tunnel. Leading their horses along the zigzagging tunnel, the companions eventually found the garage level was jammed full of hastily parked vehicles, civilian wags, motorcycles, trucks, and even a LAV-25 armored personnel carrier.

Tethering the horses to the rear stanchion of the APC,

the companions did a quick recce of the base to make sure there were no sec hunter droids hidden about, or anything else for that matter, then proceeded directly to the fifth level.

The comp room seemed the same as always, the colored lights on the control boards blinking in an irregular pattern, a lone monitor dully flashing binary code sequences.

Grabbing a wheeled chair, Ryan hastily rolled it into the antechamber, then gently placed it into the mat-trans unit and shut the door. A minute passed and nothing happened. Then they heard an odd revving noise from the comp room, and strange white mists rose from the ceiling and floor of the unit to engulf the chair...and it was gone.

"Yee-haw, working again!" Jak yelled, grinning widely.

"Wonder what changed?" Ryan growled, rubbing the long-healed wound in his side.

Returning to the comp room, the companions looked over the array of controls for the main computer.

"What deviltry is this?" Doc muttered uneasily.

"Dear God in heaven, could it really be that simple?" Mildred whispered, going to the monitor and tapping a few basic commands on the keyboard.

Instantly, the monitor sprang to life, the screen filled with scrolling alphanumeric sequences. Some of them were marked with a plus sign, while other had the symbol for minus, but most of the sequences were unadorned.

"What's going on, Millie?" J.B. asked, easing his grip on the Uzi.

"How many redoubts have been destroyed over the past few years?" she asked, sounding almost amused. "And how many homemade gateways have we learned about? A dozen, maybe more? Hell, we once found a small mat-trans unit inside an aircraft carrier!"

"So?" Ryan prompted impatiently, crossing his arms.

Mildred grinned. "I think the supercomputer was defragging the system."

"For a couple of months?" Krysty snorted, her hair flexing in annoyance.

"It's the only thing that makes sense," Mildred replied, reaching out a hand to brush the controls. "We have all noticed that the computers seemed to have been operating slower as time passed. The system was clogged with data, so the computer simply went off-line to fix itself."

"Gotta clean blaster and curry horse," Jak said with a shrug. "Guess comp same. We seen redoubt fix damage."

"Exactly. This was just some routine maintenance!"

"Never mind what happened. Works now. More important, no food here," Jak stated bluntly.

"Jak's right," Ryan said, turning around and marching from the room, followed by the others.

Returning to the top level, the companions retrieved their backpacks and bedrolls, then took the saddles and bridles off the horses and set them loose outside the blast doors. Once the animals got hungry enough, they would find their own way out of the lava tunnel.

While the rest of the companions went down to the fifth level, Ryan headed directly to the kitchen and drew a six-pointed star on the cafeteria whiteboard. Then he rubbed out the part pointing toward the dishwasher. Lifting the lid, he placed an envelope inside with a private message for Dean. Just in case.

Joining the others, the one-eyed man found everybody waiting in the antechamber. Without comment, they stepped into the mat-trans and sat on the floor. Ryan shut the door, then went to sit beside Krysty. A few moments later, the air became filled with a low hum that rapidly built in power and volume, then a white mist filled the space. As it thickly swirled around the companions, static electricity began to painfully crackle over their bodies, and they fell headlong into a thundering void of absolute chaos.

Journal Entry

AFTER DINNER, Mildred took a cup of coffee and excused herself from the table. Walking down to the third floor, she chose one of the better offices, and went in.

Sitting at a wooden desk, she extracted a small book kept hidden inside a secret compartment of her medical kit. Sharpening a pencil with her knife, she composed her thoughts, then began to write in the journal using a simple alphanumeric code.

It has been quite a few months since I last had the chance to write in my journal, and if the truth be known, I always feel a bit foolish doing so. But what the heck.

My earlier theory as to the possible origin of muties is clearly wrong. I have no idea what the damn things are—a mutated human, genetically designed weapon, cyborg, robot, or just a freak of nature. Your guess is as good as mine. The one piece of advice I can offer is to always attack them from behind. That seems to be their only weak point.

This new redoubt should be easy to identify. The antechamber is burnt pink, with black rectangles lining the floor. Highly distinctive. See drawing of location at back of this journal. The armory here is packed with military weapons of all types, LAW rocket launchers, M-60 machine guns, mortars, land mines, flamethrowers, and boxes and boxes of ammunition. Sadly, there's no food, but we're seriously thinking about repairing one of the vehicles on the garage level, an armored APC in pretty decent condition, and stuffing it to the gunwales with weapons, to do a little traveling and trading in the area.

However, be warned! There was a class four tarantula droid waiting for us inside the elevator. The laser almost removed John's head before we blew it apart with a pipe bomb. At the moment, the droid is trapped inside an Abrams tank just outside the redoubt. Ryan and Krysty welded the hatch shut, while Doc and I disabled the engine. However, the tarantula might escape someday. Remember: always go for the belly-mounted weapon first, whatever it is; laser, needler or microwave beamer. Without them, the droid is relatively harmless, aside from being able to punch a hole through your chest with one of those telescoping legs, that is.

When fighting an armored war wag, attack the driver, not the machine.

Flapjacks turn white when they're dead. Any other color, or lack of color, means they're very much alive, and merely trying to lure you closer. Beware!

A group of travelers that we met, and traveled with some, plan to start a ville along the Green River by the name of Conestoga, which seems rather fitting, in my opinion. They're good folks, and it should be a safe haven for you in times of trouble.

According to Dean, you can use the residue from acid rain to make black powder. Early in this journal, I listed directions on how to convert black powder into the much more powerful gunpowder. Take your time. The only time you should move fast is when you hear a soft hoot in the night. Then run your ass off!

As for Dean Cawdor, to be honest, we have no idea where he has gone. I read the wooden grave marker that Dewitt carved, and fully understand why Dean left. Yes, it was an accident, I think he understands that in his mind, but the heart is a different matter entirely. We will probably never see Dean again.

However, Ryan left him a map to Front Royal, so be might he there, depending upon when you are reading this, of course. Dean is a tough hombre, but has a gentle heart, and you can always trust his word.

Speaking of which, I will steadfastly keep my

word to you, unseen reader, to always be honest in this journal. Is willowbark tea good for a headache? Absolutely. Are there ancient battle satellites orbiting the moon still fighting the last war? Who knows?

Just then, J.B. called to her from down the hallway.

More later. Next time, I'll explain how to set a broken leg. That could be useful.

Closing the journal, Mildred tucked it safely away once more, then slung the medical kit over a shoulder to go join John in the shower. It had been a long day, but there was food in her stomach, bullets in her blaster and, more important, a few moments of peace and quiet with the man she loved. That really was all anybody could ask for, this deep in the savage heart of the Deathlands.

* * * * *

The
Don Pendleton's
Executioner®
HAZARD ZONE

Washington becomes ground zero for bioterrorists…

A luxury Jamaican tourist resort turns into a death trap when a vacationing American senator's daughter is murdered. When her body is then used to unleash chemical warfare on the U.S., it's clear this wasn't just a random crime. It was a message—and Mack Bolan intends to respond… even if it means bringing the battle back to Washington.

Available October wherever books are sold.

Don Pendleton's **Mack**

Bolan.

Treason Play

The Middle East crisis has a dangerous new broker...

The disappearance of an American journalist in Dubai raises red flags in Washington's covert sectors. When the tortured corpse turns up, Mack Bolan jumps into action, racing to stop the launch of a nuke somewhere in the Middle East. But this time, the masterminds aren't the usual suspects...and Bolan delivers a death warning that payback is coming in blood.

Available October wherever books are sold.

AleX Archer
CRADLE OF SOLITUDE

A treasure of the revolution…or of ruin?

It was dumb luck, really, that archaeologist Annja Creed happened to be in Paris when the skeletal remains of a confederate soldier were discovered. But this was no ordinary soldier. Now Annja is unraveling a 150-year-old mystery and a trail of clues to the treasure…but she's not the only one looking….

Available November wherever books are sold.